MUMBAI NOIR

MUMBAI NOIR

EDITED BY ALTAF TYREWALA

Published by Akashic Books
©2012 Akashic Books

Series concept by Tim McLoughlin and Johnny Temple
Mumbai map by Aaron Petrovich

ISBN-13: 978-1-61775-027-4
Library of Congress Control Number: 2011902728

Akashic Books
PO Box 1456
New York, NY 10009
info@akashicbooks.com
www.akashicbooks.com

ALSO IN THE AKASHIC NOIR SERIES:

FORTHCOMING:

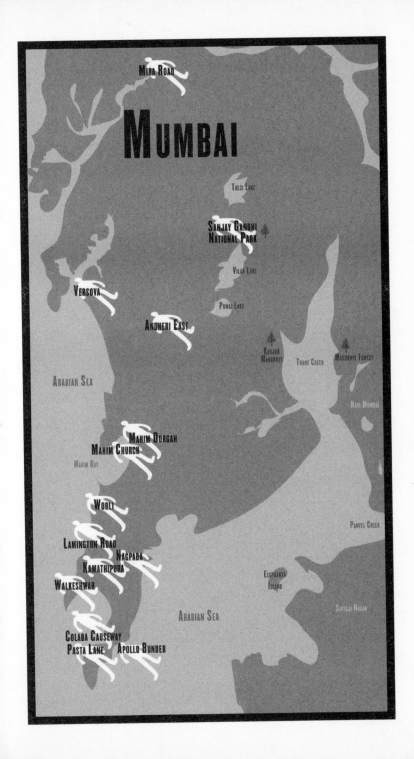

For Y.T. and D.T.—
who missed each other forever by a single day

TABLE OF CONTENTS

PART III: AN ISLAND UNTO ITSELF

INTRODUCTION
The Traffic-Choked Accident by the Coast

A boiling July afternoon. A monster traffic jam on Mumbai's tony Peddar Road. My taxi driver peers up through the windshield. Billionaire Mukesh Ambani's twenty-seven-floor home looms over the thoroughfare like a mammoth pile of Lego blocks. The cabbie remarks in the Bambaiya patois, "What building Ambani has made—right on the road. Some terrorist just has to drive by with a rocket launcher and *buss*!" He glances at me in the rearview mirror with raised eyebrows: khel khatam, game over. Looking through the passenger window, I observe, "Even an AK-47 would do a lot . . ." The cabbie is skeptical. "From the road? Angle will be difficult to sustain, saab," he says. "Plus, vehicle will have to go very slow for gunman to do serious damage . . ." I look again. The man has a point.

The traffic lets up a bit, but we continue to analyze, without a hint of irony, the vulnerabilities of the Ambani residence. Between 1993 and 2011, Mumbai has weathered eight terror attacks. Its inhabitants—12.43 million according to Census 2011—have become unwitting authorities on all the ways that an ordinary day in the city can turn out to be one's last.

Life in the island city wasn't always so chancy. Until international terrorism cast its vague shadow over the metropolis in the early '90s, the pains in Mumbai's collective neck most often had a face and a fixed address. The city's denizens knew the names and backgrounds of underworld majordomos. They were familiar with the bastions of extremist religious parties. And they tried their best to stay away.

Before the liberalization of India's economy in 1991, perhaps the only thing worth striving for was one's ability to stay on the good side of the law. Mumbai's middle and working classes were easy to recognize back then: they toiled hard, wore polyester, and fantasized about migrating to the West. Their heroic struggle to choose a righteous life over an easy life often invoked the respect of those who had done away with such bourgeois moral anxieties. The outlaw narrator of Abbas Tyrewala's story in this volume reminisces how the bhais of his time never harmed Mumbai's common folk because they were awed by their courage to live honestly and bring up children.

This promise of a "clean life" has driven millions of people over several centuries to abandon India's rural hinterland and throng Mumbai's streets in search of employment and social equality. It helps that under its urban façade, the city comprises numerous villagelike communal ghettos where people of similar religious and caste backgrounds can flock together. In Namita Devidayal's piece, the wealthy, pill-popping homemaker resides in an "all-vegetarian" Jain building, where the appearance of a single nonvegan egg can wreak havoc. Anyone who has gone apartment hunting in Mumbai will testify that the city's communal boundaries are often as impermeable as national borders.

The provincialism dictating who one's neighbors may or may not be doesn't, thankfully, extend to Mumbai's commercial life. When it comes to making money, the city has been by and large blind to caste, class, or creed, exalting productivity and wealth-generation above all else. History has shown that in its unabashed pursuit of profit, Mumbai can also be deaf to considerations of ethics and morality.

Through the early half of the nineteenth century, a large number of local Parsi, Marwari, Gujarati Bania, and Konkani Muslim businessmen were involved in the opium trade, shipping Indian-grown opium out of Bombay to China, in direct competition with the British East India Company, which exported the product out of Calcutta. While millions of Chinese sunk into the despondency of addiction, Bombay's capitalist classes grew staggeringly rich. The success of the opium trade, followed by the cotton boom in the 1860s, sparked the ascension of Bombay from a barely profitable port town to a roaring trade center. Much of the city's infrastructural development, including its lasting social and educational institutions, was paid for with the dirty money of these local businessmen. It is a historical ethical conflict that the city has never quite faced up to.

Over the centuries, crime has remained at the service of commerce in a city that was cravenly capitalist long before the rest of the nation followed suit. If a demand exists—even for something as wishful as the "elixir of youth"—you can bet some enterprising chap in Mumbai will move heaven and earth to fulfill it. Even if it means having to strip human corpses of their testes, as the elixir-peddling hakim does quite profitably in Kalpish Ratna's time-warping tale. In Sonia Faleiro's unsettling glimpse into the city's transgender subculture, death isn't even a prerequisite: the dai earns her keep by relieving sentient (and willing) men of their jewels.

Paisa pheyko, tamasha dekho. Throw the cash, watch the dance. These words from an erstwhile Hindi film song have become the de facto motto of Mumbai. Cash can get things moving in a rusty bureaucracy. Cash can help you get away with murder. Sometimes a little cash can help you save big money.

In Mumbai's dance bars, whole wads of cash must be thrown to get the women moving. Outlawed in 2005, these dens of misogyny and exploitation still manage to scrape through under the euphemistic moniker of "orchestra bars," where the concept remains unchanged: tantalizingly dressed women dance or sing in front of a lusty male audience. No self-respecting tome on Mumbai would be complete without a riff on this seedy city institution. Avtar Singh's story fulfills *Mumbai Noir*'s dance-bar quota. To his credit, Singh infuses genuine romance into an overly romanticized setting.

Like its dance bars, Mumbai too has been heaped with exaggerated depictions in recent decades. The city's chroniclers—its novelists, essayists, poets, journalists, and filmmakers—often seem overawed by the idea of Mumbai, rendering its quotidian realities in brushstrokes of grandiose narratives. What inoculates the stories in this collection from the hyperbole of "maximum city"—that much-abused term coined by the astute Suketu Mehta to describe Mumbai—are the restraints set by the noir genre, which stipulates, among other things, an unflinching gaze at the underbelly, without recourse to sentimentality or forced denouements. (But not without the courtesy of a glossary of Indianisms, to be found at the back of the book.) When viewed from a plane (or hot-air balloon), any metropolis might strike one as jaw-dropping. For a majority of Mumbai's residents, however, the city's over-crowded public transportation and decaying infrastructure fail to provide even the minimum of relief.

Unending traffic. Sparse greenery. Corrupt governance. Mumbai always seems on the verge of a massive breakdown. What keeps the city somewhat peaceful and functioning is the very thing that makes it overwhelming: the population density, which is one of the highest in the world. Mumbai's ever-present multitudes serve as eyes on the streets, pitching in during moments of crises, and at other times inhibiting acts of random violence. This has helped the city earn its reputation of being one of India's safest urban centers.

While Mumbai's civil society is remarkably accommodating to all varieties of lifestyles and individual preferences, perhaps the biggest threat to the city's famed cosmopolitanism comes from its twin banes: Mumbai's ultranationalist groups and its increasingly sectarian police force.

Bombay was officially renamed Mumbai in 1995 when an alliance of these ultranationalist groups controlled the state government. The renaming was meant as a symbolic undoing of the country's colonial past. Ironically, other legacies of the British colonial rule were left untouched, such as Mumbai's suburban rail system, its water and sewage infrastructure, as well as its enduring colonial-era architectural landmarks.

In December 1992 and January 1993, during the Hindu-Muslim riots that swept through Mumbai following the demolition of the Babri Masjid, the city's police force, possibly for the first time in its history of serving the city, abandoned neutrality and sided with the Hindus, turning what would have been a routine communal skirmish into a catastrophic minipogrom. For the citizens of the city, and for its minorities in particular, the communalization of the police was the start of Mumbai's darkest chapter. Devashish Makhija provides a heartrending depiction of cynical police officers let loose on Mumbai's religious minorities. In this story, the international war on terror is echoed in Mumbai, turning every Muslim man into a suspect following a bomb blast. Riaz Mulla takes a converse approach, delineating how an ordinary businessman can turn into a bomb-planting extremist. Mulla looks unflinchingly at how events may have unfolded leading to Mumbai's first terrorist attack.

In March 1993, in a misguided attempt to settle the score after the Babri Masjid riots, Mumbai's Muslim-dominated underworld unleashed a series of thirteen bomb blasts throughout the city. The mastermind of these blasts, Dawood Ibrahim, was a Mumbai-born gangster operating out of the Middle East. Two hundred and fifty people lost their lives in the explosions and hundreds more were injured. (Those interested in understanding the often mundane genesis of headline-making terror attacks may look up Anurag Kashyap's award-winning film *Black Friday,* based on S. Hussain Zaidi's book *Black Friday: The True Story of the Bombay Bomb Blasts.*)

Since 1993, there have been no further communal riots in the city. Instead, in a kind of outsourcing of violence, Mumbai has been targeted by international terrorists no less than seven times. Each attack jars the city out of its intense commerce-driven routines. But life resumes normalcy within hours, once the corpses and debris have been cleared out and the injured deposited in hospitals. Social commentators accuse Mumbai of a savage sort of indifference. Absolutely nothing seems to affect the city. Or maybe that's a wrong way of looking at things. Maybe Mumbai isn't just one city, but an organic conglomerate of innumerable subcities, each thrumming to its own vibe. A tragedy in one part of Mumbai barely registers elsewhere. People fall off moving trains, bombs erupt in busy bazaars, lives are made and broken in the city's daily flux, and things go on as usual.

Altaf Tyrewala
Mumbai, India
December 2011

PART I

Bomb-ay

JUSTICE

BY Riaz Mulla

Mahim Durgah

The court will now pronounce its verdict," the judge remarked plainly, as if he was going to read out the evening news.

Asghar Khan stood up in the witness box with the anticipation of a man in that twilight zone of hope when the decision has been made but not yet announced.

"The defendant has been accused of planting a bomb in the crowded Zaveri Bazaar area which killed three people and injured many."

Asghar Khan wondered whether it was necessary to revisit the circumstances; does a doctor open the incision to check if the surgery has healed?

"The court has been convinced that there was no motive behind this dastardly act but to kill innocent people and create terror."

The night came alive for Asghar and even today it seemed as unreal as it had seven years ago. He had watched terrorized from his hideout on the terrace as the distant sounds grew louder and the street was suddenly filled with a multitude of swords, tridents, and flames. The group first torched his scooter and in the light of the fire he could see them—known faces made grotesque by the flames. He had bought the scooter secondhand for twelve thousand rupees, the first vehicle of his life. As the tires and seat went up in flames, the mob broke open the shutter of his small travel agency office, Haafiz Tours and Travels. An enterprising insurance agent had once told him to get everything insured; but how does one insure against the betrayal of friends? They unplugged the phone and flung it to the ground and started to ransack his cupboards, throwing everything they could lay their hands on into a huge pile in the middle—passports and airline tickets and application papers—and he realized they were not just going to burn his office but also the small business he had successfully managed to set up. None of his clients at his budding Haj and Umrah travel agency would be able to perform pilgrimage that year; some, like his parents, probably never.

"The court finds Asghar guilty of willful murder and damage to public property."

The passports, due to their glazed cardboard, were the last to catch fire and burned the longest. That night he wasn't worried about the scooter or his business; one doesn't worry about the future when the present itself is under threat. He was worried for his life and Salma's and their first child still in her womb. She had tried to scream when they poured kerosene on the scooter. She had saved passionately for it and like every woman she was not good at taking losses. He had clasped her mouth firmly and tiny droplets of blood appeared on his palms where she bit him. She had probably realized that the present is of little significance if there is no future to look forward to.

"The court understands that Asghar suffered losses to his business and property in the riots preceding this incident."

How does one understand something one has never experienced? Even he had not understood when they first came asking for money to fight for the homeless Palestinians. After that night, when he had lost everything, they became his new friends, the only people to lend him money to buy food and treat his wife. He had asked for tickets to go back to his village in far away Uttar Pradesh, where his brothers set up grocery tents in open markets, moving to a different village each day—Dariyapur on Mondays and Thursdays, Rahimgunj on Tuesdays and Fridays, Bidwai on Wednesdays and Saturdays, and their own village on Sundays. He had tired of setting up and closing down a business each day in a new place and had come to Mumbai in search of stability. What he had never thought of was what happens when the thing that brought this stability is suddenly taken away. It was not as easy as setting up a new tent in a new village the next day and he felt a sudden longing to return to that varying yet familiar routine. His new friends, though, refused him that getaway; he had business to settle in the city before he could leave.

"But if every aggrieved person starts to take the law in his hands there would be anarchy. It is the duty of the state to provide justice."

What did the state mean by justice? Having to prove that the property which was burned belonged to him when all the relevant papers were destroyed along with the property? This was necessary to prevent fraudsters from taking advantage of the state's grant, the presiding officer had said, but Asghar couldn't decide which was a greater denial of justice: the state being cheated by a few opportunists, or the rightful being denied what was due to them. He had refrained from following the path of retribution his new sympathizers were advocating. Though he had lost all means of livelihood, the future still bode a small ray of hope: his unborn child.

"The court would like to take a strong stance in this case so that this particular judgment acts as a deterrent to all such acts in the future."

It was the birth of his son that marked the end of the future for Asghar. He was born blind and Asghar was convinced it was due to the trauma of that night. He would hold his baby, looking intently at that innocent face, knowing the child would never see him, never see anything. He decided to put a black ribbon on his own eyes for a day to feel what it meant for his son, but he couldn't keep it on for more than an hour. Salma felt it would not be as bad for their son because he had never known what sight was, but Asghar couldn't decide which was a greater loss: of having found something and lost it, or never knowing what one had lost. Six months later when their son began crawling, Asghar and Salma realized the enormity of raising a blind child. There was little Asghar could do for his son, and that helplessness was far greater than his helplessness that night when they had burned down his office. There was no morning here, no returning to normalcy. He was a fool to believe that it was all over. Sometimes when he watched his son he could see them standing outside his door laughing, mocking his naïveté.

Justice cannot be the sole purview of a few, his new friends had told him, and now he realized they were right. Who would give justice to his son? He would have to do it himself. He met them the next day and they told him the plan. All he had to do was park a scooter in the Zaveri Bazaar area during the busy morning hours. It was ironic, he felt, that a scooter was going to be the vehicle to get back at them.

"In order to provide justice to the innocent families who lost their beloved ones in this tragic incident, and to deter young people from taking the law in their hands, the court wishes to pronounce the strictest punishment in this case. Under section 302 of the Indian Penal Code, the court pronounces capital punishment for Asghar Khan; to be hanged until death."

Everyone heard the rap as the judge slammed the hammer purposefully on the desk as if hitting in the last nail. For a moment everything was quiet and then the whole courtroom erupted in a frenzy of mobile clicking; there would soon be a new segment on Breaking News.

Asghar sat back in his chair in the witness box feeling like he was the only person in the room; the judge, having delivered the verdict, stood up and left, the lawyers gathered into a huddle amongst themselves, the press got busy with their cell phones, and the police escorts waited patiently for Asghar, respecting a man's need to be with himself at such a time. It was as if he had already been hanged. He had feared this verdict and had hence forbidden Salma from coming to the courtroom today, but it still seemed unreal to hear it from the judge's mouth. How had he ended up being sentenced to the gallows? He had always wanted to be a dutiful law-abiding citizen of the country. He now realized why they had first wanted him to wear a belt of grenades and blow himself up in the marketplace. It is so easy when everything finishes suddenly, when you are still subsumed with the euphoria of vengeance. What was painful were the endless days and nights in the prison awaiting the verdict, because it gave him time to reflect, time to judge right from wrong; and when left alone with enough time, it was impossible not to see what was right and realize that some wrongs can never be undone.

Justice Talukdar picked up his papers and hurried out of the courtroom; he felt it was important for a person in his position not to get emotionally involved with people he judged. As he got out of the building through a special exit, kept locked only for a day like this, he saw her sitting under a tree, crying violently, seemingly unaware of the son sitting beside her. She always wore the full naqaab in court, and this was the first time he saw her face. She was beautiful and much younger than he had imagined, and the tragedy and youth only highlighted her vulnerability, accentuating her beauty. He felt a strong desire to comfort her but checked himself, knowing that both of them would not know what to say to each other. He had for long nights agonized over the impact of his sentence; does one human have the right to send a fellow human to death? Does the fact that society and law granted him that right make it any different from murder where the person assumed that right for himself; was that in fact the *only* difference? How was tightening a noose around the neck and allowing a person to hang to death less violent than stabbing or shooting at close range? All the agony came flooding back, and he felt less sure than he had in the morning when he arrived at the court. The law had been laid down and his duty was only to ensure that justice was delivered impartially, once the crime had been proven without doubt. There was simply no element of doubt in this case, and it would have been a gross violation of law if he had not upheld the rightful judgment. What if the father, son, brother of every person who was killed in the blast were to grant themselves the right to park a scooter full of explosives in a public place?

His car stopped at a signal, and from the backseat he noticed a temple on the sidewalk. People stopped by, clanged the metal bell hanging on the entrance, and folded their hands in a brief prayer—a plea to be answered, a wish to be fulfilled. He had never believed in temples and prayers, only in his own sense of justice and fair play. There was a statue of Lord Krishna inside the temple with the flute on his lips; playful, serene, and extremely assured. On an impulse, Justice Talukdar folded his hands and bowed his head; less in a gesture of worship, more out of respect for someone who, even in the midst of a fierce battle, was so certain about what was right and what was wrong.

Salma cried violently at the unfairness of it all—how could one incident take away everything that was valuable to her.

She had not known Mumbai or Asghar until marriage; for a girl brought up in the sleepy hamlet of Gazipur in UP, men and Mumbai symbolized dominance and corruption. Yet, after her marriage, she was pleasantly surprised by the ease with which she was accepted, as if the city and Asghar had all along been waiting for her. Mumbai was like a playful elder sister, vibrant and all-encompassing, and Asghar was unlike the men in her village—he treated her with a respect and companionship that was almost like love. She felt she had known the man and his city all along and it was only natural that now she had come to stay with them.

Asghar had set up a small Haj and Umrah travel agency in the living room of their one-room house in the predominantly Muslim neighborhood of Mahim. Five times during the day the loudspeakers from the numerous mosques would blare the adhan, and the narrow streets would be filled with bearded, paan-chewing men answering the muezzin's call to the faithful for prayers. On their way back, the men, most of whom ran small local businesses, would sit and chat with Asghar in his office, taking a pamphlet as they left. Asghar had no need to sell his religious tours; the muezzin and the preachers had already done that job for him.

As the businesses prospered and the preachers in the mosque became more effective, Asghar's business started to pick up. With the savings from their first big season, Asghar bought a secondhand scooter. He had always wanted to purchase a motorcycle but Salma was adamant about the rugged, bulky two-wheeler—a motorcycle was after all not a family vehicle. Almost on cue she became pregnant with their first child, as if all along it had been waiting for its future carrier to be purchased.

The demolition of the Babri Masjid was the first sign that the game was beginning to change. The usually cacophonic streets suddenly fell silent as if in mourning, and the loud call of the muezzin sounded eerie in the deserted lanes. The few people who ventured out to the mosque would hurry back home and the talk, if any, was full of vengeance and bitterness. Salma sensed a certain anxiety, a foreboding mixture of fear and anger, and the news of communal riots in the neighboring town of Bhiwandi only added to the unease.

They were having dinner in their house one night when there was a frantic knocking and Salma knew instinctively that something was drastically wrong—as if all that unease and disquiet of the last few days had finally reached her doorstep and erupted into those loud, hysterical thuds.

"Run!" was the only word their neighbor uttered, and the sheer look of terror on his face was enough for Asghar to drop his meal unfinished and rush out of the house. Once outside they did not know where to go; the familiar streets wore a deserted, closed look, as if wanting to shut themselves from the gory spectacle that was about to be played.

They scrambled up to the terrace and from there Salma saw a face of the city she never knew existed. The night was lit by huge bonfires and the calm would suddenly be pierced by gunshots and shrieks that reverberated long after the victims had fallen silent.

And then the mob appeared at the corner of the street, the fire from their torches reflecting from their gleaming, naked swords, disguising their identities but vividly display-ing the determination and glee in their eyes. They set about torching everything in sight as if it had all been kept there to be burned.

Like the earth, destined to its seasons, the city eventually came back to its busy, careless way of life, but Salma knew that it was only a façade, for she had seen the face behind it and it could not be forgotten. The vibrancy and the compan-ionship had died that night. Asghar lived with her but she was no longer sure what he felt or thought. He nursed her dutifully during the pregnancy and when the child was born blind he did not let his distress affect her, but this new lack of sharing pained her more than all the other tragedies. And when the police came to pick him up for the explosion in the marketplace she was numb, not from shock but from the pain of knowing that she had lost him forever.

The verdict had only formalized this. She never doubted Asghar's complicity in the crime or the validity of the judg-ment, but Asghar was not a criminal, not the heartless cold-blooded murderer the judge had made him sound. And she cried with the thought that the world and the aggrieved rela-tives of the victims of that blast would never know about it. It was a burden she and her son would have to carry to their graves.

The sheer unfairness of it all made her feel helpless. The verdict had delivered justice but it was in some way not fair to the three of them and to the ones affected by the blast. Because those present in the courtroom that day were *not* the ones who had perpetrated both the crimes; they were all in fact the victims.

* * *

Time, impartial and fair, is nature's ultimate panacea, the relief for all pain. Yet, when the court announced the death penalty for the man who had been responsible for her husband's death six years ago, Sneha felt the old pain suddenly surging back; the phone call from the police asking her to come to the hospital at once, the mangled body of her husband, the crowd at the funeral, and the sudden empty nights. It was as if after traveling a long distance to get away from something, she had realized that what she wanted to get away from was not in that place but inside her own self. And she cried with the realization that what she had lost would never be recovered by all the justice the world could deliver; that she was wrong to have thought that today with the verdict all her ghosts would be laid to rest.

But time, relentless and unstoppable, very soon regained the ground it had lost to that momentary burst of aggrieved melancholy. As she boarded the train Sneha was already thinking about her work at school and the things she needed to buy for the evening meal, and it was only a little later that she realized that the burkha-clad lady sitting opposite her in the compartment was Salma. All her loss and sense of defeat, at not having received justice despite the verdict, came rushing back and she felt a strong desire to strike back and gain some semblance of victory.

"I didn't see you in the courtroom but I am sure you must have heard the verdict. He is going to die; *to be hanged until death*," she tried to mimic the judge, and then the spite returned as she thought of Asghar. "He deserves to hang, bloody murderer."

"Please don't talk like that in front of his son," Salma pleaded, totally unmindful of the sentence and Sneha's spitefulness, as if they were natural. "He doesn't know anything."

Sneha persisted, not wanting to let go without extracting her revenge. "And how long will you keep him ignorant? His father's photo is there on every TV channel and tomorrow it will be on the front page of every newspaper. Your son would have to be blind not to know about his father."

"He *is* blind. He has never seen his father."

A fast train whizzed past in the opposite direction on the adjacent track making a loud noise, and Sneha was happy for the distraction. With a single stroke of tragedy, nature had robbed her of her right to avenge.

"I am sorry," she whispered, realizing the shallowness of her diatribe.

"Sorry for what?" Tears welled up in Salma's already swollen eyes. "You have suffered earlier and now it is my turn. It is His way of delivering justice."

Sneha wondered whether He delivered His justice in this manner; an eye for an eye, a death for a death, a widow for a widow; someone must have surely been blinded in the blast, she mused, looking at the child. The boy was staring blankly at her and she realized how in her bitterness she had failed to notice his condition, she who was a teacher at a school for the blind.

"Does he go to school?" she asked.

"School? Who would admit a blind child?"

"There are separate schools for the blind, even colleges. I teach at one."

The future always rules the present and a faint hope lit up in Salma's eyes.

"Will you teach him?" she asked, unmindful of her position, unmindful of the fact that the student's father was the killer of the teacher's husband.

Sneha needed no reiteration of the past. Their plight

united them despite their religion, despite their peculiar positions, and their truce was unsaid and complete like it can only be between two women.

"I will get him admitted to my school. Come."

The train was slowing down as it approached the station and Sneha and Salma stood up as if they had boarded with the sole purpose of getting the boy admitted to a school for the blind.

As the train stopped they alighted holding the blind child between them; two women left to live in a world where men delivered all the justice.

THE ROMANTIC CUSTOMER

BY PAROMITA VOHRA

Andheri East

O sama was sitting around in the cybercafé when our local cop, Jadhav, came in to put up a notice. It said:

Report any Suspicious Activity to the Police!
There could be a TERRORIST in your midst!
Protect the nation!

"You taking down all ID numbers and addresses in the register, right?" Jadhav asked me.

"Absolutely, saab," I said.

What I wanted to say was: *Jadhav, what about Osama here? Isn't it suspicious that he is hiding inside the cybercafé instead of standing outside at the DVD stand, just when there's a raid happening on the footpath vendors? Wonder who informed him, Jadhav? Couldn't have been you now, could it?* But it was no use joking with Jadhav. His sense of humor was Pvt. Ltd.: Only Laughs at Own Jokes.

"What, Jadhav, I heard you've bought a Nano," Osama butted in. "When you taking us for a spin?"

Jadhav walked out without answering.

"He's really bought a Nano?" I asked Osama.

"Then? You think he'll buy a Mercedes-Benz or what? Mahakali bribes are too small-time, brother."

"I don't think you should needle Jadhav so much," I said.

"Abbe, what can he do? If it weren't for us, he'd be buying a purple Scooty Pep, not even a Nano."

"It's not us, big shot, it's Haider bhai who pays him off," I reminded Osama. Haider bhai was our boss—he owned the cybercafé, all the pirated DVD stands in Mahakali, and the Starlight DVD library on the corner.

"So? We're a reflection of our boss, isn't it? We're his little bastards, aren't we? Haan? Ha-ha-ha . . . haan?"

I ignored Osama, who by now had started fidgeting at one of the computers.

I'd worked for Haider bhai since I was eight. Those days VCRs were the craze. Haider bhai had set up shop in the Mahakali area, about eight stops from Mograwadi, where I live. For a hundred rupees a month I'd deliver VCRs to the chillar class who couldn't afford to buy video players of their own. Three hundred rupees rent for Sunday, five hundred for overnight.

At that time, seventeen years ago, the neighborhood wasn't very developed. Sometimes I'd go sit on top of the Mahakali Caves, which are supposed to be some ancient temples but were basically full of pissing bats and kissing couples. From there you could see the whole area—a few four-story buildings, hutments stacked up the hill like stadium steps, and the big leafy convent next to Holy Spirit hospital. Roses and jasmines bloomed in the windows of the transit camp houses. Ladies sat outside cleaning rice, while their cats and dogs slept in the sun. Nowadays, the view from the Caves is clogged by new sixteen-story buildings coming up, one after another, in clouds of red dust. And on the other side, far below the Caves, where there used to be only jungle, the new special economic zone, full of call centers, with walls like curving sheets of white silk.

The cybercafé I ran was in a semiconcrete market opposite a big residential complex. Two hundred square feet, with a tinted-glass front and booths with lockable doors covered in orange laminate. There was nothing dangerous about our customers—I could have told Jadhav that when he came with his stupid warning sign; that would be giving them too much credit.

Only losers and misers visited cybercafés those days—the kind who didn't have their own computers or who were lying to their wives. Film strugglers from the PMGP tenements, college kids from the transit camp whose parents worked menial jobs, and unemployed fellows whose parents had managed to buy a one-bedroom place in one of the tackier new buildings. I'd read the chat histories of many. The art talk, the politics talk, the family-life talk—it all ended in some version of cybersex. No matter what, it was always the same—pretending to take an interest in each other when all you wanted was to have someone pay attention to you.

Like there was this dude, Prashant. Struggling actor, muscle-boy type. Wife had some fancy job, but the fellow still used the cybercafé. You could ask why but you don't get answers by asking questions. Walked in pumped up from the gym and sagged like a relieved addict when he logged on. He sat there doing faltu Facebook chat with people better than him to convince himself that he was intrinsically above his own station in life. When you saw a guy like that you knew he'd eventually be careless. Sure enough, one day he forgot to log out. I went and read his chat. He was talking to some woman who claimed to be a TV writer in her profile. Not a hot type at all. He probably though she'd get him work.

Prashant: Can I pay you a compliment?
Kamakshi: Gosh. Well no one minds hearing nice things,
*   so sure, why not?*

Prashant: I'm not talking about anyone, I'm talking about
   you. You know what's totally unique about you?

Kamakshi: Ha ha, okay, okay. Say.

Prashant: I think it's amazing, the way you remember lines
   from like, the most amazing songs. You know, you'll suddenly say "romance on the menu" or "sangria in the
   park" and I'm like, whoa, what a woman.

Kamakshi: Gosh, you're making me blush. But come on,
   that's not so unique.

Prashant: Trust me babe, it is.

Kamakshi: Ok, if you say so. But there's lots of people like
   that, maybe you just don't know any.

Prashant: You know that you are special. Why won't you
   let me just tell you that babe?

Kamakshi: You're just flirting with me.

Prashant: What if I am?

My mantra was Ctr+C, Ctr+V—to be read later in all
those empty hours. There were lots of people like that jerk. I
had no shortage of reading material.

"Why are the cybercafé booths orange? It's like we're
seeds inside a pumpkin." Wise words from Osama.

"I don't know, Osama. Mrs. Haider must have liked it,
she got it done up. If you don't like it, go out, no, and do your
work. I think the raid is over . . ."

"I hear Haider bhai is planning to shut down the café."

"What crap," I told him.

"Arrey, I'm telling you—Mrs. Haider is trying to persuade
him to let her put in a costume jewelery counter in here."

"As if he'll let his wife work."

"That's also there. But times are changing. And our
Haider bhai is not one to be left behind. He said it to me him-

self: *Times are changing, Osama, and we must change with them.*"

Osama was one of those guys who threw words into the wind to see how far they'd fly. For instance, his mother had named him Sadiq Osama. So he went around telling the boys he had a danger name because his mother wanted him to be a revolutionary of Islam. Then he told one documentary film-maker lady that his name was Obama and his mother had named him that before the black guy came around. So she interviewed him and he even made her pay him two grand for it. He also said various other sleazy things to her about under-garments and whatnot, but instead of being disgusted she was fascinated. That's respectable people for you.

"Haider bhai will never shut down the cybercafé," I said.

Osama laughed. "You think he loves you and won't take your little kingdom away from you, even though all the customers have disappeared? Come on, Surya!"

I ignored him. Haider bhai would never shut down the cybercafé because it was the one thing he did which didn't go counterfeit.

VCRs gave way to VCDs and then DVDs and then everything gave way to piracy—and Haider bhai may be bald and burly but he was light on his feet and he pranced nimbly like a fat fairy from one change to another. He still ran Star-light DVD library for the types who loved their country and wanted to rent legit copies of bastard Bollywood films for one-fifty a pop. For other normal people, he put three guys along Mahakali Caves Road selling pirated DVDs—fifty rupees for five films on one disk.

But in between he opened the Hai Five Cybercafé. A technology requiring English and education was here to stay, he thought, and would mean a better class of customer too. Haider bhai's son, Asif, was put in charge of Hai Five.

The technology may have stayed, but business began sliding in a couple of years. At that time I used to stand under the big tree in Sher-e-Punjab, where there was a lot of traffic of young Sikh boys in tight T-shirts wanting XXX DVDs. But we had to vacate that spot because the cops didn't have a police station in the neighborhood, so they put up some chairs under the tree and said it didn't look good if they shared the shade with a pirated DVD seller.

So I was moved to the cybercafé—which saved Asif's face. It's what I'd been waiting for. You had to get from outside to inside. Outside, there was no difference between you and the guy who sold dead fish or the guy who cleaned people's ears. You all smelled alike, of Mumbai sweat. Inside you were you, or somebody.

That's why I stuck it out with Haider bhai. The rule was simple—you had to have a maibaap in this city. This was the thing that stopped both of you from feeling all alone, the idea that you were there for each other although you may or may not be.

"I think I know Haider bhai better than you," I said to Osama.

"Accha, forget it," he whispered. "Your RC is here."

RC stood for Royal Challenge whiskey. Earlier Osama worked in one of the many dance bars around here, before they were shut down. RC was also how he referred to a girl who came to the cybercafé. He thought I liked her, hence my Romantic Customer. I told him that was nonsense. But who can stop a talker from talking?

She was in her second year B. Com. at Tolani College. Her father was a friend of Haider bhai's, so she was allowed to come to the cybercafé for her "studies." She was very thin, with the sticking-out collarbones that made you feel protective. She wore those salwar kurtas with shiny flowers that glittered at you. You could see her bra straps through the kurtas and her nails were long and pink. She wore big hoops or long dangly earrings. You could hear her nails and earrings and bangles all going *clink, tick, chink* in the booth while she typed.

That day she walked in wearing a kurta of dusky pink with gold roses. The salwar was like bell-bottom pants. Her name was Shagufta Ahmed. It meant bouquet of flowers. I had made the mistake of telling Osama and he asked me how I knew.

"She told me," I said.

"Huh? Just like that?"

"No, I asked her one day."

After that he started calling her my Romantic Customer.

Okay, yes, I liked her. I just didn't want to discuss it with that asshole Osama.

She usually came in the afternoons, when no one was around. Initially she used to stay for twenty minutes or so. After I asked her the meaning of her name, she began staying longer. Sometimes she would leave the door of the booth ajar and I could see her e-mails—cute dogs, pictures of giants that once walked the earth, religious e-mails about the ninety-nine names of Allah. It was obvious she left the booth open so I could see her and she could feel me seeing her. Because one day she glanced back when I was watching her and instead of closing the door, she smiled and said, "What are you looking at?"

I was embarrassed, so I just laughed and said, "Oh, I was just lost in thought, sorry."

She said, "What thought is so deep, Suryaji, that you got lost in it?"

I swear, I almost said something, but just then Haider bhai parked his scooter outside the shop and I pretended to drop my phone and cursed. If he'd seen me talking to her, I didn't think that would have worked somehow.

There was something about her presence in the cybercafé that made me feel peaceful. Dark afternoons, just the two of us and the sleepy sound of the fan whirring. We could be in a flat of our own almost.

I never opened or checked Shagufta's windows. You could say I was a fool. But whatever I got from the door sometimes left ajar was enough. It's not that the desire didn't overcome me at times. But the waiting and imagining gave time a reason. I knew her e-mail address: Shaghufta_91@yahoo.com. I had written her a love letter. It sat in my Drafts folder. I had quoted couplets of Urdu poetry by some guy called Shakeel Badayuni. I was going to send it once it was properly done.

That day of the raid, Osama could have left the moment Shagufta walked in, but instead the fucker sat down in a booth.

I began to hear Shagufta typing furiously. At some point she emitted a little laugh inside her booth. I smiled to myself. I didn't notice Haider bhai until he was already off his scooter. I hissed at Osama who quickly got up and went out.

Haider bhai came and looked around. "All well?"

"Yes, bhai."

Shaghufta greeted him.

"Nice to see you working hard, beta," he said. "Your father must be proud. Give him my salaams."

"I will, uncle." She smiled.

"Very good girl," he said to me. Then he looked around once more. "Surya, why are the monitors on if no one is using them? Electricity is free or what?"

"Sorry, bhai. Osama was using it."

"Arrey, how many times have I said he should not sit around here?"

"He doesn't listen, bhai." I saw no need to remind Haider bhai about the raid and make excuses for Osama.

"That boy is very nonserious," Haider bhai said on his way out.

I went to switch off Osama's terminal and saw that his chat window was open. His ID was Ghulfam88, of all the sidey things he could come up with.

> Ghulfam88: Can I say smthng? With yr permission?
> Shaghufta_91: Okie.
> Ghulfam88: I really love talking 2 u. I keep thnkng, when I see Shgfta I'll tell her this. Thoughts of U are stuck in my mind like gum.
> Shaghufta_91: I also wait for you to cm online.
> Ghulfam88: Wd you like 2 meet in real?
> Shaghufta_91: Dnt be silly. I dnt knw.
> Ghulfam88: Ok. Sorry if I said too much. You wnt me 2 go?
> Shaghufta_91: U go if u wnt
> Ghulfam88: You know I dnt want to stp tokking 2 u ever.
> Shaghufta_91: U der?
> Shaghufta_91: Hey, RU thr?
> Shaghufta_91: Can't say bye also or what?

I'd read enough loser chats in my time to know not to click on the button called *Chat History*. It wasn't a very long history—about a month after she started coming here, soon after he started joking with me about how much I liked the Romantic Customer. The first chat was just after I'd told him the meaning of her name.

> Ghulfam88: Is Shaghufta yr real name?
> Shaghufta_91: Is Ghulfam yrs?
> Ghulfam88: No.

Shaghufta_91:What does it mean then? Why did you choose it?

Ghulfam88: It means the bee who likes to suck on flowers. Bunches of flowers, Shaghufta.

Ghulfam88: Wot are you wearing Shaghufta?

Shaghufta_91: Guess.

Ghulfam88: Wot if I guess right?

Shaghufta_91: I'll give you something nice.

Ghulfam88: Ok. It's smthng soft.

Shaghufta_91: Maybe.

Ghulfam88: Maybe black?

Ghulfam88: You der?

Shaghufta_91: GTG.

Ghulfam88: But am I rite? What r u giving me?

Shaghufta_91: Ok, tok to you soon.

I remembered her black and silver kurta with a dupatta that had ghungroos on it, that tinkled along with the *chikachick-chicka* of her nails on the computer. I remembered all her clothes.

So Osama thought he was smart. He thought he could keep a secret from me, of all people. I tried to guess his password. Success on my first try. *RC*. What a surprise.

I opened a window and typed.

Ghulfam88: Hi, sorry I got DC.

Shaghufta_91: Oh hi!

I could hear her bangles clinking.

Ghulfam88: U missed me?

Shaghufta_91: Wht do you think?

Ghulfam88: U never answered me. u wnt to meet in real?

Shaghufta_91: Maybe.
Ghulfam88: What if I could be in the booth next to u and
  touch u just now?
Shaghufta_91: Cd be.
Ghulfam88: Ya? Excited?

I could hear her breathing. Maybe she could hear mine.

Shaghufta_91: U r bad.
Ghulfam88: U r making me go mad. U r putting bad
  thoughts in my head. Whole day I thnk of u, of kissing
  you, dnt be angry.
Shaghufta_91: Wat is happening to you 2day!
Ghulfam88: I have written a poem for you.
Shaghufta_91: Show.

Oh, I would show her. I opened my e-mail account and fetched that Badayuni fellow's poem out of my Drafts folder and pasted it into the chat window. I was aroused and angry now.

Shaghufta_91: Is beautiful.

Naturally it was beautiful. It wasn't written by a guy called Ghulfam88, was it?

Ghulfam88: Wat are you thinking? Y quiet?
Shaghufta_91: I am thinking if you would be next to me
  then the poem cud come true.

I stood up and looked over the partition at her. She glanced up, her eyes disoriented as if woken suddenly from a lifelike dream. She was flushed and quickly opened up some random window and pretended to be concentrating on it.

"Do you want me to come there, then? And make the poem come true?"

She went pale and looked confused. I walked into the booth and it was very crowded between the two of us.

"What are you doing?"

"Only what you want me to do—you said it on the chat." I reached out and squeezed her breast. She was shocked, but didn't stop me. For a minute I thought of doing more. But I wasn't thinking clearly and I didn't want to make a mistake.

I went out; she sat inside the booth for some time.

When she came out she said, hesitatingly, "Suryaji . . ."

I looked up.

"Why were you chatting with me like that when I was here? Why did you want to trick me like that?"

I shrugged. "Maybe you wanted to be tricked. People like that so they can pretend to be innocent."

"What do you mean?"

I peered away at my terminal. She stood there vaguely for a minute.

"I don't know how many other people you chat with, do I? Your dad tells Haider bhai you are coming here for your studies. Haider bhai doesn't charge you. And me, I'm just a fool. We are all fools."

She turned red. "How can you say something like that? Why are you behaving like this? I thought—"

"What did you think?"

She shook her head angrily and left as if she was never coming back.

I could see Osama outside chatting up some customer. He was wearing huge dark glasses and looking like an evil fly in a cartoon—they weren't his goggles, of course. He must have borrowed them from Amul Butter, his chikna friend who manned another DVD stand. I wasn't too angry with Osama. It was a matter of expectation. About Shaghufta I felt unsure. She had been carrying on with Ghulfam88, and now that I was Ghulfam88 I didn't really know what that meant to her, or to me. I felt a bit fucked up.

Then there was no Shaghufta for three days.

I was just getting used to that when she walked in on the fourth day, in the afternoon as usual. She was wearing a strange color—blue and green at the same time—in a shiny material, with some transparent bits. It was sexy. She didn't look directly at me. She went into the booth, leaving the door open. There was no one else in the cybercafé.

After some time she turned around, but I refused to meet her eyes. I stared steadily at the computer, where I was logged in on Osama's account as *Ghulfam88*. She soon logged on and sent me a message, as I knew she would.

Her: *Are you still angry?*

Me: *That makes you happy, doesn't it?*

I could hear her breath. *Why should I feel good if you're angry?*

"Isn't that what girls want? They want men to be angry because of them," I said out loud.

She laughed then. I got up from my seat, walked over to her booth, went in, and closed it behind me.

"See, you're laughing. For that very reason, isn't it?" I clutched her shoulders and she did not stop me. She was flushed. I moved my hands down and squeezed her breast again. We were both breathing very hard. I sat on the edge of the computer table and kissed her. She wouldn't open her mouth and I could feel her teeth hard against my lips. I put my hand between her legs and pushed. She groped her way up my leg. Mrs. Haider's orange laminate was blurry. Shagufta said, "Surya, Surya, I love you . . ."

"I also love you," I said between my gasps.

After I left the booth, she stayed inside for some time, the door open just a little. I watched her, openly now.

"See you," she said while leaving.

The next day there was another customer when she came, so I ignored her. But the next day and over the following days there was no one around so I went into her booth. I always positioned myself to face the door. In case anyone came I could pretend to be checking some virus problem.

After a few days I suggested that we meet somewhere else, but she said that was impossible for her, she wasn't allowed to go out alone anyplace but college and the cybercafé. I was feeling bold, so I tried to pull her kurta off, but she stopped me. She didn't mind hands under clothes, but not clothes off. Finally, she did not stop me from unzipping my pants.

It was understandable and maybe it had to happen, but that day I did not realize Osama had walked in.

"Abbe!" he yelled. Wise words as usual. It was awkward. He stood around, looking pale. Then he said, "Sorry," and fled. I quickly sorted myself. Shagufta looked like she was going to cry.

"Don't worry," I said. "He's my friend, he won't say anything to anyone."

"How do you know!" Shaghufta cried. "My father will kill me!"

"I'll kill Osama then. Nothing will happen. Really!" I touched her cheek.

She turned away. "What we are doing is wrong."

"Who says?"

She shook her head and left.

* * *

The next day she did not come, and the next and the next. A week passed. Osama didn't come in either. I tried to talk to him about it after a few days, but he just mumbled, "Don't worry, yaar . . ."

One afternoon, he came and sat at a computer and made feeble jokes. I saw him checking his chat messenger. Haider bhai paid a surprise visit that afternoon. When Osama got up to go, Haider bhai exhaled in exasperation and waved at him to continue. Osama sat awkwardly, trying to look serious while Haider bhai checked the accounts and looked over the register. "Ahmed saab's daughter hasn't been coming?" he asked me.

"No, bhai, been a few days."

"Oh, I must check with her father if she's all right."

My heart thudded and tried to get the better of me but I gritted my teeth to keep it down. As soon as Haider bhai left, Osama also sidled out. I quickly swapped my SIM card. Jadhav might have considered my extra SIM card suspicious activity. But sometimes you had to lie low and switch off your phone, so you needed a number to call from, right? I dialed Shaghufta's number. After some rings she answered. My heart unfurled when I heard her voice.

"Shaghufta, are you okay?"

She was quiet. Then she said, "Who is it?"

"It's Surya. Haider bhai was here, and he was saying he was going to check with your father if you're okay, so—"

"Okay, thanks," she said, as if the conversation was over.

I quickly said, "Shall I meet you at your college gate to discuss it?"

"Why? I will handle it." She hung up before I could respond.

My heart felt tight. I didn't think she was cut-and-dried like most girls. But she'd have to prove she was innocent if things got dicey. Which meant she might have to prove that someone else was guilty. Like me.

I thought a lot about what to do. I realized there was only one option: I would have to tell Haider bhai myself.

The following Saturday, when he came in for his evening check-in, I told him that I needed to show him something. I opened up Ghulfam88's chat history and told him it belonged to Osama. Haider bhai read it slowly and got very quiet.

Then he said, "Surya, you've been with me a long time and I know I can always trust you. Thank you for telling me this. If something had happened . . . You know, I owe Shaghufta's father a large sum of money. If this had got to him, I would have been responsible and . . . Well, son, you did the right thing by telling me."

"I've worked for you seventeen years, bhai."

He patted me on the shoulder.

I let my breath go a little; I felt safer. As Haider bhai got on his scooter outside, I saw him say something to Osama.

The following Monday, Amul Butter was at the stand, in his dark glasses and stonewashed jeans. I went out. "Oye, Amul, where's Osama?"

"Arrey, that bugger. He went to Virar yesterday to pick up DVDs from Kaana Shankar. There was a raid going on and he must have talked some nonsense, as usual. He got a solid beating. Solid. Both his legs are badly broken. Asif went, it seems, and took him to a hospital. Let's see when he gets okay and comes back."

Haider bhai, a man of the moment, had never looked back too much.

Days passed and Osama certainly was not back. I felt a bit bad. I missed having him around. It wasn't like there was much to do in the cybercafé. But mostly, I was relieved. It was peaceful without the constant distractions of Osama walking in and out. Gave me time to plan. Another year here and I would have enough to start something of my own. Once you were inside, you were in, and if you kept your head down, you could keep burrowing further in.

Then one morning, as I walked up the narrow footpath to work, I saw the cybercafé was already open. I entered warily. Haider bhai was standing with Mrs. Haider, who was dressed in pink, looking like a bubble of gum. A carpenter was measuring out some space.

Haider bhai saw me and smiled. "Arrey, Surya, I was trying your mobile since last night but it's switched off. Why?"

"No balance, bhai, so I just kept it off."

"Accha, listen. Your bhabhi here has been telling me for long to start something new. This area is also changing a lot—it's no longer full of riffraff. New buildings are coming—you know Kalpataru? It has a swimming pool even. Gentry like to buy knickknacks. You know that feng shui—Chinese frogs and bamboo and kya kya. We will start up that now. As it is, a modular kitchen shop is opening next to us so next need is good luck for the new house. Bhabhi is also at a loose end since Asif is married and his wife looks after the whole house. We can move one-two computers to the DVD shop. One can stay here for shop purposes. Rest we'll see what we get."

I said nothing.

"Frankly, I made the cybercafé with a lot of faith. But what to do—the world changes and one must change with it, eh? It's no longer a place for riffraff."

I stood quiet. He looked me up and down with a strange expression.

"Arrey, you're worried? Why? You've been with me seventeen years. You think I'll just throw you away? For now, you take over the DVD stand, and later I'll settle you somewhere."

He slapped me on the back, which made me choke. But it wasn't like I needed a clear voice to say anything.

With the feng shui shop Haider bhai finally hit the right note. Everything in it was fake from the start. How could it betray him? A man needed to be very sure about that before he put his wife to work. As for settling me somewhere else, it didn't really seem to be on his mind. After installing me at the DVD stall, he barely noticed me.

I tried Shaghufta's number a couple of times from both my SIM cards. She cut the call each time.

Under the sun, steadily steeping Mumbai sweat, I acquired a philosophical perspective on Osama. After all, why would his actions be above the level of his sleazy brain? "Ladies watch maximum adull films," he would say, standing tipsy on top of the Caves some nights, like a spare part in a gangster movie. "Because they are restricted to the house, they are pent up, so what should they do?"

"Abbe, shut up, you little rat. It's not *adull*, it's adult films. Hurry, we'll miss the last bus."

"Arrey, what does it matter how you say it? Thing is the same, is it not? Haan? Ha-ha-ha—haaan?" And he would hurtle down the slope without brakes.

When I thought of him a lot the other day, I didn't question it too much.

I went to visit him. He lives in Mograwadi too, in the backmost lane, where the later, poorer people built their lean-tos, close to the train tracks. I took along some DVDs. Adull films, of course. And some Romantic Customer whiskey.

He was really happy to see me. "I'm mending well," he said. But it didn't look like it to me. He looked awful.

"You go out if you want, khala," I said to his mother. "I'll stay with him till you come." She looked reluctant but I knew she'd have many errands that needed doing.

We drank a bit and talked of this and that. Osama asked, "So how's everything at the cybercafé?"

"It's fine." No need to tell him more than this.

"Accha. All is okay between you and Haider bhai?"

"Why wouldn't it be?"

He looked troubled. I watched him, trying to fathom his drift.

"Look, yaar, you're the only one from the lot who has come to see me since . . . you know . . ." He looked away, his eyes wet. "So I feel I can't lie to you. That day of the raid, Haider bhai called me over. He had been asking about RC before in the cybercafé and I . . . I got nervous, and I told him about you and her."

It took me aback, I admit it. I stared at him. "But why?"

He avoided my eyes. "Yaar, you know me, I don't think straight sometimes. I panicked. I thought if Haider bhai knew that I knew about you and RC and didn't tell him, then he'd have my ass. It's been eating at me since then . . . and I . . . I'm so glad nothing's happened. I'm sorry, yaar, forgive me."

Ah, Mr. Ghulfam. I wondered whether to tell him I knew his other little secret to really make him squirm. I felt tired at the thought.

I laughed. "Yeah, forget it." Haider bhai hadn't known me seventeen years for nothing, I thought. He knew whom to settle where, that's what made him a man of the moment.

I poured us both a little bit—well, a lot—of RC.

"I'm so happy you came, yaar," Osama said. "It's nice to know you have someone of your own from time to time."

I smiled and nodded. We are not alone, from time to time, that's true.

BY TWO

BY Devashish Makhija

Versova

Rahim

R ahim liked the night shift. He tilted his head back and filled his lungs with the black sooty air, as his bladder quickly emptied below. He could piss into the sea, even spit his paan into it, and no one would mind. Because at night Mumbai was a brutalized, heaving whore. She didn't give a fuck who pissed in her seas. It was during the day that Mumbai creaked and rattled like a desperate machine. And you dare not piss in a machine. It gets pissed off. And then it crunches your balls between its tooth-gear wheels. Rahim remembered telling Rahman that over dinner one day, gesticulating so wildly that the daal and rice sprayed out of his mouth, the same way that the shit had burst out of their rickshaw's exhaust pipe during the surprise PUC inspection. Rahman had looked at Rahim sternly and said, "Don't talk that way, this city is our mecca, it feeds you and me despite the lies we tell. Don't offend it. It could as well turn into our jehennum."

Rahim tired of his brother's fear of hell. *Take Langdi out at night once*, he'd gestured to Rahman, *and you'll know. By daylight even a murderer looks like he could do with a hug*. Rahman never took his advice. He grimaced each time Rahim referred to their auto-rickshaw as Langdi, the lame one. But Rahim needed to remind himself. What self-respecting man would ride a beast with three legs? A beast that doesn't gallop, instead sneaks and swerves slyly to survive. A goonga, perhaps, would. A handicapped vehicle deserves a handicapped rider.

Langdi, like Rahim, was made to survive Mumbai. She was an old machine, the kind that had the engine in the front, one that wouldn't pull it up an incline but vibrated like an electric drill. Rahim didn't mind the vibration. When he was waiting for a passenger to show up he'd keep the engine on, enjoying the tremors running up the insides of his legs like a cheap champi tel massage. Also, Langdi had a large gassy behind, just like Ammi's. If Rahim wasn't wrong, he felt in his heart that Rahman thought so too.

Rahim turned away from the oily edge of the Versova Sea and plodded through the sodden sand, not caring to check if it was the masticated remnants of the evening high tide he'd stepped into or someone's pasty turds. In the darkness it was one and the same. Rahim heaved his slight self over some rocks to get to the main road, where Langdi stood, her insides throbbing with a Himesh Reshammiya song. Rahim slid into the ghostly blue-lit interior of his rickshaw, turned the music down, grabbed the starting lever near his feet, and jerked it upward. Langdi coughed and shuddered to life. That shudder always made Rahim hard. It reminded him of the way he shuddered in the sandaas some mornings when he grabbed and tugged at himself.

"Made up for the lack of rain out there, did you?" a voice from the passenger seat barked at him. Rahim grinned into the rearview mirror—it hung out from the side of the windscreen the way a footboard traveler does out of an overpacked BEST bus. "Chhee, those teeth need a PUC test of their own," the voice squealed. Rahim now gesticulated into the mirror, *Where to?* The woman in the back leaned her powdered face out into the whipping breeze, her small blouse battling to keep her breasts inside it. "Infiniti," she told him.

The further out of the speeding auto Ramdulari swung, the further down the driver's seat Rahim slid, as if to maintain the precarious balance of the rickshaw, but in truth he did so to keep her ample reflection from slipping out of the little round window of the rearview mirror. She was his most consistent passenger. On good nights he made more money than Rahman made in a week. But he never let on how. Or Rahman would slap his own forehead so hard it would kick a *Lahaul-willa-quwat* out of his God-fearing lips. Jehennum, he would say, we'll go to jehennum for this.

Rahim hated to admit that Rahman was not entirely wrong.

They had come to Mumbai from Akbarpur, a small filth-heap of a town that sprang up along the railway tracks soon after the East India Company ran the first train across the nation's breasts. It was a town forever in transit. A quick-halt junction for mostly goods trains. As a result, all the businesses in Akbarpur centered around food, the only commodity people passing through really needed. Their father was a kasaai, a butcher with the dirtiest mouth in the town square. So dirty that he used to cuss his first wife even as he exploded inside her, cursing her for not being able to bear him any children. And then he cussed his second when she bore him not one, but two, simultaneously! So dirty was his mouth that word was he never threw away the shit that came out of the intestines of the goats he cut open; he ate it all.

But Rahim knew better. Ever since he could walk, he used to be given that shit to dispose of, along with the tree stump Abba used as a chopping block, each night, to clean off all

the little bits of rotting meat that clung to it. Rahim's childhood passed in a blur of bleating goats, morose cows, and dead
meat. Rahman, though, stayed hidden behind their mother's
abundant girth. In the hefty shadows there he must have discovered the fear of God, Rahim often thought. Abba didn't
dare inseminate their mother again, for fear that she might
bear triplets the next time around. Instead he married a third
time. Most nights when Rahim would stand alone at the rim
of the toilet bowl that was Akbarpur, and toss little bits of
rotting meat up into the air for the eagles to grab and devour,
he'd peer across the landscape, toward the west, and think
of the large sparkling city he saw in movies, where tall, angry
young men bashed in the heads of fat, loudmouthed flesh-
eaters like his father.

The night their mother died, coughing her guts out onto
the mattress, her TB untreated, as Abba cussed in orgasm inside her, Rahim grabbed Rahman's hand and ran.

He had watched films where boys running toward freedom
from tyranny simply follow the light. The only bright lights
around Akbarpur were along the railway tracks. Rahim followed them for days and nights. Until they reached Mumbai.

Through it all Rahman did not utter a word. Though between the two of them, he was the one who could speak. Rahim was born dumb, his tongue stitched by God steadfast into
the floor of his mouth.

Rahim never forgot how hard his heart had beaten when
he finally stopped running, staring at the thousands of people swelling this way and that in one of Mumbai's suburban
train stations, the choral murmur of their voices promising
him lives he could never have had in that little junction they
came from.

Rahman was heartbroken. The only person he had cared

for in the whole world was gone. He could have been tied to a post for slaughter and he wouldn't have minded.

In the many years that followed, the boys learned to care for one another. They were identical. Even their beards grew the same way and their hairlines receded in exactly the same curves. They both belched at the same moments during their meals. And if one had a cough, rest assured the other, wherever he was, was being wracked with a phlegm attack too.

Somehow Rahman always knew what was going on inside Rahim's head. And on those days when Rahim took a deep breath, silenced his furious mind, and paid attention, he could tell what was going on inside Rahman's head too.

They had spent nine months joined to one another like two nostrils. That was Rahim's favorite analogy because if one nostril got blocked, the other knew. They needed to breathe in tandem, but could breathe for each other too. Which is what they grew up to do. Having worked many odd jobs across South Mumbai, and unable to save anything they earned, Rahim hatched a plan. Which took them to the northern tip of the island city, where the land disappeared into the sea.

And took one of them with it.

Rahman

Rahman lay on the single mattress, staring at the outlines of unknown countries being traced on the walls by white ants. He knew he should sleep, but he worried for Rahim each night. He's got Abba's genes, muttered Rahman to the floor. Thank god he's goonga or he'd be cussing with every third breath. Where does all that impatience come from? Rahman had told Rahim he'd go with the pandus when they came knocking last month, but Rahim had insisted on being the martyr this time. The last time the cops had picked up

Rahman; the welts they'd left on his legs had still not healed.

The cops had been getting increasingly frantic over the last few years. Bomb blasts had begun to hit the city with the frequency of public holidays. Before the police could wrap their heads around a bomb that blew out of a tiffin carrier near the Gateway of India, another splattered limbs from a scooter near Dadar. Casualties were far too many and suspects far too few. It seemed that Versova, the land's end, was inoculated from this virus. But then six months back a taxi blew up in Vile Parle. The wheel that sprang free from the blasted cab rolled past many police thaanas and teetered to a halt near Versova Koliwada, the fishing village, where the RDX landings were suspected to have occurred. It was only logical, the media had insisted, because after the '80s when Versova used to be a smuggler's favorite place to weigh anchor, it had fallen off the radar, and the state's watchful eyes had since turned to places as far off as Panvel and Mumbra, red spots on the map of the 1993 terror attack trail.

Why would these fishermen fill their catch with bomb-masala? thought Rahman, upset at the state's insinuations. And even if they had, what did a poor migrant auto-rickshaw-walla have to do with it?

Last night Rahman had been quiet. Rahim had poked him in the ribs to squeeze a sound out of him. The jab was futile. Rahman had finally been convinced that being picked up by the pandus five times now in less than a year was God's way of telling them that He did not approve of their deceit. *On the contrary*, gestured Rahim, amused, *look at it this way—if I got locked up, you would be free forever, because you would not officially exist.* Rahim had gurgled with the exertion of his gesticulated explanation. But Rahman had felt his heart sink even further.

* * *

Rahman had never been too keen on Rahim's "plan." Rahim had applied for a single auto-rickshaw license. They'd found themselves a little kholi out here in Khoja Gully, in the heel of the fishing village, so far from even the skeletons of the decayed boats that on most months their landlady forgot she owned this little shack that she had to come collect the rent for. No one here knew there were two of them. They emerged one at a time. Rahim drove the rickshaw by night. And Rahman—as Rahim—drove it by day. The owner who rented his auto to Rahim had never in his thirty-year rickshaw career seen one man drive an auto both shifts, seven days a week. He was initially skeptical, worried Rahim might belly-up his three-wheeler if he fell asleep at the handlebar. But over time Rahim had convinced him of his "inasmonia," explaining to him in a badly spelled brief essay scribbled on the behind of a restuarant menu that he never got sleep, so he'd rather make a living all the time.

This wild lie had one downside. Rahman too had to be mute to the world outside. Which meant he could only talk to Rahim. Who could only talk back in gestures.

Rahman was starting to forget what a real conversation felt like.

Rahim slept soundly by day. Rahman tried to sleep at night, but the weight of this falsehood pressed down so hard on his heart that it kept his eyes sprung open, till the threat of dawn would inject some urgent fatigue into them and they would grudgingly close for a couple of hours each morning. This made Rahman tired. Of this life. Of being alone in what he felt. Of this strangely imposed burden of muteness. Of this unforgiving city. And the auto.

He didn't trust the people who climbed into the rear passenger seat every day. Most never even noticed him. He could be a mere machine. They could slide money into a slot in the back of his head and he would drive them to wherever they wanted to go. The few who acknowledged him did so only to haggle about the meter being tampered with and pay him less. To these people he was Rahim, hence mute. All he could do was glower at them, hoping his stern silence would make them cough up what was his due. But silence in this city is an alien commodity. Not only is it painful in its near-total absence, but exhibiting it seems to connote to people a capitulation so complete that they step on you like you are a foot-pedal brake.

Afraid that if he ever blew a fuse a verbal projectile might launch itself out of his mouth without warning, Rahman decided to keep his passenger interactions to a bare minimum. To aid which he had recently bought a small slate and some chalk. Since the old meters never showed the actual fare, which had to be read off a small chart kept tucked above the windscreen, he had started writing the fare on the slate and holding it up for the passenger in the back. This small but determined action seemed to deter some of them from an impulsive haggle. The habitual hagglers needed to be fed the chalk, thought Rahman, copious amounts of it! But he banished any violent thoughts as soon as they entered his head. He might be pretending to be Rahim, but he didn't want to become him. Not yet.

Also, Rahman could never figure why Rahim would need a box full of chalk every second night when Rahman could manage a whole week on a solitary stick.

The first time Rahman had been picked up by the pandus for interrogation was when bombs had ripped through the local trains. He remembered spending all evening ferrying the injured from Khar Station to Lilavati Hospital. He remembered not charging anyone a single paisa. He remembered telling the cops all of that, answering their long violent verbal questionnaire with countless humble nods and shakes of the head. And he remembered the subinspector—Doglekar was his name—saying in Marathi that all you Muslims are loose-tongued liars. And anyway, how could the police take his word for it when he didn't even have a tongue to give his word with? Rahman was let off with a warning that time. The cops kept his license with them, the one that referred to him as *Rahim*. He remembered returning at two a.m. to see a panicked Rahim waiting for him beside two cold plates of food. Rahman had walked in silently, sat down, and they had eaten. One rice plate. By two. Like they always did. No fuss. No regret. No anger. Just fear. And a prayer. That tomorrow might bring a little more rehmat than today.

In exchange for a week's earnings Rahim collected their license the next evening.

Sometimes, when Rahman feared for them, his nostrils would fill with the stench of dead flesh. The same smell from his father's meat shop. The smell that Rahim reveled in, but Rahman couldn't stand. It made all the fluids in his gut rise up together to his throat. Every last drop. Sweet. Salty. Bitter. Cold. Hot. Sharp. Bubbling. And his head would swim. It was the stench of death. And in those precise moments what he'd regret most of all was this plan of Rahim's.

To help himself through such times he'd gotten into the habit of keeping a small swab of cotton soaked in ittar behind his left ear. He'd scoop it out and slam it to his nose. And he'd be able to breathe again. But the ittar lingered on his whiskers, and Rahim, sharp fellow that he is, would catch a whiff the minute Rahman walked in at night. And then he'd rib him about having a woman stashed away in Juhu and keeping it secret from his dumb twin. Rahman was never amused by such talk, and earnestly defended himself, saying firstly he'd never do such things outside of marriage, and more importantly he'd never ever hide it from his brother. The smallest secret between the two of them could get them caught. And then he'd proceed to tell Rahim every last detail of the day. It was a habit they'd cultivated from when they'd gotten that rickshaw license. Since they were to be one person by day and night, they needed to know all there was to know about each other, so they'd never get caught off guard.

But there was one small embarrassing detail Rahman never shared with Rahim. On those days when even the ittar was of no use and he felt himself shivering in a fever of fear, Rahman would end his day early, park the auto behind the abandoned boats outside Khoja Gully, lift the backseat, empty the little chamber there of their tools, climb in, and slide the seat back into place above him. Scrunched up in a fetal position in there, he'd think of Ammi and the nine months he had spent inside of her, and of which he had no memory. For those few dark, breathless, unending minutes that womb would be his alone, not shared with one exactly like him. His ammi would then be alive, and he'd be unborn, waiting to live. Sometimes he'd lie there till he gagged. Sometimes he'd lie there till his legs cramped. Most times he'd just lie there till he could weep no more. And then he'd climb out, his fear washed off, his mother's death accepted, replace the tools, the seat, and drive back home.

As Rahman lay watching the first few fingers of dawn slowly taking hold of his eyelids and pulling them down, he had a sinking feeling. I hope the cops don't take Rahim this time, he muttered into his shapeless pillow. Ever since they interrogated Rahim the last time he's been so short-tempered and distant. *If they come knocking I'll find a way to reason with them. And we'll leave this place. This gully of the lost. This city of the unfortunate. We'll run again. I'll lead this time. And where we go we can live fearlessly as two. Not one, by two, like we do here.*

And just as his eyes slid shut, a key rattled nervously in the lock on the door outside. Rahim, shaking, tumbled in, and with his hands doing a manic dance in midair he signed out: *Bhai, there's been a blast in Borivali.*

Ramdulari

The first time Rahim had gone missing from the streets he'd taken his hands off the handlebar in response to Ramdulari's query, and joined his fingertips to gesture *home*. *And where's that?* she had asked, snapping her powder-case shut, not convinced. *Far away*, Rahim had indicated dramatically in the rearview, *a small railway junction where no one ever stops.*

The complete opposite of Mumbai, she had added, *everyone's last stop*. Rahim had smiled triumphantly. He had taught her the sign language over the many months he'd known her. And she had learned well.

The second time he had gone missing he'd signaled to her that he had been sick. *What with?* she had asked with concern. He paused. It was a cold night. He fogged up the rearview with his breath and with his finger scrawled *loveria*. Ramdulari had taken over a dozen customers that night to spite his blatant lie, and watched his drawn face in the smudgy rearview with one eye as she got fingered and squeezed.

Both times Langdi had been off the roads for a few nights.

"Rahim" never missed work if he could help it. In the hallowed circles of the rickshaw-wallas he was nicknamed Duronto, after the new nonstop long-distance train to Kolkota. Now this Rahman didn't mind. All said and done, it felt powerful to be the possessor of a secret that no one else in the whole world would ever be privy to.

Or so he thought.

The last time Langdi disappeared, Ramdulari had heard that Rahim had been picked up for pooch-taach in connection with the bomb blasts that very day. Fist-fucking the right havaldar revealed to her that Rahim had been a usual suspect, picked up by the cops every time there was a round of interrogations. She went cold down to her tailbone. The five times she had been compelled to hire another auto as her mobile "full-tension-release" shag-pad had each coincided with bomb blasts in the city. Not only were customers hard to come by on those nights, she even had to pay by the meter, something Rahim never made her do. She had a lot to be pissed with Rahim for.

When Rahim had returned last month, he sidled Langdi up to Ramdulari at the corner of Panch Marg and tried to apologize for disappearing. *My house got washed away in the high tide*, read his slate as he held it up in front of her face, his smile a precarious mix of cocky and earnest. She had looked past him at the mobile police patrol motorbike cruising by across the road; she turned and hurried away. She didn't want to be seen with Rahim. The hafta she already owed the cops far exceeded what she'd made in the last week. If she got caught in a terror suspect's auto they might harass her. And she'd heard of how they tortured female suspects. The havaldar had told her, as she gave him a hand job inside a broken-down car behind the chowki, getting off on the memory of the last time he fucked an upside-down woman with his lathi. Though he did add he'd hate to do something like that to Ramdulari, there was no remorse or mercy in his voice when he spoke of the suspect, emphatically adding that the minority needed to be hung upside down and straightened out. At that he had ejaculated, spitting venom all over the dusty dashboard.

Rahim followed Ramdulari down the street, braking to a halt every few seconds to clean his slate and scribble a new request on it with chalk, before revving up again, gliding alongside her, and holding the slate up in front of her face, begging her to get inside, saying he'd drive her around for free tonight. She ignored him completely, a knot forming in her chest, her face flushed. But Rahim kept at it. He kept at it till he ran out of chalk. And then he hit the brakes, wiped his slate clean, and sat still, watching her disappear down the street, his hands starting to ache as the flat rectangular piece of night they held grew heavy with the weight of its own wordlessness.

After that night, every night, for nearly a month, Ramdulari kept her distance. Rahim would catch glimpses of her in other rickshaws, as he ferried drunk young boys, watchful dupatta-covered women, and zombielike call center employees back and forth. When his shift ended, tired and irritable, he'd make do with the fast-fading memory of that meager morning. The one in which Ramdulari had stepped out of the circular margin of the rearview and invited him into the backseat.

It had been the night after his first reappearance, and customers—scared by the terror unleashed on Mumbai's streets—were nowhere to be found. Strapped for cash and feeling unwanted, Ramdulari had suggested she pay Rahim in kind. Rahim had never dared to insinuate that to her. He had been both thrilled and terrified at the invitation. He hadn't touched a woman before, and he shyly indicated that to her. She had simply nodded. He'd parked Langdi right in the center of an abandoned field amidst a far-off cluster of cottages in Aaraamnagar. The risqué move had made Ramdulari hot. As the moon slipped out of the sky, he had slipped into her. But he'd finished even before the cock crowed. She had sighed "premachoor," and patted him on the head. He didn't know what it meant, but knew it didn't bode well for his future with her.

And he was right.

He often hoped she'd make that offer again, give him another chance to prove he could gratify her. But she never did, pretending instead like that morning had never existed. Ever since though she had started talking more, telling Rahim about her life, and why she thought "tension-releasers" like herself were so important in Mumbai's scheme of things. He didn't care much to listen, but listened well, in the hope that one night she might feel some love and send it his way.

"If it wasn't for us," she would say, "there'd be many more old women with knives in their bellies and young girls lying raped in alleys. We Ramdularis help release the beasts you men keep locked up inside you." With that she'd light her only cigarette of the night, lean out of the auto, and leave a trail of smoke like a sad, small cirrus cloud.

Over the course of the month Rahim started to simmer. It wasn't a feeling he was familiar with. But it wasn't a feeling he could help either. Rahman noticed it. But the few times he attempted to talk about it with Rahim, an invisible door was slammed shut in his face. Rahman felt scared for Rahim. They had never been this far apart before. "The next time the cops come for us, if, God forbid, they do," he had told Rahim, "promise me you'll allow me to go." Surprisingly for Rahman,

Rahim readily nodded. He even looked relieved. Rahim had not forgotten how he had smarted when that subinspector, Doglekar, had abused his community. Rahman had it in his heart to forgive and move on. Rahim possessed no such reservoir inside himself that he could dip into. He signed a *thank you* to his brother and got up quickly so Rahman wouldn't see the film that had spread over his eyes.

The brothers decided to carry on with their normal life despite the Borivali blast. Disappearing now would make the cops unnecessarily suspicious. Not like they needed a reason anyways. Rahman stopped by the Yari Road masjid thrice to pray that day. He felt confident God was having a change of heart.

But the next morning Rahim didn't return.

Rahman, though restless, his heart beating like the drums of Moharram, stayed put at home. The smell of death returned stronger than ever to his nostrils. He tried to shrug it off, talking to himself, telling himself that the stench must be from all the dead fish being dried in the fishing gaon. But his voice couldn't convince his ears.

On the second day there was a sharp rap on the door. Rahman's breath froze; he didn't respond. The knocking continued. A voice, scathing with authority, called out, "Rahim?" Rahman clenched his eyes shut. A part of him wanted to know where Rahim was, and perhaps this voice could tell him. But the other part of him told him to not expose himself. What if this was a trick, aimed at blowing their cover? "Damn the plan, damn me, why did I ever listen to Rahim?" Rahman muttered into his cold sweating fist.

On the third flurry of knocks, Rahman, shaking, opened the window. To see Doglekar outside. Rahman's throat went dry when the subinspector, his eyes hidden behind cheap plastic shades, pointed at the lock on the door outside and asked, "Trying to avoid the landlord, haan?" Rahman mustered a weak smile and nodded. Doglekar handed him the license and said, "You left it at the thaana that night." As Rahman gently took it from Doglekar, the policeman seemed to peer at him as if searching for a piece that didn't fit.

And then he turned and left.

That night Rahman emerged, feverish and fearful, gagging on the imagined smell of rotting flesh. His cache of ittar had vaporized awhile back. He now needed some sea air to wash the stink away. Worse, all the Bisleri bottles inside the room had already filled with his piss, and now he needed to shit and get something to eat. To get his mind off Rahim, he tried to remember the taste of daal and rice. All he'd eaten in two days was stale pav and dried chilis. He took the beach path out, so that he'd be seen by as few people as possible.

Returning with a rice plate packed in flimsy plastic, the thought of dining alone was starting to depress him when he saw her at the mouth of Khoja Gully . . . Langdi, leaning slightly on the raised footpath, as if waiting for him.

Langdi

Rahman inhabited Langdi on the third day. He had tried not to, but he had run out of money, and the rickshaw owner had sent him a warning to drive or go fuck his mother. Missing Rahim desperately, he gave in and for the first time ever he spoke to the auto, calling her Langdi just as Rahim used to, hoping that being friendly with the lame one at last might make her spit out a clue to his brother's whereabouts. When Rahman lovingly wrenched her starting lever, black and yellow Langdi spat out nothing except for a thick vomit of smoke from her rear. She was overdue on her PUC check.

The smell of decaying flesh now burned through his entire being. That evening on his way back after a fruitless day spent waiting for passengers in the October heat, he had screeched to a halt before the large tree in the center of the road and puked all over its roots. He desperately wanted to crawl into the auto's belly beneath the backseat but Langdi seemed oddly unwelcoming. In the face of her uninviting stoicism then, Rahman said to himself, *I have to be brave. I can't get weak now. What if Rahim needs me?* And with that thought he denied himself the coziness of his ammi's imagined womb.

He bought himself full rice plates every night, and saved exactly half of everything, packing it back up in the little plastic bags that the sabzi, daal, rotis, rice, onion, and pickle had come in. *You never know when Rahim walks in through that door*, he'd say to himself. *What if he's hungry?* With the passing days, the packets of stale food began to accumulate, stacked up in a messy corner of the single-room kholi like a miniature memorial to the missing twin. In time, the room began to smell like something had died inside it.

A passenger commented on the stench one evening. "Did someone die in here?" he asked as he squirmed in the backseat.

Rahman, stunned, said aloud, "You can smell it?"

The old man nodded, staring at Rahman as if he'd seen a ghost, then asked, "You can speak?!" And Rahman realized what he had done. This was a man who hailed his auto every Saturday—his off-day—to take him to Juhu beach, to let the sea wash away his desiccated solitude. And now, in one brief moment of confusion, Rahman had destroyed what Rahim and he had taken nearly four years to construct.

They continued their journey in a strange cloud of silence. When the man got off, he paid Rahman and waddled away, vigorously dusting his hands, cleaning them of the dirt of deceit he had been party to for so long. Rahman was done with the day.

The next time Rahman took Langdi out it was at night. And as soon as he turned the corner near Hanuman Mandir, he was flagged down by Ramdulari. He tried to drive past; Rahman was choosy about who he allowed into his vehicle. He was not going to let a sex worker sit atop his mother's womb. But Ramdulari seemed desperate—she didn't just stick her hand out like others do, she stood square in his path. And scurried into the auto before Rahman could change his mind. Rahman sat still for several long moments wondering if he should ask the sex worker to get off. Ramdulari sat still for several long moments too, feeling guilty, unable to phrase the beginnings of a conversation inside her head. Just as Rahman turned to her, his cheeks smarting, she sputtered, "I'm sorry." Rahman's eyes went round. There was a dark tinge of familiarity in her tone. *Rahim!* She must know him. She might even know where he is. So Rahman veiled his ignorance and enthusiasm and gestured, *What for?* "I know you must be mad at me," Ramdulari said. "I was scared. Scared the cops might implicate me if they saw me with someone they suspected of being a terrorist." When he heard that, Rahman couldn't veil his sadness. "I'm so relieved to see you," she continued, looking genuinely pleased. "I thought they might have . . . might have . . . you know, encountered you or something." And her gaze dropped to the floor. A long moment slowly passed between them, thick and heavy with their private despairs, and then Rahman gestured, *Where can I take you?* and gifted her a gentle smile. It was unlike any smile she had ever gotten out of Rahim. She said, "Aaraamnagar," and smiled back mischievously. Rahman, confused, turned back to the handlebar, twisted the accelerator, and made his mind speed through all the possible ways he could broach the subject of Rahim without arousing this lady's suspicions.

Ramdulari made Rahman stop in the center of the field. She reached over and killed the engine, her breasts spilling onto Rahman's frail shoulder. Rahman protested, but she shut his mouth with a kiss, unlocking their lips as soon as she had locked them, shying away and waiting for her "Rahim" to take it from there. What she heard instead was a loud, alarmed, "La-haulwillaquwat!" and looked up to see a red-faced Rahman, his eyes bursting with furious tears, his lips trembling, glaring at her with an agitated mixture of distress and shock.

"Y-you can sp-speak?!" she asked, on the brink of tears.

It was the second time in as many days that Rahman had been slapped with that question. But he didn't realize this then. Instead, he stuttered and gesticulated in a confused attempt at coherence, "Rahim a-and y-you . . . you a-and Rahim . . . ?!" Before Ramdulari could figure how to react, he said, "Please . . . request . . . get off . . . please!" And she did. Standing alone, cold and bewildered, she watched the man she thought was mute rev the auto up like a raging beast and lurch into the darkness. She didn't know what had just happened. Her heart squeezed so tight that she didn't know if she ever wanted to know either.

How could he not tell me? shrieked Rahman silently. *How could I not have figured it out?* He used to be able to read Rahim's mind. Rahim had admitted it. That's why, perhaps. The sly chutiya, he had made that admission to make me overconfident, so that I'd think I could read his mind, when in reality he hid things in its little corners that I'd never be able to reach. Unless he allowed me to. And now Rahman had found out that Rahim never did allow him.

For nearly an hour Rahman drove around like a crazed bull, missing ramming into cars and buses by mere millimeters. When he was spent, the fuel gauge nudging *E*, he killed the engine, glided down the sandy incline to the far end of Khoja Gully, braked hard behind the dead boat, muttered, "I can't take it anymore," and stared at the backseat, urging himself to step inside his ammi. And as he lifted that seat, he saw inside—scrunched up in a fetal position—Rahim, decayed almost to the bone.

Khoja

The stench was unbearable.

But Rahman, curled up on Langdi's backseat, was getting used to it. He inhaled long and deep. He didn't even care anymore about how Rahim had died. In fact, what he felt in greatest measure right now was rage. A suppressed implosive rage. At the betrayal. Not only had Rahim hidden the most important part of his life from him, he had now snatched away his last refuge, their mother's womb, the only thing—the only thing in the whole world Rahman had coveted as his own. Not to be by-twoed.

Rahman pushed the auto, its fuel tank run dry, to the same turning where he had found it last week. He stepped back and looked at it one last time, leaning on the pavement, waiting to be found again. And when he peered above it he saw a sign that read, *Khoja*. Lost.

Who am I now? he wondered aloud.

Rahim?

Rahman?

Neither of the two?

Rahim alone had been proof that Rahman was real. With him gone, who remained? The Rahim Rahman pretended to be? Or Rahman, who no one knew—or would believe—ever existed.

Rahman wondered. Louder and louder. Not caring if anyone heard. He was done with being mute. He spoke all the way back to his little hellhole. And once inside, he continued to speak. For all the years he hadn't spoken. About all the things he always wanted to say, but never could. He spoke. And he spoke. And he spoke. Through fits of hacking cough. Through day and night. Through hunger and a raging fever. He spoke.

Until there was a sharp knocking on his door once again.

Doglekar

The Borivli blast had left Rahim terrified. At the crossing of Seven Bungalows, the images of blown-up bodies tumbling through his mind, he had jumped a signal. So distracted was he that he didn't even notice when a pandu on a bike started to trail him. It was only when the bike angled its nose sharply across his path that he hit the brakes, and he felt his heart freeze with fear.

In seconds his license was gone. In minutes he found himself before Doglekar once more. The name on the challan popped up in the system as a suspect in the blasts. And the RTO had spun him around and sent him to the same chowki Rahman and he had already visited five times that year.

Standing before the raisin-faced SI once more, Rahim didn't know why but he thought of Ramdulari, and how this time when he returned to the streets with Langdi, she would never turn to look at him ever again. His mind wandering, once again he lost track of where he was. By now he had missed answering two questions shot at him by the SI. And even as he collected his wits, a heavy palm slammed into the side of his face. Bouncing back off the floor, burning with indignation, Rahim didn't know why, but he slapped Doglekar right back!

The next thing he knew he was being beaten by a rifle butt, a different bone cracking under the weight of each blow. Growing dizzy with what must have been the loss of blood, he did what any normal person would do. Any normal person who had broken the law. He confessed.

At first he gesticulated feverishly, trying to tell Doglekar that there were—not one—but two of them, yet Doglekar understood nothing. So Rahim, his mind a blur of red rage and yellow fear, desperately lunged for a notepad and pen on Doglekar's desk. At which point the SI slammed the blunt edge of the rifle into Rahim's ribs. Rahim hung by the precipice of the desk's edge, numb to the hammering, choosing his words one by painful one, pinning them down on the paper, trying to tell Doglekar in the only way he could that he . . . and his identical twin . . . drove one rickshaw . . . by day and by night . . . only for some extra income . . . and that they were not terrorists . . . and that he was sorry . . . very, very sorry . . . for breaking the law . . . they would pay for it . . . swear to God . . . but please stop beating him now . . . or he might die. At that Rahim had slipped off the edge and crumpled to the floor, the pen's nib puncturing the page.

The last thing he remembered was Doglekar kicking him in the mouth as he lay smashed and bleeding on the floor. Doglekar had simply said, "Liar."

And then Rahim's broken heart had stopped ticking.

For a good minute, heaving from the exertion of his workout, Doglekar didn't realize what had just happened. Then he bent over and checked Rahim's breathing. There was none. "Bhenchod!" he had muttered, his blood going cold. And then he had lunged for the sheet of "rubbish" the "pimp" had scribbled on, and as he frantically made sense of it his back slowly straightened and a sigh of relief nudged out from between his raspy breaths.

By Two

Rahman answered the door. Two policemen stood outside, grimacing at the stench. "Rahim?" they asked. Rahman felt the strong urge to shake his head. He nodded. "Is that your auto?" they asked, pointing at Langdi, half-hanging from the hook of a tow truck. Rahman nodded. "We found a dead body inside," one of the cops said. To which Rahman nodded again and muttered, "That was Rahman," and held his hands out to be led away.

CHACHU AT DUSK

BY ABBAS TYREWALA

Lamington Road

Every night, as the last train leaves a station that used to be called Victoria Terminus, and the last club closes its cop-smeared doors, nothing melts out into the night. No secret city slowly takes over the darkness, lit by naked bulbs that cast more shadows than light. No creatures of the night, whose silent nods to each other hold more coded information about weight, rank, and pecking order than any Internet research could ever hope to find. Frightening place, this city now. A city of law-abiding folk. The night belongs to their expensive, million-PMPO car stereos and the screaming bikes of hyperpubescent idiots.

Fuck the day the Mumbai evening dimmed into a night that was no longer Bombay.

How did they douse the city in so much antiseptic? How did they get it so well behaved? Really, how do you turn Bombay into the least sexy city in the world?

One of these days, I'll have to get a job. Give up on the night. Give up picking on this nocturnal scab, hoping to see something that still makes sense, something that gives a man a sense of his place in the world, hoping to wake up one day at sunset to find I'm back home.

They offered me a job in the early days of the new city. A parody of my earlier job. From guarding the door of the small gay drug-den pretending to be a nightclub to guarding by day the franchise coffee shop that replaced it. The landlord of the dilapidated building was trying to be kind. I know because he never had a sense of humor; certainly not one so cruel.

Food. Few places remain where a man can still eat a meal cooked by human beings. Café Olympia. Holding out. For how long? Already citizens wait for tables, elbowing out the taxi drivers, who, by the way, already have the elbows of private air-conditioned cabs and pollution norms tucked well into their ribs. A dying breed—this tough, sleepless, uncouth, entertaining transporter. Black and yellow. The last remaining colors of a fading city.

The waiter comes to my table. "Yes?"

Yes? Yes?! Motherfucker, one of these days you'll meet your real father, and he'll hate you. You served me yesterday. And the day before. The same thing every day. And the day before that I was at that table being served by . . . that fellow—there! What's his name?

Fuck. I don't know either.

What's your name?

I don't know.

It's just the fucking times. It's just the damn city.

"Mutton masala fry. Pav. Thums Up."

"Thums Up finished. Pepsi?"

Fuck you and your whole family. "Okay."

I saw *Guru* the other day. Nice film. Bachchan's son. I cried. They showed Bombay empty. Like the old days. Marine Drive with no cars. No buildings so ugly that you want to kill anyone called Contractor. Don't know how they shot it. Must've done it with computers.

It's how Bombay looked the day I first came to work with the Pathan. Khansaab to many. Lala in his absence. Or Lalajaan, as my cheeky friend Shamim called him with a face so straight, he died a natural death many years later. I called him Abbu, for the few years I drove him around in his white Ambassador.

Shamim had taken me straight from VT to Marine Drive. My first sight of the ocean. After twenty unblinking minutes, I turned to him and shook my head in amazement. He smiled.

Then he took me to Lamington Road to meet Lala.

I still remember the first time I met Abbu on a terrace, semireclining, a quivering man standing before him. Lala gently explaining that he had been avoiding violence toward him all these days because he was a simple man. A clean man. And the greatest protection of all, a family man. "The shop doesn't belong to you. Yet we offer you a fair sum. I have given my word that this will be done. Don't force me to hurt you. There is nothing I would hate more."

A forgotten man in a forgotten time, like many before but none since, he meant it. They had waited seven months before grabbing the man by the collar and dragging him up to the terrace. Not because anything or anyone protected him. In fact, precisely because nothing did.

The bhais of my time were loath to harm common folk. The rich were fair game. The poor were slapped around without a care. It was the middle class that they held almost in some kind of reverent awe in those days of scarcity. They never forgot the courage it took to live a clean life and bring up children. If anything, they almost felt responsible for them.

The proprietor of Eagle Tyres once told Afroze, Lala's closest aide, to fuck off. Though rather grand-sounding, this was actually the smallest shop on Lamington Road and Eagle seth, as he was generously called, was the total staff of the eighty-square-foot establishment—its owner, salesman, and mechanic rolled into one.

Afroze had gotten the worn-out tires of his pig Fiat replaced with secondhand ones that Eagle seth had cut fresh grooves into by hand. After a few months, one of them had burst. Afroze wanted it replaced free of cost. Eagle seth asked if he was insane. A new one cost ten times more for a reason. Afroze was livid. Threatened to do many things to Eagle, all of them involving death and bloodshed. But the bald, swarthy, belligerent man offered to give as good as he got. Afroze asked a neighboring shopkeeper if Eagle seth knew who he was. The shopkeeper nodded. "Probably. But he's crazy. Let it go."

Afroze walked off. Went up to Lala and told him about the episode. Abbu laughed. Afroze shook his head. And that was the end of that.

Until Bakr'a Eid, when Lala sent Eagle seth a small packet of mutton from his qurbani.

When Abbu retired, his soul was tired. A new order was claiming the future; there was little honor left amongst thieves. New friendships were like today's marriages: for life or convenience, whichever ended first. The Word was as solemn as a beauty cream's promise. Women found shame sitting heavy on their heads and shoulders and began to shrug it off.

The old Pathan discovered two things unchanging in life: the warmth of the sun and the Word of Allah. He spent the remainder of his days basking in one, comforted by the other.

Early afternoon, and again I can't fall asleep. I look at the weathered HMT on my wrist. Just late enough to miss *Dilwale Dulhaniya Le Jayenge*. No other tax-free movies around. I stay in bed.

I no longer visit theaters to watch films. But back in the day, we all did. Abbu frowned upon them, but we loved them. When Bachchan started playing us, we laughed at first.

Dressed like that, in those cars, preening like a woman. But soon, the bhais found themselves fascinated with this portrayal. This was how they could—should—appear. And so was born a new generation of "Dons" who tried to live up to the image that those two Muslim writers created. Dressed in suits, wearing dark glasses, driving around white Mercedes with glamorous women on their arms. Glamorous stars in their coterie. Crystal glasses in their hands. Gold-filtered cigarettes in their fingers. From Families, they turned into what that crazy film director called Companies.

And they were no longer Pathan.

Pathans did not need titles or inheritance to be convinced of their own indisputable royalty. Royalty was inherent in their solemnity, their larger-than-life ideals, their need for utter peace with their own conscience in a life lived outside the law. They blessed. They dispensed justice. They sent men without honor to their graves. They took their honor to theirs.

The new bhais were converts from different communities. Konkani and Gujarati Muslims, whose lives had not been lived for generations with the lofty ideals of the mountain peaks, but on the shores of the ever-changing, ever-diabolic ocean. Survival demanded lightness of weight, and flexibility of plan. The ocean demanded emptiness contained in wooden hearts—golden hearts would drown. It's how the underworld turned treacherous. You could be killed simply because it was advantageous for someone. And dying, you wouldn't know with any certainty why.

Now, I go to the theater, not to the film.

Cinema halls were cheap, air-conditioned places to sleep away three and a half hours of an unbearable life. So, of course, the new city went to work on them. Now they're small, claustrophobic, cost five times as much for two hours' worth. And filled with The Kids.

The Kids. The frightened lifeblood of this moribund little island where everyone has learnt to be afraid. Aged fourteen to forty, some older; dressed in identical T-shirts and jeans and sneakers. A generation of vapid boy-men and hysterical girls, to whom friendship and love and connection with the universe at large is through increasingly smaller electronic screens. Their thumb muscles now the most athletic part of their bodies. Their need to be loud a defiant shout against the absolute pointlessness of their lives.

Every film, every horrible TV show, every magazine, and every restaurant desperately trying to reach out to the supposed psychology of this soul-sterile species. The twigs that keep aflame the sad fires of an impotent hell.

In my time, boys were men by fourteen. Else they died boys. They shoved and pushed and postured and carved a little place of the area for themselves—the adda—where they were the kings. But the changes were already visible when the gangs migrated.

As the new bhais moved away from Islam, they moved closer to Musalmans. Dongri, Mahim, Agripada. Muslim bastions where the bhais, surrounded by mosques and Believers, felt cocooned from the Judgement of Allah. Quickly, their fluid moral code started flowing through the streets. The less honorable the bond, the more loquacious the vows of friendship by the young men over games of carom. All night, they nibbled bhuna-gosht and discussed exaggerated deeds of bravado, their daily reiterated fearlessness, the dire but perpetually pending consequences for those who had incurred their wrath.

The Companies had a certain regard for the those who

had served the Pathans. When your own brother could no longer be trusted, we who could be were a luxury. Old-timers in the gang were like vintage cars. A status symbol. A suggestion of class. Not terribly practical, but still a reminder of better days. There was great demand for our services. I was still young. Yet they started calling me Chachu. In a world that was now being filled with sobriquets like Kasaai, Tamancha, Cutting, and even a Halkat, mine conferred upon me a benign veteran status, one that elicited unlikely nods from the Bosses. I stopped driving cars and began receiving and accounting for the hafta from the street operatives.

Hafta. The weekly cost of life. Paid voluntarily to the old Pathans for protection from cheap thugs, local goons, evil landlords, even the police. Now demanded by force for protection from the demander. Each one offering their own bit of protection, depending on how much harm they could arbitrarily inflict. The goons. The cops. The new packs of street mongrels that did nothing except not hurting people. For money.

On the terrace, Lala shook his head slowly on that Sunday evening I visited him. Trying to understand. Failing. "Protection from themselves? Really? And people pay? Lahaul-villa . . ."

His words would have been even stronger had he learned I had fallen in love with a girl from the Night Bird dance bar.

Afreen. Afreen. Afreen. My soul sang the song long before Nusrat did.

Having started to make some money, I had nowhere really to spend it. In the new localities, no one asked us for money. They laughed and coughed awkwardly if we offered to pay, looking around invitingly for others to join the joke. The more money we made, the less we were expected to pay for anything. Just like the movie stars of today.

Without the fear of Abbu's censure, I gave in to the darker lights of my soul. Nights were when we came alive. Met. Spoke business. Ate. Even drank—an unthinkable a few years ago. Came to dance bars, like thrilled teenagers whose parents had finally stopped asking where they were going. And what wonderful places they were. What a testimony to a woman's power.

Not a flash of skin. Not the hint of touch. You squandered your fortune for one more glance. Or, at least, a glance more than the adjoining table received. Entire sagas of rivalry, jealousy, love, hatred, betrayal, and vengeance played out wordlessly every evening, against the backdrop of the most popular film music. Every night, you went back for your fix of life lived in looks.

There were just two rules. Don't touch. Don't fall in love. The first got you in trouble with the house. The other could—would—destroy you. I broke the second rule. And spent many months and most of my savings trying to break the first.

Six months and many thousands of rupees later, I started to receive mock-exasperated smiles. Preferential attention was no longer in proportion to the currency notes I flung. The odd pleasantry at a table—a certain sign of a man of consequence. The odd drink replenished at her nod, without my asking—a sign of virtual royalty.

A year later she deigned to meet me outside the bar. It was much, much more expensive. The drama became far more intense. I no longer needed an opponent to feel the gamut of emotions from desire, hurt, hope, betrayal, self-loathing, and rage. There was no longer the cool solace of stepping out the doors, no adrak chai the next afternoon to wipe the heart clean and start afresh the next night. It was now a drama that stayed in my heart, in my head, growing and simmering and festering. It was life itself.

She only condescended to let me buy her gifts. The odd lunch. A walk by the ocean was a privilege. A movie rare. When it became clear that she would never, ever fall in love with me, I mustered up all my courage and asked her how much it would cost for her to sleep with me. She laughed. She laughed without malice, without mockery. She laughed caught genuinely unawares. Then she stopped and looked at me with the most hatefully kind eyes.

"How much do you make?"

She made more.

I went home. Stayed there.

Everyone had heard about my sad, silly, broken heart. The no-exit clause of the Underworld Charter was overlooked for sad old Chachu, who could no longer do the math of life. I was out.

I cried. For many days, many months. I cried alone at home for my Afreen who would never be mine. I never saw her again till she died. But my heart died with her.

When the vote-lusting politicians who could afford private dance parties pulled yet another plug from the city's life support, the Night Bird became the Sunshine Air-Conditioned Family Restaurant.

No families ever went there. It was a haunt for sorry old loners to listen to old film songs sung live. Songs of love lost, love broken, love shattered, love killed. We sat moist-eyed, mourning affairs that never were and marriages that were. I sat there, knowing what no one else knew. We were all singing a dirge to a dying city.

And to my Afreen, who was buried with the city's spirit in the December of '92. The chaleesma was spent indoors, in fear, in January '93. And we finally stopped mourning her a hundred days later in March '93.

The bhais became terrorists. The underworld fled overseas.

I fled to Colaba, one of the last places where the city that never slept tried to stay awake. It was drowsy already. The denizens seemed wired and wide-eyed, as if prised open with caffeine and determination. Somnambulant swagger became the body language at dusk.

Citizens started encroaching the territory. They came to enjoy the grunge, impress giggling bimbos with it, feel cool amongst its charcoal grills and roasting meats. They had learned the joys of the nightlife in a city that could barely keep from snoring.

To dispel the beckoning slumber, the city learned to party. Hard. Through the '90s, Citizens joined the nocturnal celebration that was Bombay. Discotheques, those mysterious places where exotic people went for erotic escapades, suddenly sprouted everywhere. You no longer caught your breath in the brief period it took for long, slender legs to emerge from expensive cars and walk into those fascinating dark spaces as fluorescent thumps leaked out momentarily when the doors opened. The doors were thrown open to all.

I stood outside one such door and kept watch; occasionally the peace. There are no bouncers better than ones with dead hearts. Unafraid of pain, unafraid to hurt, unafraid of the consequences, I observed the city grow stupid and weary with youth, watched the mating dance lose grace and imagination, saw The Kids destroy The Juice.

Juice. That thing that once flowed through the narrow, street-lit veins of the city, keeping her alive, sexy, alluring, dangerous, juicy, safe. The Juice began to dry up. No one knows how or why. No one knows who turned the generator off, or which fucking moron channeled the same energy to a giant cloning machine that churns out the coffee-shop chumps. If I had a bomb, I'd strap it to my chest and walk into that machine. Or at least a Coffee Day.

When, in November 1995, we were told that there was no longer a Bombay, we never fought. We never refused in outrage to turn off the lights. We just went to bed as told.

But I couldn't sleep. It was just too dark.

Somewhere, lost in my sleepless dreams, is a Bombay that many have never seen and many more have forgotten. She was like a beautiful mistress whom you could ill-afford, but she was worth frittering your job, marriage, and life away for. I catch a glimpse sometimes; at least I think I do—in a nod that carries a forgotten respect, in a brief look from a window before it shuts, in a rumor of The Juice still flowing on some nights, in some haunts. But never anything that I could reclaim, never enough to take me home.

I still roam the city looking for The City. I still walk the nights searching for The Night. Searching for my Afreen. Searching for anything that gives a man a reason to live.

Or at least a chance to die.

PART II

Dangerous Liaisons

NAGPADA BLUES

BY AHMED BUNGLOWALA

Nagpada

The muezzin's call reverberated in the air, exhorting the faithful to the evening prayer, as I was entering the bustling Nagpada police station on a tricky assignment. I wanted some information for a client. She was understandably shy of publicity, considering the nature of her business. I don't sit in judgment about what people do for a living. My client operates in a gray area of the watered-down underworld—once, not so long ago, headquartered in Nagpada. Now it has gone global.

Inspector Konduskar's welcome was just short of Antarctica. We exchanged some banal pleasantries and I got down to business.

"Can you tell me where I can find Salim Chingari, for old times' sake?" I put it to him.

His dour expression didn't change. He looked at me squarely with his bulging eyes and intoned in a typical, languid coplike manner: "You have some nerve, Gomes, walking into this police station enquiring about Chingari. We're not an Ask-Me service for washed-out private detectives nursing delusions of being crime busters."

I had expected this reaction from him. It was an act he had to put on for my benefit. I hardly needed to refresh his memory of the time, about six months earlier, when I had put a couple of leads his way in the sensational and brutal massacre of three eunuchs in Kamathipura—the notorious red-light district adjoining Nagpada.

Konduskar got a promotion for "cracking" the case in an "expeditious" manner. I got nothing. Now it was my turn for a little payoff. You see, what the cops didn't know was that the hacking to death of the eunuchs was a mere red herring to camouflage a much bigger crime—which included, among other things, one of the biggest land grabs this side of the equator. You must have read about it in the papers. It was in the news for almost a month before some fading actor made waves with the dramatic announcement that he was ready to bid "the long goodbye" to Bollywood to take up the cause of improving living conditions in the slums of Dharavi. What his publicist called the three S's of social transformation—schooling, sanitation, and sympathy. Of course, there hasn't been much progress to report, except that many residents of Dharavi were spotted wearing a "free" T-shirt with a picture of the star, juxtaposed with an uplifting message: *I will be there.* He was there, once, for a photo-op with a local politico in tow. The pictures splashed in the papers showed the two talking to a small girl with a bewildered expression on her face. It was pathetic.

My interest in Salim Chingari was hardly academic. I wanted to make his acquaintance for a number of reasons—the most important being that he could put me in the right direction for the case I was on for my publicity-shy client, Hawa Bai.

It took the tough Nagpada cop a long time to make up his mind. He finally muttered, "Let's go and eat some kebabs at Sarvi."

We walked across the street from the police station and settled down at a corner marble-top table with typical fake

Irani chairs—the real ones are collectors' items with the Page 3 denizens of Mumbai.

The waiters knew I was with a distinguished personage and the service was extra prompt and courteous. A few morsels of the well-marinated kebabs—for which Sarvi is justifiably famous—mellowed the big cop's mood a little and he asked me tentatively: "Why are you interested in Chingari? And don't play games with me, Gomes."

"He can connect me with someone I'm looking for. And I don't play games with cops, especially the ones attached to Nagpada," I said. "Too rough on the nervous system."

Konduskar allowed himself a half-smile—something strictly rationed in the Indian police force. Something to do with a morbid fear of appearing people friendly, I guess.

He didn't say anything and ate another mouthful. He could almost be the brand ambassador for Sarvi kebabs!

I could tell he had a lot on his mind besides the whereabouts of one of Nagpada's most infamous residents—frontman, bagman, lookout, district collector. A man of many parts.

"It's strictly off the record." I put some real persuasion in my voice. "And I have no retirement benefits. I need this job." I wanted to add a bit of emotional appeal.

He chewed on another kebab and on what I had just pitched to him.

"Okay. This is the last time and then we are quits. I believe he's in a safe house somewhere, which belongs to a financier who lives in Pali Hill. You get Chingari and I will book him. I don't have the time or resources right now with all this bloody bandobast duty almost daily. Anyway, the commissioner wants bigger fish." Konduskar was outsourcing his small problems. In a way it was good for me.

"Name and street number?" I ventured.

"Try the local police station. You might get lucky," he said dismissively. It was clear that was all he was willing to tell me for old times' sake and the kebabs. Or probably that was all he knew.

"Thanks," I said, picking up the expense-deductible bill.

Before figuring out how to work this Pali Hill lead I decided to drop in at Sameer's for a drink. The old thirst was acting up. Sameer runs a tough watering hole in Nagpada but I am a welcome "outsider" at his place. About two years ago I saved him a lot of grief by warning him about an impending excise raid on his place. When the raid did happen, Sameer had transformed his place—overnight—into a funeral parlor. Pure artistry!

A couple of days later it was back to business as usual—the drinking business.

Sameer's place ought to be be a tourist attraction. It's colorful, to say the least. His clients drink hard and talk loud. And they don't carry business cards. The walls are adorned with posters of flashy cars which are a passion with Sameer—though he can't drive any of them. In the old days he used to serve only battery juice in his joint, but globalization has caught up with him.

Sameer came over to my table with a half of Rasputin vodka and put it on the table.

"This is on the house, Shorty. How's the detective business?"

"If it gets any worse I'll have to ask you for a bartender's job."

"Anytime," he said. "What brings you to Nagpada all the way from Dhobi Talao?"

"An old flame who's feeling sentimental about our tryst in Khandala," I lied.

"Okay. See you around." He ambled away, shuffling his prosthetic foot. He'd lost his right leg in a bitter intergang war in Nagpada, about twenty years ago.

Over my second drink I got into stock-taking mode.

Things were not going too well for me in Mumbai—where there's no dearth of crooks, crime, and sleaze. Business was slow and I was getting all the bottom-of-the-barrel jobs. Like this one from Hawa Bai to trace her favorite trick—Jasmine—who had disappeared mysteriously after spending a night with Chingari, a week ago. The cops were not too keen on finding another lost soul in Mumbai's flourishing flesh trade. Hawa Bai had promised to be generous with the money. It helps with paying the bills, you know. The influential madam obviously had a soft corner for the girl. I could understand why. The picture she had shown me—handing me some "expense" money—was of a twenty-something girl, full of hope and idealism. Part of the reason I was on this job was to relive how it had felt to be young and idealistic. I feel like this about once every ten years.

Goa was a great place to grow up, but I was destined to move to Mumbai. A builder tricked my ailing father into selling our ancestral Cortalim home for a song. It rankles me even today, after so many years.

I did a lot of drudgery jobs in Mumbai—waiting tables, selling water filters, working for a courier company—before I answered a "trainee operatives" ad for a place called Aces Private Detective Agency. Their motto was: *Don't Worry, Be Happy.* Bizarre. The things I did as a trainee I would like to forget. What I did when I was employed as a regular operative I would like to forget even more—waiting tables is much more honorable and you live longer. That is, if you want to live in this soulless metro-retro city which belongs only to the rich and powerful who flaunt their jaded lifestyles by living in baroque maximum-security homes with "intelligent" toilets and travel by private jets to meet their boutique mistresses in the capital. Of course, to carefully coincide with well-timed, ego-massaging visits to some sympathetic ministers and bureaucrats to influence policy and decisions. *Crime now sits in high places—insular and mocking.* I can't remember who said that. Must be the vodka.

I resigned from the detective agency for what is euphemistically known as "personal reasons." The truth is, we had a terrific row over the case of a big-ticket industrialist who wanted the criminal charges against his profligate son dropped or diluted. He—the son—had mowed down six people in a drunken stupor while driving his flashy SUV after a late-night party. The agency was hired by the parents of one of the hapless victims who were killed. All the evidence I had painstakingly gathered was dismissed by the boss of the agency and the cops as "fanciful conjectures of a drinking detective." I felt lousy.

The decibel level at Sameer's place was getting a bit too loud for my liking so I decided to call it a day. I walked up to the bar where Sameer was in an animated discussion with a pock-marked guy who had the telltale look of a contract killer.

"Thanks, Sameer. Rasputin was smooth."

"Drop in again. Try the Havana rum next time."

"I will. Who's your beautiful friend?"

"Does a few odd jobs for me."

"Like what?"

"Garbage disposal."

"Good night. When do you close?"

"We never close—we're in the service business." He grinned. "Good night."

I took a sagging and smelly black-and-yellow cab to my dingy pad in a rundown building on a narrow and filthy by-lane of Dhobi Talao to get some much-needed sleep.

It was a pleasantly sunny December morning when I got off—or more accurately, was shoved out—of the harbor-line local train at Bandra station. I took a rickshaw to Pali Hill. The garrulous driver mistook me for a tourist and kept up an unsolicited commentary on the famous and infamous residents of the Hill. He pointed to a big bungalow and said: "That's where I dropped him last night. His car had run out of gas on Carter Road. He was tight and gave me one hundred rupees as a tip."

"Who?"

He looked at me in amazement. "You mean you don't know?"

"No," I said.

He did an imitation of an actor to jog my memory.

"I give up."

He did another imitation, this time more elaborate.

"Pass," I said. "And I'll get out here." I gave him a five-rupee tip; he gave me a pitying look. "I am not in the movies," I explained.

I walked for some time—uphill, taking in the sights and smells—till I came to the building I was looking for. My destination was the Pali Hill Association for the Ethical Treatment of Residents.

If you lived here you had arrived, or at least you got free invites to fashionable book launches and fashion shows where they serve cheese and wine—that is, if you could sit through the dreary readings by earnest authors of trivia or the silly posturing of starlets in ridiculous outfits conceived by designers with a very tenuous grip on reality.

I rang the bell of the third-floor apartment with an ornate door depicting peacocks in bas-relief.

Two dogs started a barking chorus.

The door opened and a sixty-something white-haired man—in a designer maroon kurta and wooden beads—appeared. He had a look of mild annoyance or disapproval on his face.

"Good morning," I said, raising my voice above the dogs' din. "Are you the chairman of the association?"

"Yes, I am." He was curt.

"My name is Bharat Kumar. I need some information on Pali Hill residents. May I come in?"

"What kind of information?" He was leery. "Come in," he added reluctantly. The most difficult part of a private detective's job is to get entry. The rest is usually a cakewalk.

"Thank you," I said entering the large living room, as the two Labs—black and beige—jumped all over me. They were happy to have company. I petted them to calm them and they quickly settled down, panting, near my feet. I parked myself on the overstuffed sofa—probably Italian, though I wouldn't bet any money on it.

"My dogs like you," he said in a softer tone.

"Yeah, I like dogs. They are very instinctive."

"Do you have dogs?"

"No, but I know some in the neighborhood very well. I feed them."

"And what neighborhood would that be, Mr. Kumar?" He was trying to size me up.

"Altamount Road," I said glibly. It was the first thought that popped into my head.

He looked at me skeptically but didn't say anything out of politeness. "You wanted to know something about the residents here," he said instead.

"You see, Mr. Chairman, I am scouting for a quiet property here. Altamount Road is getting too crowded and crass for my liking. Too much one-upmanship."

"I agree," he said.

"I was wondering if you have a list of the residents of this enchanting place. It would be nice to know who our neighbors are going to be." I was playing the long shot. You have to in this business.

"What's your budget, if I may ask? I am also a real estate agent." That came as a surprise; it was not part of the script. But I should have known better. Every third person in this city is either a stockbroker, realtor, or insurance salesman.

"Five," I ventured. I was thinking in thousands but he presumed I meant crores. That suited me fine.

"Would you like something to drink?" Another unscripted surprise.

"Sure. What you got?"

"Anything ever bottled or canned. You name it."

"I'll settle for a Heineken." After all, what the hell, I live in Altamount Road, the world's tenth most expensive address, where the residents buy islands in the Caribbean as a hobby.

"Heineken it is," he said expansively.

He got me the can of beer from the kitchen fridge and poured himself a large Teacher's from the ornate bar across the sofa I was slouched in.

"Cheers. To Pali Hill," he intoned in a deep Bogart voice.

"Cheers," I said. "To Pali Hill."

After a full hour and a half of this nonsense of raising toasts to Pali Hill, I managed to get the list from him. It was touch and go. But I've been there many times. I promised to contact him—to look at the "once in a lifetime" properties he "exclusively" represented for his "reputed" clients—as soon as the missus was back from her shopping trip to Dubai. I patted the dogs—he had named them Google and Yahoo!—and got up to leave. They gave me doleful looks, almost imploring me not to go. But I had work to do. Find Jasmine—dead or alive.

"Thanks for the beers." I made a quick exit.

At a cybercafé down the road I printed out the list he had given me from my flash drive. It made for fascinating reading: a Page 3 *Who's Who* of Mumbai. Or was it, as a journalist once wagged at the Press Club, the *Who's Why*? The list was long and methodical—name, occupation, religion, sex, age, club membership, vegetarian or nonvegetarian, details of pets, names and domicile of domestic help, owner or tenant, duration of occupation, etc. The only information missing in the list was whether the residents—dominated by the Khans, Kapoors, Shahs, and Patels—preferred the missionary position or the Japanese one.

For the next two hours, over coffee and sandwiches, I scrutinised the "occupation" column of the Excel sheet—the listing of film financiers was far too long for my liking. Salim Chingari could be under the benevolent protection of any one of them. I needed a short list of three for a fighting chance of finding Jasmine.

I knew just the right man who could help me do that. I was going to use my social network, again, which I have assiduously cultivated over the last thirty years. A private detective is only as good as his contacts.

"This is a surprise, Shorty! Where the fuck have you been recently?"

"All over town."

"Looking for something?"

"Yeah. Love and sympathy."

"Forget it. Even the Salvation Army is out of stock."

"Got to be somewhere. Dalal Street?"

"Something on your mind?"

"Need to find a film financier."

"Don't choke me, Shorty. Are you thinking of making a movie about your life, *Jab I Fart?*"

He laughed outrageously at his own witticism. I let him have a little fun at my expense—I'm not touchy. Besides, Rafique Irani knows everyone and his uncle in the city. I was at his spacious sea-facing office in Nariman Point. The corpulent and jovial Irani is India's Recycling King and his life's ambition is to be on the *Forbes* list of Asia's richest entrepreneurs. I am sure he will get there. Besides collecting truckloads of old newspapers, plastics, and bottles every day and sending them to China by the shipload, he's also a personal collector of antiques—especially *Titanic* memorabilia. He has quite a collection which he showed me once at his Worli residence.

One of his kinks—in a long list—is that he doesn't like neighbors. So he bought the whole building and converted it into a private museum with the top floor as his residence. He's one moneybag in Mumbai I have a sneaking affection for. He has a sense of humour—the Parsi kind—and doesn't take himself too seriously. I got to know him because I had once given him a hot tip that a certain liquor baron was moving in for the kill to buy a rare pair of Roman wine goblets from a source in Istanbul. Rafique Irani beat him to it in a photo finish. I was at his house that night when he opened one of the rarest single-malt bottles on earth—to celebrate. I really couldn't figure out what all the fuss was about. It tasted like booze.

After he had calmed down a bit, I showed him the list and gave him a camouflaged outline of the case I was on. I urged him to identify the three most likely film financiers with underworld connections. He studied it for five minutes, picked up a pen, and circled a name. "Here's my shortlist of one."

I looked at the name he had circled in red—*Dr. Prem Pardeshi*. I wondered about the subject of his thesis.

"You're sure?"

"As sure as the sun will rise tomorrow and a politician will take a bribe."

"Do you know him?"

"Nope. I know about him from my business sources."

"Thanks. Anything I can do for you?"

"Yes, Shorty. Get me the Kohinoor diamond. My fiftieth birthday is just round the corner." He burst into his boisterous laugh again.

"Sure," I said. "Give me a couple of days to talk to the queen."

For the next four days I was busier than a pandit during marriage season. I was on Pardeshi's tail like a man possessed. I wanted to bring an honorable closure to this case to salvage my self-esteem—I was not ready yet for Konduskar's description of a "washed-out" private detective.

I used every trick in the trade to shadow him. Pardeshi was a man you could easily lose in a crowd—fiftyish, short, frail, and nondescript. I hired a retired policewoman to help with the shadow work. She is very good at tailing people in the guise of an old woman selling flowers. Part of her old police work.

By the third day we had a good fix on Pardeshi's routine. He would kiss his tired-looking wife goodbye at the door of his apartment at Buena Vista in Pali Hill and head straight for a sleazy massage parlor in Santa Cruz called Tasty Bites.

Two hours later he would be on his way to a bar in Andheri named Natasha's Nest. I followed him inside on the third day. I was in disguise—wearing thick specs—and sat at one of the distant barstools sipping a Bombay beer, the least pricey one in the joint. He had a forlorn expression on his face—typical of afternoon drinkers. He ordered another drink and something to eat which looked like omelet and bread. I ordered a grilled cheese-and-tomato sandwich to while away the time.

His next stop was at a building in Lokhandwala complex—one of the biggest concrete jungles after Gurgaon. He was there for barely forty-five minutes—presumably in his office. Maybe the film finance business was at a low ebb; how much of the same old shit can the public really take? Then he got into his heavily tinted black Accord and was most likely headed home—for a well-deserved siesta. I followed him in my hired-for-the-day rickshaw to the base of the Hill, like I had done the previous two days. I have used Mustafa's services on tailing assignments before—he doesn't talk much, is the soul of discretion, and is an expert driver in Mumbai's saturated traffic. And, as a bonus, his rickshaw is spotlessly clean. I like that.

On the fourth day I got the break I was looking for. Pardeshi skipped his massage—or whatever—and was heading toward Juhu beach. He seemed to be in a major hurry judging from the persistent honking. I had a strong hunch he would connect with Chingari—on orders from his bosses in Dubai, Karachi, Colombo, or god knows where.

My hunch was right. He drove into a gate of a two-story bungalow which had all the signs of a safe house—still, quiet, eerie. We waited across the road and Mustafa pretended to change a tire so that we wouldn't attract too much attention. I gave him precise instructions.

I was on edge but ready with my act.

In about fifteen minutes the black car came out of the gate. I couldn't see too well because of the heavy tint but I was reasonably sure there was no one else in the car except Pardeshi and his young driver.

I made my move. I was going to make a very high-risk pizza delivery.

I entered the gate, walked up the driveway, and rang the bell next to the heavy door. Nothing happened so I rang again. Now I could hear some activity inside.

"Who's that?" a gruff voice said in Hindi.

"Domino's Pizza, sir."

"I haven't ordered any pizza-wizzah. Get lost," the voice barked.

"This is a free promotion offer, sir, of our new kheema and karela pizza." I recited this in an American BPO accent.

The door opened. No one can resist a free pizza!

It was Salim Chingari all right—all dressed up to make a quick exit from the safe house. He didn't get very far; I had him right where I wanted him. He was looking at the barrel of my licensed gun in extreme close-up.

"Sorry about the pizza, sir. The promotion just expired."

Though grouchy, Konduskar kept his promise. He booked Chingari on multiple charges—extortion, assault and battery, unlawful confinement, among others. The next day Chingari spilled the beans and begged for a fix of heroin. He was not so tough after all. What worried me was that he was an escape artist—from jails. But then, I am not his keeper, only his finder.

The Nagpada cops and I traced Jasmine that night—not in very good shape but alive. She had been kept as a "prisoner of obsessive love" by Chingari—the hophead fixer of Nagpada. She was in a nursing home in Lower Parel—why there's no Upper Parel, I have no idea—shot full of sedatives to ease the pain inflicted by a horsewhip. When Jasmine was well enough I took her "home"—to Hawa Bai's high-class whorehouse where she belonged. She didn't have anywhere else to go. The story of so many young and hapless girls, from all parts of the country, who are tricked into this business by ruthless agents working for entrenched establishments like Hawa Bai's.

It was a touching reunion—even for a hardened private detective pushing fifty.

"Come and spend a night with one of my girls when you're feeling blue, handsome," Hawa Bai said in her imperious tone, handing me the rest of the money.

"Maybe." I took the cash and left.

The next morning I called up Rafique Irani at his office.

"Mr. Irani, the queen has graciously consented. She wants to present the rock to you in person. When would be convenient?"

"Tell her majesty I'll be there before she can say East India Company." I could hear the guffaw.

"The case is closed. I found the girl."

"Good for you, Shorty. Was it worth it?"

"Yes."

"Come over for a drink tonight. I want to hear the details. This raddi business is getting me down."

"Sure," I said. "And I'll pick up some biryani from Altaf's on my way."

He's a big pushover for gourmet biryani. In his private museum there's a set of vintage copper and brass biryani cooking handis from the Mughal era.

Rafique Irani had company when I walked into his penthouse. His lady love, I presumed, from their body language.

"I am Behroze Ichaporia," she introduced herself. "And you're Shorty Gomes, of course. I have heard so much about you and your exploits from Raf."

"Don't believe a word of it, Miss Ichaporia. It's pretty dull stuff: all in a day's work. Our friend here exaggerates and embellishes things to make my work sound interesting, like advertising."

"You are being modest, Mr. Gomes." She had a pleasant resonance in her voice.

"No, I am not. I am being realistic."

As the evening progressed, I discovered she was a self-made Mumbai woman—independent, smart, empathetic, and full of life. Another collectors' item for Irani. After we were suitably oiled on the expensive cactus juice—she had a good appetite for the stuff—she pulled the old, hoary question on me: "Tell me, Mr. Gomes: if you were not a private detective what would you be?"

"An undertaker," I said. "The business is steady."

Two weeks later I was drinking my second cup of tea at Kayani's, glancing at the headlines in the morning newspaper—full of scams in politics, sports, agriculture, defense, industry, finance, entertainment, you name it. The same old pasteurized story—with monotous, clockwork regularity. How much more of this brazen looting can the people take? I wondered. Compared to these plunderers, Genghis Khan was a rookie just learning the ropes. There was little point being a "crime-buster" in these loaded, free-for-all times. As Konduskar had implied at our meeting in Nagpada, what was the sense of putting the small fry behind bars?

As I was punishing my brains with these weighty questions, a minor news item in the inside pages caught my attention. The headline read: *Dreaded Criminal Escapes from Judicial Custody*.

Salim Chingari had done it again. His MO was the soul of simplicity. While being taken for a court appearance in a police van he had faked a very convincing fainting fit—frothing from the mouth and all. The two flustered cops drove him to a nearby hospital for emergency treatment. Chingari made his escape from the hospital brandishing a surgeon's scalpel. The two cops were suspended, pending an internal inquiry. You know what that means.

So here I was, back to square one. Easy come, easy go, I ruminated. It made my day.

That afternoon I packed my meager possessions from my flophouse and decided to go where I belonged.

My old landlady was very understanding. Waiving the half-month's rent, she said: "Bring me some Goan sausages if you decide to come back, Shorty."

"I will, Mrs. D'Costa," I said. Though there wasn't much chance of that.

I took the night Volvo to Goa and slept like a baby. The vodka-and-lime mixture helped.

When I landed at Panaji, I felt alive and ready to start all over again.

THE BODY IN THE GALI

BY SMITA HARISH JAIN

Kamathipura

Radhana's hamam was as disgusting a place as I had expected. Located at a petrol station in Panvel, near one end of the Mumbai–Pune Expressway, it was a haven for lonely truckers and sexually transmitted diseases. Subhash Mehta was found in a gali behind the eunuch bathhouse, lying in a large puddle of his own blood, which was still trickling from his groin when my men got there. His genitals had been hacked off, leaving him with only a two-inch penis stub and parts of his scrotal sac.

By the time my havaldar and I drove to the hamam, the gali was cordoned off with police tape. On the outside of the barrier, a handful of reporters who had found their way to the remote location jockeyed for camera position. On the inside, a group of garishly made-up women, residents of the hamam, pleaded with a constable to let them return to their guru, insisting they hadn't seen a thing; khaki-clad officers took measurements and collected samples from the body and the area surrounding it, recording each item in a notebook and placing the samples into small plastic bags for analysis.

I worked my way through the activity, toward the narrow space where Subhash lay—spread-eagled on his back, naked.

"Bloody hell, yaar. Who would do this?"

The senior constable, one of the small minority of Indian Christians living in Mumbai, crossed himself and mumbled a short prayer. Other constables walked near the body to take a closer look at what had become of their colleague, a rising star in the Mumbai police crime branch. Some uttered a short blessing; most checked themselves below their belts.

A group of constables remained on the periphery, craning their necks to see over the shoulders of those surrounding the body, but keeping their distance. There is an even divide in Mumbai between those who believe in the power of the eunuchs and those who don't. Hijras were believed to be honored ascetics, conveyers of holy power, custodians of procreation; and what is more important than that? Not a surprising sentiment in the second most populous country in the world.

"Eh, come here!" I shouted. I was as disgusted by the hijra culture as those constables, but a member of my branch had died, and someone was going to pay. The gali snapped to attention, and the senior constable scrambled to meet me.

"Sir, we have secured the area. There is one witness; we are talking with him now."

I turned in the direction he indicated. Two constables stood with a slight man wearing an '80s-style safari suit and a terrified stare. One constable jotted notes on a small pad, as the other tried to coax more information from the textbook salesman. A.J. Reddy had stopped for petrol in the middle of the night, on his way home to Pune.

"There is one woman only—older, wearing a sari. She tells the men what to do," the witness said.

"How many men?" one constable asked.

"It was dark. I'm not sure." He closed his eyes, as if to envision the scene. "Must be five or six."

"Then what happened?"

"One man, he has a knife. The lady says, *Make the subinspector pay.* Then she leaves. I run, before they come after me.

I hear a man scream. So loud, it is." He stopped to catch his breath. "I run faster to my car, but the women . . . the people from the hamam come outside to the gali. They see me and scream that I do this. But I don't do this!" His voice broke, and he looked at the constables, frightened.

I left them to finish the interview and turned back to the senior constable. "Where are the others?" I asked.

"Some we have questioned and released. The rest are inside."

I motioned my havaldar to follow me, and we made our way to the hamam.

The cement walls and corrugated roof of the crumbling structure smelled of urine, sweat, and desperation. A sign on the outside advertised a menu of offerings: *Tea—Rs. 6; Cold Water—Rs. 8; Toilet—Rs. 2.* At the bottom of the list was a painted picture of a condom with no price next to it—safety, with room for negotiation.

My havaldar inspected the grounds while I looked around the inside. I stood as close to the door as I could, opting for the smell of gasoline over what was waiting for me in there: pink walls sporting pictures of the available hijra prostitutes, seductive smiles on their faces. I wondered about the type of men who came here.

"Inspector?"

I turned to find the head prostitute, the one called Rani, standing in the doorway of the room she shared with three others. I moved inside, pulling my feet under me with each step.

The space was divided into four makeshift cubbies—on one side, shelves stacked with personal belongings; on the other, a small mirror and makeup table. In the back, a woman finished dressing; near her, another made her bed. Sex workers covering up their night's work.

Rani saw my lips curl and came to her sisters' defense.

"It wasn't always like this. We hijras used to be respected. People welcomed us to bless their sons and their marriage unions. Then the nakli ones came, the fake ones. Men who can make children, but who want to enjoy our success. So they dress like us and act like us and come to all the marriage and birth functions, until we are left with no other way to make money, but this." She raised both hands in a wide stretch that indicated the whole room.

I looked around the austere space, filled with only what was necessary for the eunuchs to ply their trade: beds, makeup stands, and a rack of beaded and glittery clothing straight from a roadside shop in Bandra. My stomach lurched.

"How did Subhash Mehta come to be in your gali?" I asked, ending her diatribe and returning us to the reason I was there.

The others in the room stopped what they were doing and focused on Rani. Her lips quivered, and she bit them to keep them steady. She lowered her eyes before answering. "He came often, he took care of his business, then he left."

"Are you saying Subhash Mehta was a . . ." I stumbled over the word, "customer?" An image of Subhash lying in the gali, turned into a eunuch, flashed in my mind.

Rani turned her head, but not before I saw her exchange a quick glance with the other two hijra prostitutes in the room. All three remained quiet.

Before I could stop myself, I raised my hand and brought it down hard against Rani's cheek. She collapsed to the floor.

"Haramzadi! Bitch! Tell the truth!"

The other two took a step in her direction, but stopped when I raised my hand.

I dropped to the floor, ready to strike Rani again. She crossed her arms in front of her face and buried her head under them. I recoiled at the sight of what I had done. It was common practice amongst my colleagues to take advantage of the uniform, but I had always avoided such confrontations. Subhash's brutal murder changed things. I stood and moved away from her.

After several moments, she looked out from under her arms. "Inspector, we are not the ones you should be investigating." She spoke softly. "It is the fake ones who are responsible. We are like this from birth." She pointed to the area between her legs. "My brother and I used to pull on it, to try and make it bigger; but this is how God wants it." She swiped at a tear that rolled down her cheek.

Once the God card was played, there was no room to disagree.

The practice of prostitution in hijra bathhouses was known to my higher-ups, and they turned the other cheek—some of them, rumor had it, in the bathhouses themselves. But Subhash . . . it didn't make any sense.

I had enough to file a first information report, but the real story of what had happened to Subhash in the gali last night remained hidden.

Two weeks before his murder, I had scheduled Subhash to work with me, to cover the state elections. Bahujan Samaj Party activists were expected to confront Shiv Sena–BJP members, in an effort to disrupt what was being predicted as a landslide victory for the latter's candidates. The issue on everyone's mind was safety. The increase in the migrant population of the city was having far-reaching impacts on infrastructure, crime, and even health care. Without proper representation at the state level, funds could easily go to other parts of Maharashtra and away from Mumbai. Every available member of the Mumbai police force was deployed for crowd control. Subhash and I were assigned to the Shiv Sena rally at the Parsi Gymkhana grounds.

"What took you so long?" I asked Subhash when he finally arrived at the Azad Maidan police station in Colaba, forty-five minutes late. Despite the nearly twenty-year difference in age, ours had been an easy collegiality.

"Late night," he said with a grin.

Despite my irritation at having to wait, I had to smile at his boyish gloating. On many occasions, Subhash had filled our ears with stories of Bollywood starlets he'd met at some big director's house party, or socialite girls whose fathers had been only too happy to see their precious daughters with a member of Mumbai's finest. The class division, otherwise rampant in the city, didn't seem to touch Subhash.

It was ten o'clock in the morning, so traffic was still light as we drove to Parsi Gymkhana. Some businesses were opening their doors; many others remained dark. We drove three kilometers north on Marine Drive, looking at hotels and residential buildings on our right and the smog-coated view of the Arabian Sea on our left.

The exteriors of most buildings were covered with black and dirt—the city's beauty hidden under decades of slow decay. Scooters zigzagged between cars; their drivers kept helmets within reach, in case they spotted a policeman. Beggar children came to the car: "Saab, I want to eat. I'm hungry. Mahashay." High-rises, some of the more prominent of the city, sported clotheslines threaded across their balconies, the day's wash fluttering in the breeze coming from the Arabian Sea. Untethered men hammered eighteen stories up, building even more structures in an already filled skyline. Pigeons squatted on rooftops and fed along the shore.

Everywhere signs and billboards told you what to do: *Stay in Your Lanes*; *No Honking Unless Necessary*; *Stick No Bills*; *Don't Answer the Call of Death: Cell Phone or Hell Phone?* Most people ignored the street signs. Even the red-light timers on many traffic stops, to tell cars when to turn off their engines— an effort to keep down petrol costs, pollution, and the road rage created while waiting for the light to turn green—did little to calm the constantly frayed nerves of Mumbai drivers. Here, tradition and modernity, fertility and asceticism, excess and poverty lived within the same city limits.

Two cricket stadiums and a hockey stadium later, we turned right onto the grounds of Parsi Gymkhana, an open-air lawn and clubhouse commonly used for public functions, press conferences, and weddings. Cylinders filled with liquid propane gas clustered in a corner outside a collection of sheds set up as temporary kitchens, where food for the day's events would be prepared.

I parked in the makeshift lot at one end of the large field where the rally was to take place. The lawn was packed with Bollywood elite, media, and state officials. The average Mumbaikar was barely represented, reflecting the city's low voter turnout of the past decade and a half.

Despite pleas from Mumbai's glitterati, most of the city's residents shunned local politics. State officials tried to claim that school exam schedules, high temperatures, and the busy April–May wedding season were to blame for the poor showing at the polling stations. The reality for many Mumbaikars, however, was that their lack of interest was a function of apathy and indifference—a belief that their vote wouldn't result in the change they wanted, so why bother?

Those who did show up at the Gymkhana came with an agenda. Protestors carried signs accusing the Shiv Sena–BJP alliance of everything from defamation to violent attacks. Sena backers showed their support by screaming obscenities at the opposing group. Police constables watched the proceedings closely, lathi charge sticks at the ready.

At the front of the rally, local Shiv Sena leader Mukesh Sinha worked the crowd into a frenzy. The majority party leader had already discussed the potential loss of infrastructure support funds if BJP candidates weren't sent to the state assembly, and he had moved on to health care.

"When we consider the alarming rate at which AIDS is spreading in the city," he said, "we can easily identify the culprit—the growing hijra community of prostitutes and sex workers. We must make an example of them and those who keep them in business."

The onlookers applauded their assent. This hard-right sentiment was exactly what this crowd had gathered to hear, the same conservative pandering that had brought the Hindu nationalist party to its current position of power.

"We can set an example for the other cities of India, and even of the world." The crowd erupted again and added cheers to its applause. The leader of the largest local presence of the Shiv Sena–BJP alliance was as militant and ambitious as they came. With the elections looming, the dissolution of the hijra gharanas in Mumbai had become a hot-button issue, and many politicians saw it as just the feather in their cap needed to win seats in the state assembly. What lengths would he go to to win? I wondered.

* * *

Radhana's hamam, like so many in the city, was under the jurisdiction of one guru, Rekha Devi. As head of the most powerful gharana in Mumbai, she would have the answers I needed.

The drive to Kamathipura took us to the only place in the city more seedy than the truck stop. The galis of Kamathipura, Mumbai's oldest red-light district, boasted every manner of sexual gratification imaginable, from conventional prostitutes to eunuchs to the area's crowning glory, child virgins.

The late-morning April air was thick with heat and pollution. My havaldar and I traveled in noisy air-conditioning along Mahatma Gandhi Marg until we picked up Kalbadevi Road near Metro Cinema in Dhobi Talao. Just past the cinema, the usual mixture of people waited outside the red-painted plaster façade of Delhi Darbar, home of the best biryani in Mumbai.

Along the way, we passed more mandirs than we could count, making the godlessness of our destination a mirthless joke. All around us we saw traders hawking their wares in shops lining the streets—watches, steel cutlery, books, ready-made clothes, designer saris, bicycles. Two lanes, one in each direction, became three or four, as cars made their own passing lanes. Buses, trucks, cars, and auto-rickshaws shared the road with cows, goats, stray dogs, and even an ox cart; dogs crossed the street with the same nonchalance as pedestrians, a casual look over their shoulder to acknowledge the honking horns but not to obey them. During peak hours, Kalbadevi Road could rival the daily traffic of Peddar Road.

Our descent was a gradual one. We passed the Cotton Exchange building, Paydhuni Jain Temple, and parked in Iqbal Chowk, from where we walked—through Bhindi Bazaar, Null Bazaar, Chor Bazaar—until we reached Kamathipura. The changing images along our route peeled back the city's secret: a cosmopolitan veil hiding layers of desperate reality.

Most of the hijra prostitutes worked out of Gali No. 1, on the south side of Kamathipura; but Rekha Devi made her home in Peela House, site of the notorious hijra cages of Kamathipura.

Once in the gali, we were accosted by the compounded smell of garbage, urine, and feces. Open drains, naalis filled with excrement, lined both sides, the air thick with the suffocating odor. Ramshackle structures stacked two high offered glimpses of the activity inside: cots with thin mattresses and no sheets; cloth curtains separating one-meter by two-meter spaces, with room enough for two people in a horizontal position; bare walls revealing nothing about the sex workers who rented space by the customer.

Nearby, a group of women wearing loud Maharashtrian saris—jeweled greens and fuchsias and sapphires—their nails painted in gaudy colors, thick coats of lipstick, kaajal, and powder covering their faces, tried to cajole money from passersby.

One of the hijra women pressed a button on a large, portable sound system and, as soon as the music started, she and the other eunuchs began their dance, sexually suggestive to the point of burlesque, even going so far as to include audience members, whom they coaxed with come-hither gestures and forced hand-holding. They danced with abandon—hairy, muscular arms waving about in a frantic and jubilant display.

One hijra teased the small group that had gathered by grabbing the front of her sari and lifting it ever higher, grinding her hips to the music, the motions seductive enough to make me forget what she was.

Most people in the gali stood—this was a place to transact business, not sit and rest. In every square meter, prostitutes competed with street vendors and shops for their share of visitor money. Eunuchs, dressed in only what was necessary to advertise their wares—jeans and cropped tops, ghagras and dupattas, saris barely disguising the absence of a blouse—called out to the passing men, promising unheard-of delights available only in Kamathipura.

When we arrived at Peela House, we were greeted by the head of the commune, Rekha Devi herself, who was wearing a white sari and little makeup. I guessed her age to be about forty-five.

"Come with me," she said, leading us toward a small shack outside.

We walked along a dirt path behind Peela House, watching eunuch women in various stages of transformation. Two of them sat laughing, grabbing at each other both playfully and sexually. In another spot, a eunuch sat on a stool holding a hand-mirror, plucking out her facial hairs one at a time; others along the way brushed their long hair in the open air; painted their nails, examining each one as they finished; and gossiped.

I watched as a large, thick woman pushed two balls of cloth down a young boy's blouse and shaped the clumps into breasts. Her hands massaged the area under the boy's shirt, caressing what was in there. When she was done, she drew her hands out slowly and cupped the boy's face.

"These will do until the medicine starts to work," she said. "Then you will grow your own." She was almost maternal in her touch—maternal and sexual, at the same time.

"Inspector," the guru said.

I looked away and found that we had arrived at the shack.

Once inside, we sat on folding iron chairs—the guru's in the center of the room, my havaldar's and mine across from her. In the corner, several hijra women sat in a cluster, listening.

"None of my chelas would do this, inspector," she said, indicating the women. "They are all my daughters. They are not involved in what you're investigating."

"A witness saw several men in the gali outside your hamam, taking orders from a hijra," I reminded her.

"Anyone dressed like us could have entered the gali," she countered.

"Are you suggesting that hijra imposters castrated Sub-hash Mehta? Why would they do that? Putting you in a bad light puts them in one too!" I resented her quiet confidence, her silent ridicule, her unspoken certainty that I couldn't touch her.

Rekha Devi summoned one of the hijra women to her. The chela sat at her feet and placed her head in Rekha's lap. Her face was covered with knife cuts, the red color suggesting they had been made recently.

"What happened to her?" I asked the guru.

"She tried to run from one of the nakli ones, one who was trying to sell her to his friends. So he made sure she couldn't work for anyone else. She stays with me, but she does not talk of the incident. He cut out her tongue, called her a whore, told her she was good for nothing else."

She rubbed the chela's head with slow strokes. The two women sat in quiet misery, eyes closed, the guru rocking them back and forth. Then, as if remembering I was there, she re-sumed our conversation.

"We are not the zenanas, inspector, homosexual men who join our ranks only to enjoy relations with other men, or to profit from their own deviance. We are true ascetics, who sur-vive so we can carry out our divine charge. Many men come to us—old and young, married and unmarried, fathers and those with no children—because God has given them a taste for what only we can give, so hijras can survive, so we have a way to earn a living."

"Doesn't carrying out your charge mean growing your numbers, creating others like you?" I recalled what had been done to Subhash in the gali and found myself shouting at her.

"Those who come to us come of their own accord. They undergo the nirvan, the emasculation, by choice."

"You have hundreds of daughters . . ." I hesitated at my use of that word, "in the city. How can you be sure none of them were involved?"

"Perhaps you need to see the nirvan to understand. Come back in two days' time, and you will know." With that, she stood and left the shack.

My havaldar and I made our way back to our Qualis. Outside, we passed three hijra girls sitting across from an older eunuch. They watched intently as she explained the proper use of a condom, using a wooden dowel.

I returned to the Azad Maidan police station to file my report, such as it was. My team had worked nonstop since the discovery of Subhash's body three days before. Despite eyewitness testimony, extensive lab work, expert analysis, and test identification parades, my investigation had turned up nothing. With no hard evidence, no way to identify the author of the crime, I had yet to file a single charge sheet.

The next day, with no other leads to follow, I set about the task of cleaning out Subhash's desk, reducing his career to the contents of a plastic bag. His keys and other personal effects sat in an envelope on the top of his desk. I pulled out the small chain that had been on Subhash's person from the time he joined the crime branch. Only one drawer was locked, the big one at the bottom.

I reached in and removed its contents—a sheaf of papers with columns of writing, four wads of thousand-rupee bills, and a stack of about twenty eight-by-ten full-body shots of eunuchs in various stages of undress, posed to attract a certain audience. On the backs of the pictures, in Subhash's hand-writing, were notations: *Rs. 6,000, 4 hours. Rs. 15,000, full day, multiple visitors.*

I felt the blood drain from my face. Names I recognized—Bollywood royalty, political kingpins, even members of our own crime branch—crowded onto three pages from a school composition book, each announcing their preference: *Vaginal tattoos. Two at a time. Children.* The pictures fell to the floor as I tried to process the clashing images before me: a decorated police inspector, a trusted colleague, a willing felon.

By the time I arrived at Peela House, the sun had already been up for four hours. Groups of young men were gathered across the road, casting surreptitious glances at the house, likely hoping for glimpses of what happened behind its infamous walls. Next door, two men stood by a movie banner under the sign for the Alfred Cinema and shared a cigarette. Nearby, a bicycle waited for its owner at the VD clinic offering *100% cures* for AIDS.

I made my way along a dirt path on one side of Peela House lined with cages, where fifty rupees would rent you a sweaty bed and a eunuch for fifteen minutes. The path ended at a locked, wrought-iron gate, where two hijra women granted me access to the main compound. I ducked under a rough canopy of neem trees into a small courtyard, hidden from the prying eyes in the bazaars along the roadside.

Rekha Devi and her chelas were assembled there, awaiting my arrival. They were dressed not in ceremonial clothing, as I had expected, but rather in everyday salwar suits and saris, in muted colors and modest styles. Rekha Devi nodded, and a group of hijras started their dance, moving in a circle, chanting the name of their mother goddess, Bahuchara Mata. One man stood naked in the middle, his head lolling from side to side, as if he was drugged. A woman stood before him, a dark metal object in her hand, a knife whose blade had lost its glint many nirvan ago. The chanting grew louder, and I watched the knife wielder sharpen her instrument on a large stone. She did not clean it before she used it. In one quick motion, she grabbed the penis and testicles of the man before her and swiped at them with the blade. One precise cut removed all the genitalia. The body parts fell to the ground, and the women moved around them in a frenzied state. Two of them clutched the arms of the newly emasculated man and walked him around. Blood poured out between his legs. The chanting reached a fever pitch, and I turned and vomited till there was nothing left inside me.

When I came back up for air, they were still walking her around, shouting for all the maleness to bleed out.

Rekha Devi took a slow, deep breath. "My daughter," she whispered. After several moments, she turned to me. "You see, inspector. Our cuts are clean. No one will look at Subhash Mehta and believe we had anything to do with his death."

She smiled and reached her hand out to me. She knew.

A SUITABLE GIRL

BY ANNIE ZAIDI

Mira Road

To understand food, you have to eat out in the Petrol Pump area. The city is mostly dead to food. Bandra-Versova is all sho-sha. I lived there, so I know. Most people go to restaurants because they don't know what else to do when they go out. They sit on hard chairs and keep calculating whether or not the bill will be worth it. Do film stars eat here? Has anybody said in the papers that this place has good food?

In Petrol Pump, I know people who go out to eat because there is nothing to eat in their houses. Or because it is some-body's mother's birthday. These are sensible reasons to eat out.

No place has good food in Petrol Pump, yet all the restau-rants have people eating in them. This is the great thing about Mira Road. Great cities are built of this quality—the necessity of being here and people's grudging acceptance of situations. If you fuss too much about how bad it is, you will not survive it. And if you don't survive, what does?

Daddy wasn't so hard to deal with before he started rationing. I always thought that after Mom died and I left the house—I wonder why I was so sure it would happen in that sequence—he'd go to pieces. He'd drink too much. His liver would go bust. He wouldn't eat. The maid would see all that food choking up the fridge and she would stop cooking. I might drop by unexpectedly and scream at her. Some day, I imagined, I'd make Daddy eat well—fruit, salad, steamed carrots, boiled halwa for dessert. He might even eat it, nostalgic for what we meant to each other, and missing Mom's scolding about his health.

But things never work to a plan, do they? Mom died and Daddy grew afraid of dying. Now he carefully measures out a generous shot of rum and drinks it slowly, a sip at a time, mixed with warm water. He's begun eating sprouts for breakfast. He even exercises in the balcony. Pranayams and surya namaskars. I can't stand it.

One Sunday morning, I gave him my practiced speech. I said I wanted my own property. Property needs watching, so I'd have to leave for a while. I'd still come by every other day. I wanted to do my own thing. So I needed a home-office type of place.

I wasn't looking at him while I spoke because I thought he'd get senti and start saying stuff like, *But where's the need?* or he might offer to let me use the guest room as my office. I had an excuse ready. I was going to say that I couldn't possibly put him through it—strangers visiting, ringing the bell all day. Besides, he was allergic to fur.

But Daddy didn't get senti. He just said I should find a man quick, that was my only hope.

I would have packed my bags that Sunday. But there was nothing under thirty lakhs on either side of the Western Express Highway. Brokers heard my budget and they all said the same thing: Mira-Bhayandar.

I was resigned to staying on at home for another year and starting my business slowly but then Daddy upset my plans again. Last week, he said it a second time: "Find a man, then do what you want."

This time I snapped back. I said I wanted to live on my own terms, not exchange one bully for another.

His brows went up but the hand holding his bottle of Old Monk didn't shake. He poured a little into the glass, added warm water, took a sip. Then he asked: "Where are you off to? Mira-Bhayandar?"

She is always forgetting. The first time we met she forgot her umbrella in the bucket outside Ruff Ruff. I called after her. Four times. Madam, madam, oh madam, hello madam. But she walked straight on.

Then there was the day I sat beside her. I thought it would be easy. Everyone joins the line, calling out their street names. Petrol-Petrol-Petrol Pump? Sheetal-Sheetal-Sheetal?

When three people have said it, they point to each other, fall into the pact of a shared ride, and wait to find an auto. All three squeeze in, thigh against thigh. One of the team barks "Sheetal" to the driver. The auto jiggles, swerves, bumps along. Three people rub shoulders, elbows in each other's waists, thighs aligned, riding in total silence for ten minutes. Then we fumble for five rupees, and then it is over. It should have been easy.

But in life, nothing is easy. I waited outside the station for six days, between nine p.m. and midnight. I had already noted that I never see her in Mira Road before nine. Train after train went past that day, and for four days after that. But I didn't see her. On the sixth night, I finally spotted her. I rushed forward, got in line ahead of her, and began calling: "Sheetal-Sheetal?"

She just stood there, sullenly staring at the big round eye of oncoming autos, blinded. My heart sank then. She wasn't willing to share!

There are such people in Mira Road too. They don't share.

I have been here thirteen years and everything was okay until five years ago. Now, some girls are too sensitive. They glance around wild-eyed, worried about who they might have to share an auto with. What's the worry? A man will not eat you. But such women will not respond when you call out. They wait for other women to start calling—Lodha-Lodha-Lodha, Sheetal-Sheetal.

This girl is worse. She doesn't want to share an auto even with other women. For a moment, I was very angry. But I didn't give up. That is one of my good qualities. I don't give up easily. Because I know how life changes you. Everything that was impossible yesterday will become possible tomorrow.

I kept watching her, kept waiting for her at the station. Since the monsoon started, the roads are worse and people don't form the unwritten pact-of-three to share a ride back home, nor do they patiently wait in line. Everyone lunges at the gleaming eye of autos juddering up. They grab the metallic skeleton of the auto and almost hurl themselves in. Even the buses aren't spared. There is always someone else—stronger, fatter, more aggressive—who cuts into the line ahead of her. Someone like her doesn't stand a chance.

Poor girl. I feel sorry for her. She stands in the rain, biting her lower lip, tears rising to her eyes as auto after auto gets hijacked by packs of commuters who bring a ferocious urgency to their hunt for transportation. She cannot bring herself to race against them, or elbow aside the competition.

For a week after the rains began, I let her suffer. When I thought she had learned her lesson, I decided to try again. I joined the line and called out loudly: "Sheetal-Sheetal!"

Small as a mouse, her voice struggled over my shoulder. "Sheetal?"

I turned and looked at her face closely for the first time.

She was standing less than a foot away. I nodded and we stood side by side, waiting until another man called out: "Sheetal?" A white-cap man with a beard. He climbed into the auto first. She hesitated and glanced at me. I got in ahead of her, then she too bent her head and climbed in.

We rode together for ten minutes. Her hips were warm against mine and so were her arms as they gathered up her chest. She did not turn to look at me though. She didn't remember seeing me at Ruff Ruff. But everything has its time and place. She will have time to remember afterward.

I often step out with the feeling that something is missing, or about to go wrong. Doesn't that happen? You pause at your door, keys in hand, waiting. For the phone to ring perhaps. Or you suspect you are forgetting something. Umbrella? Glasses? Wallet? Tiffin? Chewies? Mobile? Hair band?

It happens a lot to me these days. I peek into my tote, check for items I cannot afford to forget. Then I shake my head vigorously and pull the door shut. I have to stop being paranoid. It isn't like I have to swipe in at work. If I forget something, I can always turn around and go home. Nobody's going to e-mail an office memo. My KRAs won't slide.

It's brilliant. I don't have to worry about leave or promotions. As long as I can find even two clients a month, I'm okay. But the salary mentality doesn't disappear so easily. I tell myself, Daddy's there, worse comes to worst. But Daddy has the most terrible job in the world. No hope of promotion or raise, no holidays. Still, I can always go back to the house. And he wouldn't let me starve if I returned.

If only I could work from Juhu. Mira Road makes everything harder. Just getting out and coming back crushes the sanity out of me. Like last night, when I tried getting on the 10:21. The crowd was manageable, but one aunty tried to push past me. I got up on the footboard and blocked her with my arm. Other women scrambled on and off, but I stood obstructing half the doorway until the aunty swung her bag at me and boarded, screaming, "Where are you from, man? Where do all you people come from?"

I occupied the fourth seat, turned my back to her, but she kept at it, all the way to Mira Road. As she was getting off, ahead of me, I stuck my foot in her path. She tumbled onto the platform and lay there panting in a heap. I ran up the stairs but stood watching her from the overpass. She lay there for a good two minutes before someone hauled her to her feet.

I found her outdoors, buying carrots. I was standing in my usual place near the laundry. She did not recognize me.

I don't mind. Why should she remember a man she shared an auto with? She didn't even turn her head to look at me, not once. But I like her more for it. It is a sign of character. It is a good sign.

Or maybe she is farsighted. I think I would like it if she was. I can imagine her being fifty-five years old and picking up a letter from the doormat, squinting at it helplessly. I could then take it from her and read it out loud.

If Mom was alive, she'd have been disappointed. Actually, if Mom was alive, things would not have been this way. She'd have objected to my quitting the bank, objected to my moving out, objected to sharing autos.

This—sitting outside the airport at four in the morning with two hundred rupees in my bag—would have caused a panic attack. Three cups of coffee down, no sign of the flight. I could go inside and wait in the lounge, I guess. I have the permit letters and everything and the customs guys know me well already. But the coffee inside is twice as expensive. And the customs people always ask too many personal questions: Why animals? Why not banking? In that case, why not an NGO? Don't NGOs pay well nowadays? But how will you get home at this time of the night? Pet transportation is all very good, but who will take care of you? Hahaha! Who is your boss? But who is responsible for you then? Where does your father live? He must be worried. Unmarried daughters . . .

I think I can do without all that. It is so much simpler meeting the animals. If you say hello, they just say hello back or ignore you. And that's fine with me. Thank god it is a dog this time. It is supposed to be a black cocker spaniel with one white ear. In a rectangular basket, painted white and sprayed with Lyla's linen perfume. Apparently, Lyla douses her sheets and curtains with perfume before using them. Santa Barbara lifestyle, I guess. The dog has his own deodorant too.

I should have charged more for this. I can still tell Lyla there will be extra expenses for the night I spent waiting at the airport. Plus taxi fare. I'm hoping the flight will be delayed another half hour, then the night rate won't apply.

Daddy is getting so difficult. He's stopped asking if I need anything. I'd usually decline, but he'd offer me five or ten thousand anyway. He'd say, "House-warming present," or, "Overdue birthday present." But he can be nasty about it.

Once, I dropped in when his old colleagues were visiting. Later that afternoon, I had an appointment at the Karjat dog farm, so I got up to go. Daddy told me to wait and handed over some money. He winked at his friends as he held out the cash, and said, "You better find another man to mooch off. I'm just a pensioner now."

Daddy must have thought Mira Road would straighten

me out, that I'd come running back in a month, suitably chastened about harsh realities and rational choices. But now that I've stuck it out five months, he's stopped giving me money. He doesn't even ask Anwar, the driver, to drop me home. I have to ask.

It killed me to ask last time but it was forty degrees outside and I didn't have money for a cab. Daddy finally sent the car but he made a big production out of it. He first asked if he could call a car service instead. Then he shook his head despairingly and finally he rang Anwar, but insisted I wait until the driver had eaten his lunch.

I said I'd wait. But Daddy didn't ask if I wanted any lunch. So instead I asked him if he was hungry. He sneered at me and said I could go ahead without him.

I went to the fridge and stood with my face against the open freezer. My face felt hot and my eyes brutally dry. I fixed myself two parathas from the ready dough, which I spiced up with coriander and chilies. Finally I crushed a pill into the chutney. I spread the chutney on two slices of toast and told Daddy he should eat it or he'd get acidity again.

Daddy just doesn't leave me a choice. I keep wanting to make him eat better, and I visit regularly, but he doesn't understand my need for space. I too have some rights. I've always had to fight for everything. Even to choose my work. He was the one who gave me Montu. He should understand why I want to work with animals. But no, he will never understand. I will have to fight him forever.

It is easier to fight with pills though. He doesn't know we're fighting and it doesn't hurt either of us. He just falls asleep for a while. I prefer to leave our Juhu house while he is asleep. Anyway, it doesn't hurt to sleep a little extra at his age.

* * *

I finally found out where she goes when she stays out late at night. I kept wondering what she does and then I decided to follow her. She heads to the airport to deliver goods, or to wait for some delivery. I don't know what is inside the packages yet, but sometimes she waits for hours.

It was really distressing to think that she often doesn't return to Mira Road until after midnight. It was painful just to think of where I might find her, and how I'd explain to her that it was not right. I was worried that she would be like the Bandra-Versova girls, standing on the road in knickers, or like that one who had grown up in Mira Road and still would not listen to me, though I tried for so long to explain that it was not right to hang around in the market after dark. For some women, there is no cure except to keep them locked up. But this one is different. I have always known it in my heart. She only stays out late because of her work.

I was just a few steps behind her when she hailed a taxi. I heard the driver ask her, "Domestic or international?" and she said, "International." So I knew she was going to the airport.

I followed in a bus. She could have taken the bus too. A bit of a wastrel, but she will learn. Once we have kids, she will definitely learn to save. I am pleased to see that she isn't irresponsible. Look at the way she goes to visit her father once a week at least, even twice a week sometimes. It is a sign of character.

She takes good care of her old father too. She makes the auto wait while she picks up a bottle at the wine shop, and something at the medical store, each time she goes to visit him. Every day I grow more convinced that she is the right one. A good, responsible girl.

I think her father is very understanding also. He does a

lot for her. The driver drops her home. And the last few times she walked out of his house, her handbag was so full that her shoulder was weighed down by it.

Yesterday I followed her all the way up to her building. She lives on the first floor. I found a ladder and climbed up until I could look into her window. She was pulling things out of her bag. A carton of milk. A bag of basmati rice. Her father is so thoughtful. It is a good family. A solid family.

She is a proud type though. A little too stuck on independence. A lot of girls are. But she knows her limits. She buys alcohol for her father but never drinks herself. I have been watching her trash can and the grills on her windows. There are no empty bottles. She is a really good find. Once I have explained to her about not taking so many taxis, she will learn to save. Together, we will manage.

I glanced at the photo again. Mini's beautiful. She's bitten someone only once, but that was because Juneja had been shouting at her. Dogs take cues easily. When I was given Montu, I was just two and a half. I couldn't talk properly, much less give orders. But Montu mostly knew what I wanted from him. He obeyed my gurgling, my pointing, my screaming.

That's the amazing thing: dogs just know. They do whatever you want; they almost kill themselves trying. In comparison, what rubbish human relationships we drag around. Mom was supposed to love me. Daddy says it even now, after he's had his nightly ration: "I love you, sweetie-pie." Sometimes, it makes me snarl on the inside.

Daddy used to say that Montu spoiled me. I think he did. Loved me so much, nobody measures up. Some nights I lie awake wondering what Montu felt. Him sitting at home, waiting for me to return from school, me petting him for ten minutes, then rushing off to play with other kids. It makes my heart ache to remember Montu.

I'm glad I have to go to Karjat. Being at the farm will be good for me. Juneja won't be there until later and I will have plenty of time to get to know Mini.

I watch her waiting at the airport. She drinks a lot of coffee. I must teach her to switch to tea. Made from fresh cow milk. I still don't know what she is carrying in those big baskets. I have tried standing close to her but she never sits near a crowd. She moves to a corner and sits alone with a cup of coffee from the Nescafé booth.

I stand with the taxi drivers and hotel boys, and hold a placard so I can blend in better. Once or twice, she has looked up in my direction, but she never recognizes me. I even choose a name that I take from the envelopes I find in her trash. Lyla from Santa Barbara. Katie from Sydney. But she never notices.

Some of the drivers who wait with placards at the airport have begun to know my face. They have started asking which hotel I work for. I always name a company in Pune. I say I wait for company officials. Up and down, once a week. That satisfies them. I say Pune because I know the place a little. When I worked in Versova, I was with one Pandit who had a big farmhouse outside Pune which he sometimes rented for film shoots.

Once he took me there. There was a special kind of party and he needed a trustworthy guard. I was supposed to warn him if I saw a police vehicle. I did too, but most of them were so far gone, they didn't run or hide. So they were rounded up and some tested positive for drugs.

The police wanted me to become a witness, identify whose party it was, who came, who left. Pandit found out. He was on bail when he called me to the office. I just kept saying, "What will I do now? Where will I get another job?" He would take care of me, he said. He went on and on about how I should leave Mumbai. He would give me a gold chain and one lakh.

A lakh was nothing. There was nothing even in Mira Road for a lakh. But I didn't want to argue. I promised to leave the city and asked Pandit to give me his blessings. But before I left, I took the keys to his office. There wasn't much kept there but even small things add up to a lot. There was a petty-cash drawer. There was a silver idol of Ganesha. There were names and addresses in a diary. It was enough at first.

I called a few people who were at the party, found addresses. I learned to wait, and to follow. Over six months, I asked for only a little bit. One should not crush people with greed. Like Bapu has said, the world has enough for human need, but not greed. All my small earnings added up to a one-bedroom flat near Petrol Pump. Just six months' work and everybody was happy at the end.

The trouble with people like Pandit is that they don't understand the worth of small things. Small jobs, small savings, small deals, small shops. That is what life is about: Small things. Small connections. Small appetites. It keeps the world healthy.

Juneja turned out to be such a bastard. First, he wanted me to sort out his hound within three days. I asked for a week because Mini was taking longer to respond to the trainers. She took to me like a magnet though. I even called her Montu once or twice, instead of Mini. The farm people asked me to help train her, so I did.

She's got such a gentle heart; I really like her personality. Such a pity Juneja wanted her trained to attack. But then he was paying a lot—me, as well as the Karjat farm. So we were training her to attack strangers whenever we let out a low whistle. In another day or two, she would have been ready to be handed back to Juneja.

But now he's just abandoned Mini. I tried to convince him but he's refusing to take her back. He's got a new Doberman apparently. The farm is feeding Mini at my expense.

I've been calling my clients but it doesn't seem like anyone has room for a hound in this city. My last resort was Daddy. The house is biggish and there's Juhu beach for exercise. I told him I would take care of the grooming and so on. Everything could work out. But he is refusing to take in a dog, saying Anwar will object.

I'm glad Mom isn't around to watch this. Daddy's priorities are so warped. He's more bothered about the driver's religious beliefs than my happiness. And Anwar doesn't really mind. I talked to him about Montu and my work and he even helped me fetch a dog in a basket last week, while Daddy was asleep.

But Daddy's decided to be difficult right now. The mess in the house makes everything worse since he cannot think straight when things aren't in order. He's fired the maid, accusing her of stealing rice and milk cartons. I tried to tell him he was mistaken, that he's never known how much rice there was in the kitchen at any point. But he insists there's some hanky-panky going on. The latest thing is that there's a dangerous man hanging around. Daddy thinks someone's planning a burglary and the maid is in on it. He's afraid she is poisoning the food as well.

When he told me, I just rolled my eyes and called Anwar. I asked, "Do you feel ill when you eat lunch here?"

Anwar said, "Of course not."

Then I shook my head at Daddy. He seemed sort of frightened. But that doesn't stop him from being bull-headed, does
it? He still won't agree to take in Mini.

She wasn't at the airport, arrivals or departures. She doesn't
take the train back home these days. I waited last evening at
the station from six, right up to half past two when the last
train arrived. I even went to her father's place. I put on my old
watchman's uniform and stood outside the building. But there
was no sign of her.

She could have gone out of town for work. I don't know
where though. This is a disturbing thought—I don't know
where she goes, who she meets. It isn't right.

I even thought of going up to her father's flat, but in my
watchman's uniform it was not a good idea. Nobody would tell
me anything.

I spotted the man myself. Daddy took me to the window and
pointed him out. I was exasperated. I said, "He's a watchman,
Daddy! Of course he hangs around; that's what he is paid to do."

But my father wasn't convinced. He kept muttering that
the fellow is always looking at the house. "Directly here. He
knows an old man lives alone."

Daddy was still suspicious about the food. He was hardly
eating. It's like he had an extra sense, though nothing changed
except that he was sleeping two hours in the afternoon and
another hour at night. He felt more tired, that's all. No other
side effects.

I took him for a check-up anyway. Doc said it was just age
and told him to eat better. Daddy began to complain to the
doc about the maid and the planned burglary. Me and the doc
exchanged a look. I rolled my eyes. Then I offered to cook

and keep food stocked in the fridge whenever I visited. Doc turned to Daddy and asked, "Happy? That's what you wanted, right?"

Since then I've been visiting every other day. When I cook, he eats better. But sometimes when I am watching TV or waiting for Anwar to return from some pointless errand, I glance up and find Daddy staring at me. He looks piteous, like a scared kitten.

I usually smile vaguely and leave soon after. Sometimes he calls at night, asks how I am doing. Then I ask if he is okay. He keeps asking what Mira Road is like. I keep telling him he could see for himself, but he refuses. With a great, pretend shudder, he says, "Never! It is on the other side of the world. It is night to Mumbai's day."

She came back to Mira Road last night. I knew because I saw her father's car parked outside her building, and the driver waiting for her. She didn't stay long though. She left with a big bag. Seemed to be in a big hurry.

It is time to move to the next level. Trust cannot be stretched this far. I let her go out at all times. I let her do whatever she does, without asking questions. But every girl has to understand that there are limits. She has to take some responsibility too.

I'm taking Mini. I talked Daddy into it, saying it was the only way to make the house secure. He kept refusing, but I told him it was settled. I made sure we talked in front of Anwar. Daddy said, "He will quit; you wait and see."

I looked at Anwar, who kept staring at the wall. I asked for the car keys then. I said, "Anwar doesn't have to drive the dog around. I can do it myself."

* * *

I followed as quickly as I could. It was a good thing it was after five. The traffic was slowing down and it gave me time to catch an auto.

She was driving the car herself. It felt strange to see her drive. I don't know how I feel about it. I must talk to her. The highway is not easy. Big trucks. Bad drivers. It is avoidable for a woman to drive a car.

Smooth, smooth, smooth. Life is smooth as the highway today.

Daddy's resigned to the idea of a watchdog. He even asked what kind I'd get. Not a very furry one, I promised.

Once Mini settles in, things will get better. I'll keep the Mira Road property. It's useful to have a second place. Daddy will be glad to have me back. Rent from the Mira Road flat will help when business is down.

It has been too long since I traveled. I had no idea how fast things move outside Mira Road, or how slow. The auto trundled on our roads slower than a tonga, and her car soon moved out of sight. But by the time we hit Ghodbunder, I realized I knew where she was going. I've seen envelopes in her trash, addressed from some farmhouse in Karjat. So I got out of the auto and took a bus to Panvel.

She has to come back via Panvel. Better not to talk to her in Mira Road. Nor Juhu. A midway place where people stop only a few minutes. Yes, Panvel would be a good spot.

He just came up out of nowhere. I was at the Panvel plaza, getting fuel, taking a bathroom break. Then I decided to get a samosa-pav.

I stood outside eating, keeping an eye on the car. I'd left the windows open a crack for Mini's sake. That's when I saw him, prowling around. I wanted to call out a warning. Because Mini can be really quiet and she has been trained to attack suddenly. But just then, the man turned and looked straight at me.

"Is that your car?" he asked.

I called out from afar, "Yes, why?"

He began walking toward me, saying there was a flat tire. I kept looking at his face; there was something familiar about it.

I'd had the tires checked barely two minutes ago, as I drove through the petrol pump. But I waited for him to walk up. He was smiling a bit, almost like he was familiar with me. I didn't want to say anything yet, not until I remembered where we'd met.

He asked if I wanted help with changing the tire. I shook my head. He shrugged and said, "I'll do it if you want."

I said, "There's a petrol pump right here."

He began to chuckle softly. It was unnerving. Then he said, "That's where I'm coming from, Petrol Pump."

I glanced over at the pump. The fellow who checked my tire pressure was not in his place. I was certain this man was not the man who had checked my tires just two minutes ago. But he could be working at the same pump. Maybe I remembered his face from previous drives.

We both walked toward the car. I opened the trunk and got the spare tire out. While he changed it for me, I stood there, all the doors open, leaning against the backseat. He kept glancing at me. At one point he said, "So, you're headed back to Mira Road now? Or to your father's?"

Mini's tongue found my hand and I let her lick it. She was just a black shadow in the car. Except for her pink tongue, you couldn't see her at all. I patted her head, then stroked the side of her mouth. It was our signal for silence.

I asked, "How do you know?"

The man grinned. "We've met before. I own a house in Mira Road. Don't you remember? At Ruff Ruff, the shop near Sheetal? We even shared an auto once. Don't you remember me?"

I stared.

He was talking in short bursts, asking questions, "So what's your business like? Mira Road is growing so fast, isn't it? We never had people like you moving until a few years ago, but it is so advanced now . . ." And he kept saying, "Don't you remember where we met? But don't worry, it happens."

He asked for tissue to wipe his hands. I handed him the box from the dashboard.

He wiped his hands and said, "I'm going back tonight. I would have taken the bus but since you don't have any company, I can come with you. Anyway, it is not so good for a girl to be out alone at this time."

I drew my breath in sharply. He laughed in my face, then said he'd make himself useful.

It was odd, the way he stressed that he "owned" a house, then saying he was from Petrol Pump. For a moment, I wondered if he was telling the truth. Is it possible we'd met? Mira Road was a blank in my head. There's the house, the train station, the bank, Ruff Ruff. I must have met vegetable sellers, salesmen, pet owners, watchmen, newspapermen, dairymen, plumbers. It is possible I met him and then completely forgot.

As I was putting it away in the trunk, I looked at the flat tire carefully. There was a three-inch gash, clearly made with a knife or a big piece of glass.

I got into the driver's seat. I could say no and drive away. But he was going to follow me anyway. He'd take a bus and go to Mira Road. He'd be in the area and, who knows, share an auto with me another day.

He was leaning into the car now, returning the box of tissues to the dashboard, smiling at me.

But why did we share an auto? If he lives in Petrol Pump and I live in Sheetalnagar, why did we share the auto?

I turned the key in the ignition. Mini's supplies of food, the rag-basket, a blanket, my training whistle, a doggie windbreaker, all were piled on the front passenger seat.

He was still leaning in at the car window. So I said, "Come, but you will have to sit in the back because I have so many things here."

He got into the back at once. I took off at a roar before he had even shut the door. In the rearview mirror, I could see his face. He was grinning and his eyes were red like a demon's, thanks to the reflection of the headlights on the highway. He hadn't noticed Mini.

I knew her quiet, aggrieved breathing because I was listening for it. She's a good, patient dog. The traffic thinned and we rode in silence until the creek approached. It was past midnight when he leaned forward, put an arm around my seat. His hand was nearly touching my cheek when he said, "I have been waiting to talk to you. All my life, I waited for someone to arrive . . ."

I recognized his face then. It was the man hanging around outside Daddy's flat in a watchman's uniform, the same as the one he wore at Ruff Ruff. I let out a low whistle.

She is a hard-working girl. Educated too. But I have a lot to teach her. She must see that it is only a question of changing. Night and day follow each other. This is fixed. As time moves through the sky, it moves through everything else as

well. Prosperity follows struggle. Cities grow like wildflowers
they flourish like weeds and finally they are ruined. Calm fol
lows storm. Love follows hate.

Her life will change soon. Mira Road, my house, her face
our worth in the world—all of it can change. But she mus
learn patience. She must hold her life, and mine, tightly lik
a rag doll. Grasp it around the middle, so she does not chok
its mouth, nor leave its hands too free. In her hands, she wil
see life change and then she will lose the fear that it is slipping
away from her.

TZP

BY R. RAJ RAO

Pasta Lane

For over a week now, two policemen have posted themselves on the street below my building, and keep looking up at my third-floor flat. I have stopped going to the balcony as a result. I hide behind the curtains of my living room and watch them. They patronize a cigarette stall, buying fags and guthkha, as well as a chai tapri a few feet away. As they finish drinking their tea, and roll tobacco on their palms with their thumbs and index fingers, the policemen look up again. Sometimes they talk to the others who hang out at the cigarette stall and the chai tapri. They glance up as they talk. I get the feeling they are asking these men if they know anything about me.

The policemen arrive in the morning, when the workday begins, and leave in the evening, shortly before dark. They are not there at night. I thus go down to buy provisions and such only after sunset. The college where I teach is closed for the holidays, so I don't have to leave the flat during the day. Even so, I move around stealthily, stopping every now and then to make sure the cops aren't hiding behind the row of parked cars that line the street. The presence of the policemen has made me so paranoid that I have started having nightmares. I woke up screaming one night as I dreamed they were strangling me with fingers that were really talons. They laughed demonically as they throttled me, their claws buried in my flesh, my blood streaming down my neck to soil my white shirt. I rose from bed, switched on the table lamp, and glanced at my watch. It was four a.m. I tried to go back to sleep, but couldn't. So I went to the kitchen to fish out a cookie and make myself a cup of coffee. I then exercised for a bit. This is how I killed time till the newsboy rang my doorbell.

My flat is situated in Mangaldas Mansion, a five-floor building off Colaba Causeway. The street, Pasta Lane, is notorious for the pimps and rouge-smeared call girls in miniskirts who frequent it after-hours. It is said that call girls own half the flats in Pasta Lane.

If that's the case, shouldn't the policemen be keeping a watch on them rather than me?

I inherited my Mangaldas Mansion flat from my parents who are both dead now. I certainly cannot afford a flat in Colaba at today's prices, considering I'm only a lecturer by profession. I have often thought of selling my flat and going to live in distant Borivli or Virar, where the prices are cheap. That way I would be able to stash away cash for my old age. Though I'm in my forties, I'm single and live all alone. This is what terrifies me about the policemen downstairs. What if they come up in the middle of the night to put handcuffs on my wrists? Who will come to my rescue?

Living alone does not mean that I don't have casual visitors popping into my flat. They are usually disheveled strangers whom I meet in washrooms and bring home for sex. My neighbors and the watchmen of the building see these men come and go. They disapprove. But no one, in Pasta Lane of all places, has the guts to say anything to my face.

The question that nags me, however, is what is it those cops want? Is being a homo a crime even if one's in the rough trade? Or could it be that one of the men I brought home is a criminal? I never bother to check their backgrounds. How can I? Are people going to tell me that they are rapists or murderers? Several of the men display criminal tendencies by demanding money from me after we finish. I immediately open my wallet and pay them whatever they ask for (it has never exceeded a thousand rupees), because I'm scared shitless that if I don't pay them they might simply refuse to leave my flat. The profile of the fellows I pick up makes this very likely. They are far beneath me in station, and in age, and earn much less than I do—if they have jobs, that is. By occupation, these men could be taxi drivers or car mechanics or carpenters, or just plain unemployed. The majority of them live in Mumbai's slums and chawls, and haven't made it to flats. In bed they are all penetrators who dislike the use of condoms. The mere suggestion that I would like to fuck them for a change instead of being sodomized, or that they should use a condom, can make them violent, as with a nhavi who once attacked me with his shaving razor. Ironically, this was the very razor with which he had shaved me in my bedroom just a few minutes earlier.

"Gaand maro!" he'd yelled, as he took his money and slammed the door, locking me in. It was only after an hour or so had passed that I was able to call out to the watchman and ask him to unbolt my door.

The policemen stare up at my flat again. They have now gone a step further, and point with their fingers and batons. A small crowd of spectators gathers around them, and they look up too.

Who lives there? the policemen are probably asking the hangers-on, who know me because I have been living in Mangaldas Mansion since the day I was born. And the answer would be: *Saab, wo bahut bada gaandu hai. Aapko chahiye kya?*

A thought crosses my mind. Should I take the elevator

down and go confront those cops? *Why are you keeping a watch on my flat? I'll ask them. It's me who lives there, and I am a respectable gentleman who teaches in a college.* But then I dismiss the thought; it seems foolhardy to me, like walking into a lion's den. The cops might whisk me away in their jeep to question me about my immoral lifestyle, as if Pasta Lane is the holiest place on earth.

The phone rings. It's one of my pickups, Sunil by name, who wants to know if I'm free tonight. "No," I answer, though Sunil, who's a waiter, really turns me on with his lewd ways. Like the others, he hates wearing a condom (which he generically calls "nirodh"), but his explanation is bizarre!

"I want to show the world that I'm so virile that I can even make a man pregnant," he says in Hindi while fucking me. "How can I do this if I wear a nirodh?"

Sunil hangs up, disappointed. I'm unhappy too, but I don't wish to take in lovers as long as those creepy cops continue to shadow me.

This thing has been going on ever since Robert came to my flat last month. Robert is Steve's long-haired, blue-eyed partner, and he is in Mumbai to teach English to destitute kids. Three months ago, Robert landed at the Mumbai harbor in a cargo ship, because he's afraid of flying. The voyage, on an American vessel, lasted over a month, and when Robert finally set foot on Indian soil he was full of complaint. For one thing, his luggage had been pilfered. For another, he was mobbed by riffraff as soon as he stepped out of customs, and they pestered him for foreign liquor, cigarettes, and even jeans.

I met Robert at Ballard Pier and drove him in my Santro to his rented digs at Byculla, where his school is located. It was his first trip to India, and he could do precious little to hide his discomfort. Mumbai, according to him, had every-thing in excess—people, heat, automobiles, stray dogs. *Then why are you here?* I wanted to ask him. This was never clear to me. All Steve had said in an e-mail was that Robert, who is thirty-three, had finished a certificate course in English-language teaching somewhere in New York, and wanted to put it to meaningful use by working in a third world country. But at what price? A week after he began classes, Robert was attacked by snarling street dogs and had to take a regimen of antirabies injections. Then, he hated Indian food, which he said was too spicy and gooey, and was perpetually on the look-out for McDonald's and Subway-type restaurants where he could feast on french fries, burgers, and sandwiches to satisfy his cravings.

"You are too much of an American to be happy in Mum-bai," I told Robert.

Yet I was impressed by his commitment. All the more so when he told me how much the school paid him as a salary.

"How do you manage on such a measly amount?" I asked.

"Well, Steve and I have a joint account," he replied. "I take some whenever I need more."

Robert may not even have got the job had it not been for a recommendation letter I wrote on Steve's request to the Holy Cross School for Orphans.

"They are not convinced by testimonials from foreigners," Steve had said in a phone call from America. "They want an Indian to vouch for Robert's abilities."

I wrote a glowing letter, although I knew next to nothing about Robert, and addressed it to the headmistress of the school, a matronly lady named Mrs. Bhattacharya. She got back to me right away to inquire what sort of visa Robert possessed.

"A tourist visa," I replied.

"That suits us," Mrs. Bhattacharya said.

When Robert came over for tea to my Mangaldas Mansion flat wearing a sleeveless T-shirt, he had already been in Mumbai for three months and was beginning to get used to the tempo of the city.

"The taxi driver tried to cheat me," he grumbled, after settling down on the sofa and wiping beads of perspiration off his forehead. "Can you believe he tried to charge me five hundred bucks from Byculla to here?"

"How's school?" I asked, attempting to break the ice.

"Great," said Robert, his eyes brightening at the very mention of the word school. "The kids are sweet. They are quick to learn. It's a pity they don't have a single good teacher." Robert paused before adding, "Indian children are just so, I don't know . . . gracious. It's a pleasure watching them."

Robert showed me photos of some of the kids on his mobile phone. They were malnourished adolescents who looked cheerful in his company.

I went to the kitchen to make tea and serve the pastries and cookies I had bought from a trendy Colaba boulangerie. Steve had informed me about Robert's sweet tooth.

Robert took one pastry and one cookie, and asked me to wrap the rest in tissue paper for his students. I telephoned the bakery and ordered a whole cake for them. It was delivered within half an hour, my goodwill gesture pleasing Robert to no end.

Then he surprised me by declaring he had plans to stay in Mumbai forever. "I'm in touch with an immigration lawyer Steve knows," he explained.

I wondered how Robert would cope with the myriad problems that characterize Mumbai life.

As we chatted, I noticed that he had a tattoo on his upper left arm. At first I mistook for a swastika. However, on observing it closely I realized it was a set of horizontal and vertical lines that made for a stylish geometric design.

"Does the tattoo signify anything special?" I asked.

"Nope," he answered. "It was one of the designs in the tattoo-maker's book that I liked." He added that he had chanced upon the tattoo shop in Bandra while exploring Mumbai in a BEST bus.

Tattooing monopolized the conversation for the rest of the evening, till Robert got up to go. He pointed out that tattoos were expensive in America, so he was glad to have found a good shop here. Americans, he explained, are crazy about tattoos and sometimes cover their whole bodies.

"I know," I said. "I watch *LA Ink*, it's one of my favorites."

"You've got to be white, though, for the tattoo to suit you," Robert blabbered.

I let that pass.

Steve and I have known each other for ages. Steve loves Indians because he hates extremities of complexion, and Indians, according to him, are just right, neither too pale-skinned like the Europeans, nor too dark like the Africans.

Steve was the first man I ever came out to, and it was because he's white. Indians like myself are comfortable discussing our sexuality with the white man because he lives far away and is unlikely to out us. He is also without morals.

Steve lives in upstate New York. We met when he was on a six-month fellowship in Mumbai to study Bollywood films. A common gay friend brought him to my college one afternoon. Although I was publicly closeted, what fascinated Steve, on the face of it, was that both of us were lecturers, though his subject was film studies and mine social anthropology.

"I don't know too many gay academics outside the West," Steve told me when we met. "We are going to get on famously."

That night we went to Testosterone, a swanky gay bar behind the Taj, and got drunk. Steve told me all about the gay subculture of America, and I told him a little about Mumbai gay life.

"India is so much more exciting than America," Steve said. "America is so sterile."

Then he asked me a question some would consider obscene: "Are you a size queen? Because I'm one."

"You bet!" I replied.

We became buddies after that. Not lovers, because we simply weren't each other's sexual type. We trusted each other completely, and soon discovered we had other passions in common, such as our preference for working men. In queer politics parlance, we became "sisters."

Steve is over six feet tall, slightly bald, and ten years my senior. But he learned the art of pataoing from me, and claims he owes all his escapades with Mumbai's masseurs, taxi drivers, and bellboys during his frequent sojourns here for conferences and film festivals, to my tutoring. I would tell him how to go about it and he would blindly obey. He became promiscuous, though fortunately he did not test positive when he took an HIV exam recently.

Steve has been to Mumbai so many times that he regards it as his second home. He even speaks Hindi with flair.

"You spend a bomb on hotels every time you come here," I said to him one day. "How about we pool our resources and buy a house together?"

My parents had just died in a blizzard at the Vaishnodevi shrine in the Himalayas, and I had inherited some of their savings. The rest of it, as per their will, was to be given away in charity. My inheritance was insufficient for me to be able to buy a house on my own.

I expected Steve to be skeptical about the idea. Instead, he was jubilant. We thought of various possibilities, and zeroed in on a house in Panchgani, where we could retreat for the weekend.

Mumbai was ruled out for three reasons: One, the ridiculous real estate prices. Two, Steve preferred the salubrious air of the hills over Mumbai's humidity. And three, Steve could always park with me in my Mangaldas Mansion flat when he was in Mumbai. "My house is your house," I had told him.

This is how Steve and I came to own the Panchgani cottage, employing a battalion of lawyers to overcome obstacles that prevent foreigners from purchasing real estate in India. One key to the house is with Steve, the other is with me, and we drive down whenever he is in town. At other times, the house is kept locked.

After a series of hits and misses with Indian boyfriends from Orissa, from Goa, from Rajasthan, all migrants to the City of Dreams, Steve finally hooked up with Robert in America. For a while, Robert was merely Steve's tenant who inhabited the upstairs rooms of his two-floor house in New York. Then they fell in love.

Robert began accompanying Steve on academic jaunts, though he wasn't college-educated himself. At such gigs, it wasn't uncommon for old-fashioned dons to inquire if they were father and son! Eventually, Steve married Robert in Massachusetts, not because they saw eye to eye with the pro–gay marriage lobby, which was active, but because it enabled Robert to get a fee waiver to complete his graduation.

"Are Robert's folks okay with this?" I asked Steve. I knew

for certain that his own sister had a problem with Robert.

"Robert doesn't have parents," Steve explained. "He only has an old granddad who lives somewhere on the West Coast."

Steve made Robert the heir to his estate, which included his bank balance and his house. I thought this was going a bit far, but I never said so to Steve. Yaars though we were, we never got in each other's way. Besides, Steve could always turn around and allege it was a case of sour grapes: I couldn't see him in a committed relationship because I had never managed to be in one myself. None of my sexual encounters had blossomed into anything permanent, where I had someone to care for me when I was sick, or perform my last rites when I kicked the bucket.

Steve bemoaned the fact that Robert wouldn't travel with him to Mumbai for the honeymoon of their lives, because India was halfway across the world and the only way to get there was by plane. Once Robert was supposed to follow Steve to Mumbai on an Air India flight from New York. Steve and I went to Sahar Airport on the night of Robert's scheduled arrival, but he was nowhere in sight. Robert telephoned later to say that he had boarded the aircraft all right, but developed cold feet just before takeoff, and insisted that he be off-loaded. The airline thought he was a terrorist and handed him to the police, who released him with a warning.

"Daft!" I said to Steve, whose reply was that Robert was his honey and honeys had a right to be daft.

When Steve returned to the States, Robert promised that he would go with him to India some day, but it would be on a ship. There were no passenger liners to India anymore, though apparently there were merchant navy vessels that allowed civilians to sail with them, provided they paid for their passage and helped with chores on board. All one had to do was go online and check out their schedules.

Robert kept his word. But he's in Mumbai alone now, not with Steve, teaching in the school. Last month, he was at my house for tea. And today policemen stand below and point up at my place. Who can say if the two things are related?

Late in the evening, the policemen ring my doorbell. Accompanying two of the constables who watched my flat is a high-ranking officer who introduces himself as Inspector D'Souza. He is such a maverick, graying at the temples, not enslaved by bureaucracy and red tape, that at one stroke he alters my impression of policemen forever. He also knows English.

"Excuse me," he says in a clipped accent, "are you Mr. Lal?"

"Y-yes," I stammer.

"Be at ease," he says. "We're here to ask you a few questions about Mr. Robert Miller."

I was right: their trailing me does in fact have to do with Robert.

I invite the policemen inside, serve them water, and tell them whatever I know about Robert, which does not amount to much.

"Did you write a testimonial in his favor, addressed to Mrs. Bhattacharya of Holy Cross School?" asks the inspector.

"Yes."

"I'm afraid you'll have to come with us. We will release you soon."

The word *release* sends a shiver down my backbone. Does it mean they're going to arrest me?

Sensing my reluctance, Inspector D'Souza tries to calm my nerves: "No harm will come to you. You can take my word for it."

"Okay." I shrug my shoulders, afraid that if I resist the policemen may use force. I lock the flat and follow them down in the elevator. It makes funny noises and I wonder if we're going to get stuck.

We get into a waiting Qualis with a blue beacon light on its roof. The neighbors are at their windows watching us. I expect to be taken to the police station, but soon discover that we are headed to the Mumbai-Pune Expressway, out of the city. I panic. It is dark by now.

"Where are we going?" I ask Inspector D'Souza.

"You'll know soon," he answers.

It isn't long before I realize that we are on the road to Panchgani. We stop once for tea and snacks—the policemen offer me whatever they eat, but I politely decline.

After a six-hour drive, during which Inspector D'Souza works on his laptop, we're at Panchgani before dawn.

"We're going to the house that you and Mr. Steve Anderson jointly own," he informs me.

"I figured that out long ago," I reply. I wonder how he's already managed to discover so much about me.

The Qualis negotiates the serpentine roads with ease. The sun is about to rise and the views of the valley below are breathtaking. Mist hangs in the nippy air and the flowers are in full bloom. Inspector D'Souza hums a film song.

> *Dil dhoondta hai*
> *Phir wohi*
> *Fursat ke raat din*

The driver asks the inspector for directions to the house. The inspector in turn looks at me; I show them the way.

When we reach the house and get out of the car, I'm shocked. The lock on the front door is open, but the door is bolted from inside. Steve never comes to Panchgani, or to Mumbai for that matter, without letting me know in advance.

At this stage, I notice something uncanny. A figure has been drawn on the door. I scratch my head trying to recall where I've seen it. Then I get it: it's the tattoo I'd seen on Robert's upper arm. This meant Robert was inside. Steve must have given him his key. But why didn't they keep me in the loop?

Inspector D'Souza knocks on the door but no one answers. He knocks again, then again, and finally thumps on the door with his fists.

Still no answer. As the inspector contemplates breaking down the door, we hear the latch click from within and the door opens. Robert steps out groggily, and closes the door behind him. He's dressed only in Bermudas, the kind sold on Goa's beaches, with bright red flowers on a yellow background.

"Yes?" he says to Inspector D'Souza, pursing his lips.

The inspector does not think it necessary to give Robert explanations. He pushes him aside and enters the house with his men. I stupidly follow. After all, I'm a joint owner of the property. Robert is dumbstruck.

We head to the room upstairs and find foam mattresses laid out on the floor. Six boys, aged around twelve, are asleep on the mattresses. Inspector D'Souza yanks the blankets off their faces. They open their eyes and frown. Like Robert, they are all bare-chested and in Bermudas. They appear to be the same boys whose pictures I saw on Robert's mobile. Some of them sit up in bed, and I see something that makes me queasy: they have the same tattoo as Robert on their upper left arms.

Robert has joined us upstairs. Inspector D'Souza turns around to face him.

"My students," Robert explains. "We often come here from Mumbai for the weekend."

Everyone is asked to pack up and get ready to leave. One of the boys starts crying at the sight of the policemen. Robert protests, but Inspector D'Souza silences him: "Shut up! Tell us whatever you want in Mumbai. And give me your passport . . ."

One of the two havaldars is made to wait with Robert and the boys for the van that will arrive to take them back to Mumbai, because the Qualis cannot accommodate all of us. The other havaldar, Inspector D'Souza, and I sit in the Qualis. Inspector D'Souza collects the keys to the house from Robert and puts them in his pocket. We drive off, the inspector and I seated in the back.

"You're educated," he says to me after a while, as we descend the ghats. I am distracted by Panchgani's famed paragliders floating in the air without a care, like mammoth birds. "I don't have to tell you the word for Robert's crime."

He then confirms my worst fears, giving me gooseflesh.

"Since the house is partly in your name, and its coowner is Robert's partner, you become a sort of accomplice. So we will have to arrest you. I'll make sure, though, it's a bailable warrant."

I feel betrayed. How could Steve do this to me? It's possible that he was in the dark as well. But then how did Robert manage to lay his hands on Steve's door key? In order not to worry myself sick, I doze off for most part of the ride home. Still, I'm a nervous wreck. The world will see me as an abettor of Robert's doings. My shady sexual life will be exposed. I too might be regarded as a pedophile, and lynched.

Back in Mumbai, I spend three days in the Colaba police station lockup, sharing cell space with the city's taporees: dons, bootleggers, thugs. They know I'm a novice in the world of crime and treat me like a bachha. But Inspector D'Souza keeps his word and I'm released on bail.

I desperately try to call Steve in America, but only reach his answering machine.

A week later Inspector D'Souza drops in to return our Panchgani keys. He's dressed casually in jeans and a paunch-revealing T-shirt. Though I'm depressed and on tranquilizers, I open a bottle of Royal Challenge and we talk. He's actually here to give me dope.

"It was one of your neighbors in Panchgani," he begins, "who blew Robert's cover."

Apparently, this short-haired Parsi lady whom I've never met saw Robert visiting the house with the kids every Saturday and roaming about scantily clad. She grew suspicious—she's a teacher in one of Panchgani's residential schools.

"We contacted Mrs. Bhattacharya," Inspector D'Souza continues, "and she informed us that though they had wanted Robert to teach junior college, he had insisted on teaching seventh-grade kids. He grew very popular with them, and took them out on overnight jaunts without the school's knowledge."

"But did he actually have sex with them?" I ask.

"I can't say," Inspector D'Souza replies. "Sex, of course, isn't just intercourse. When it comes to minors, a bad touch is enough to render a person guilty. And going by what your Panchgani neighbor said, Robert seems to be quite an exhibitionist. The kids were totally noncommittal when we asked them what went on."

The police officer then proceeds to tell me something very odd. The boys, it seems, nicknamed Robert "Michael Jackson." And he, in turn, began to call our Panchgani place "Neverland." He gave them electronic toys and chocolates.

"Why do you think Robert came to Mumbai in the first

place?" Inspector D'Souza asks me, as I pour our second drink.

"To teach English."

"No. Robert came to Mumbai to preempt arrest in America. It was a well-planned move because he was sure the American authorities would someday get him."

He tells me a story, the long and short of which is that Robert belongs to a banned organization called MANLAB that advocates intergenerational sex and child pornography, which are looked upon with great disfavor in the States. By contrast, he thought of India as a country that turned a blind eye to such crimes.

"Why, otherwise, would a man go through the ordeal of spending more than a month on a cargo ship before ending up in a strange city where he hates the people, the food, the weather, and is mauled by stray dogs?"

Inspector D'Souza's reasoning, I must confess, makes sense to me. But there's more to come.

"That sign that you saw on your front door, also tattooed on the arms of Robert and his boys—what do you think it is?"

"No idea," I say. "I was intrigued by it and thought of it as some kind of emblem. At first I mistook it for a Nazi swastika."

"Well, it's none of these things," Inspector D'Souza laughs. "It is the letters *TZP*. And Robert got it tattooed on his arm, and on the arms of the boys he took to Panchgani, at a famous tattoo shop in Bandra. His aim was to brand as many boys as possible. He wanted to beat the record of a notorious Indonesian pedophile, a toy salesman the same age as he, whose tally is ninety-six boys. When we searched Robert's apartment in Byculla, we found a brand-new Handycam there. I suspect he wanted to use it to film the boys for a child porn ring."

"What do the letters refer to?" I ask.

"*Taare Zameen Par*. I guess you've seen the film, in which

Aamir Khan plays a schoolteacher who's different. In the notes we found in his desk, Robert describes the film as a pederast's delight."

This is disgusting. Proof of the fact that firangs are sick. They see sex even where it does not exist. The pitiable dyslexic kid in the film isn't spared either.

"Where is Robert now?" I ask Inspector D'Souza.

"He will soon be deported," he says, lighting a cigarette. "In any case, his visa expires shortly, and will not be renewed. He may attempt to sneak into countries like Sri Lanka or Thailand."

"And me? Do you think I'll be in trouble?"

"Just pray that the Panchgani lady doesn't take the matter to court, holding both the school and the owners of the house guilty. I believe she has clout."

"The bitch!"

Inspector D'Souza pauses. He gets up and heads to the bathroom. Over two hours have passed since he arrived.

"A bit of friendly advice," he says when he returns, fiddling with his fly. There's a dark spot of urine on his jeans. "Sell the Panchgani house and break off with Steve."

I move to the window. Pasta Lane bustles at night. There are roadside stalls selling pav bhaji, egg burji, and masala dosas. An open trash can lies near the stalls, where a fight has broken out among dogs for the leftovers. On closer scrutiny, I find that the dogs aren't quarreling over food, but over the lone bitch whom all the males want to fuck. The lucky one, who's entwined with her, gets it from the others who try their best to disengage them.

I walk back to the sofa, where Inspector D'Souza is on his sixth peg. When he pats the sofa and asks me to sit next to him, I oblige. He hovers his hand over my crotch.

"Even I can be gay," he says, and bursts out laughing. It's a laughter that does not cease until late in the night, when he passes out on the sofa.

PAKEEZAH

BY AVTAR SINGH

Apollo Bunder

Imagine if you will, said the drunk across the table: two men at the seawall. The one down there, he gestured. They sat by the edge of the terrace, the drunk and his interlocutor, under the last bit of tent that wept and billowed under the weight of the evening wind and the rain up on the roof of the old hotel. They could both see the road four stories below and the pavement across it bounded by the wall, the crashing sea beyond that. Boats in their monsoon rigs wallowed miserably in the harbor. Mumbai's last horse-driven carriages rolled by on the street, ferrying tourists ignorant of the terminal condition of their rides.

The clouded gunmetal sky loomed closer and closer to them and then it was night. Cars swept past the building, their lights picking halos out of the rain, ephemeral angels surprised mid-errand in the city by the sea.

Can you see them? said the drunk.

The other man raised his eyebrows. Those two? he said, pointing to a table over in the corner, where two men such as themselves huddled against the wind and the spray over their glasses, hard by the wall of the terrace.

Well, allowed the drunk, men like them. Down there. By the wall. Next to the Radio Club.

The listener looked through the rain at the slick patch of pavement the drunk had indicated, where the road from the Taj ran into the perpendicular length of Arthur Bunder. Tourists and touts carried out their ragged commerce as the last horses of that strand discharged their bowels and bladders around them, and no, he didn't see any two men in particular, but he saw men aplenty and so he nodded his head.

You see them? asked the drunk again.

Sure, said the tourist.

Then you're a fucking liar, because the story I'm telling you is fifteen years old. You still want to hear it?

Sure, repeated the other man equably, as one will when a stranger buying your drinks starts to get obstreperous.

Okay. Then listen, said the drunk.

This young man. Call him Ravi. He came to town to work at one of the many things that people came to Mumbai to do, back then and now. Was he a banker, a consultant, a shipping agent, a realtor? One doesn't know. Back then, this was what distinguished Mumbai from India, that other country across the bay. Nobody asked you what you did. It was enough that you were young and fun and a good guy to have a drink with and perhaps play a game or two of squash against. There was enough room at the bar of the Bombay Gymkhana for all sorts of itinerants and wanderers and young fools and some of them are still there, hair gray or gone and squash a distant memory, but they're still good value when the booze is flowing.

Nobody cares who you are, said the drunk, boozily reflective. That was this city's myth. It still is.

You don't believe it? said the tourist.

The drunk continued, as drunks will, as if he hadn't heard.

Ravi was clearly a child of privilege and evidently hadn't seen twenty-five. He spoke with the right accent, lived in South Mumbai in a flat with a view of the sea, and owned the only key to the door. He was athletic and clean-cut and had a nice smile and a car and inevitably found his way to the right parties. It was a world before the ubiquity of the Internet and there were hardly any cell phones and cable TV was still new enough to be remarkable. People called each other at home or the office and told each other what was happening around the bar. He liked his little set, which was in reality rather a big set, and he enjoyed the smiles and the easy laughter and the small joys and subterfuges of lives lived in cozy incestuous bubbles.

But he was, after all, an outsider. Or perhaps that had nothing to do with it.

One night, stumbling out after a few hours inside the nightclub at the Taj—a few steps that way, motioned the drunk—he was accosted by a woman with an improbable hairdo and a short skirt and a cigarette hanging off one corner of a thin painted mouth. He was amenable to what she suggested, paid her what she asked, and was led by her down Mereweather Road—behind us, waved the drunk—and up against a wall. By the by, she had him turn his face to the wall, his trousers still around his ankles, and went to work on his crack. This, she'd claimed, was her specialty, and he had no reason anymore to doubt either her claim or her expertise. He cradled his head on his crossed arms against the wall and barely noticed the lights of the occasional passing car. Her hand, outstretched through his legs, matched the rhythm of her tongue and before he knew it, his seed was going where so much urine had already been, splashing against a wall in the night behind the Taj.

It wasn't until he was stopped at a picket down the road and was groping for his license that he realized his wallet was gone. Later, in the station, he explained what had happened to the officer. The discovery of a chance few hundred rupees in the glove compartment meant a few cups of tea and an only marginally impolite policeman. His apologies were waved away, protestations of having been wronged indulged. A constable, taking it easy on a wooden settee off to the side, sniggered occasionally under the slowly moving fan. Ravi always remembered the hue of that encounter: the tube-light above, the smoke of his cigarettes in his own mouth and those of the cops and the slow curl upward, the plastic reflective paint on the walls, and outside, through the open door of the station, dawn; first a pale pink promise, then a fleeting reality and too-soon bright hard day. It was hot—hot, said the drunk, June-hot, just-before-the-monsoon hot—and the nights were barely better than the days, but still it mattered and registered that the sun was up.

You be careful now, said the cop.

I will, nodded Ravi ruefully. But what about my wallet? Some sentimental value?

Not really, said Ravi. But I'm pretty attached to the money inside.

You can kiss that goodbye, laughed the law. We can get you the wallet back, but that's as far as it goes.

But what about the money? said Ravi, as the officer led him out to the station's door, a hairy arm around the younger man's fit shoulders.

That's not my job, murmured the cop. But you had a good time, right?

Sure, nodded Ravi. There's that, at least.

Yes, nodded the other man. I've heard he's very good. He smiled at Ravi, threw him a two-fingered salute, and was gone through the swinging door.

So there it is. Ravi wanted neither his wallet pinched nor the cold touch of a man's tongue up his ass again, but the dark is a powerful draw. A joint in a car with a friend, a line or two of coke in a corner of a nightclub, an almost-fight with an acquaintance with no likelihood of either party getting hurt: genteel, entry-level transgressions that weren't even worthy of the title, no more so than a blow job in a car somewhere from a young convent-educated Bandra girl. But the city seethed around him and bulged with opportunity, and temptation rose off it like the sweat under his shirt. The monsoon was late that year, and the city smoked under the sun. He tried to resist the sound of the barkers as he walked past them in the Fort and let his eyes skate over the health and beauty center advertisements in the papers, but his will was weak or perhaps he never wanted to put up too much of a fight, and so he hearkened to the waiting pimps in the arches and the women in the shadows along the streets behind the Taj, and he thought he could smell them as he drove past with his windows down, a humid precise stink that was, in a moment, the savor of the city itself.

Was it not—said the listener, an eyebrow archly raised—just the wind blowing down from the fishing trawlers at Sassoon dock?

The drunk affected to ignore this and elected instead to study the plume left behind by his cigarette as it dissolved into the mist and the rain beyond the shelter of their umbrella. The two men at the table in the corner, still in muted conference, stoically made their way through their own measures of alcohol as the rain now came down in earnest. The tourist noted the size of one of them, a burly beast of a man well into his middle-age but still imposing even while seated. The other one was lighter and younger, but that was all he could make out and so he turned back to the drunk.

It got hotter, said the drunk. It got so hot that the water dried in the lakes up north. So hot that you thought the sweat itself would dry on your body. So hot that it was hard to think and so, one night, after a few hours in an over-air-conditioned bar where they played Latin music, if you can believe it, in this city, Ravi left his wallet in his car, parked it along the causeway—back there, gestured the drunk—and putting what he thought was just enough money in his pocket, wandered down Arthur Bunder.

It didn't take him long to meet the man he was looking for. That gent took him through an old doorway, which gave way to a lane between two buildings. A dank, ancient staircase opened up on the left, with sleeping forms off to the side and a courtyard in front with pushcarts at rest and rats at play. The wood of the stairs was warped and bent and the banister was real wood and rubbed to a sheen and the only light was a bare bulb above a door two floors up. They knocked on that door and were let in, where another man watched TV and waited on an overstuffed couch in an overly cold room. He bade Ravi sit next to him after the other man had been given his tip. He sized up his client and shouted for the girls to be brought in and then they were there, ten of them against the wall. Ravi chose and paid the sitting man who put the money to his forehead and his eyes, kissed it and put it away in his pocket, and then proceeded to ignore Ravi completely. Ravi followed his girl into the mean little plywood cubicle with the sheet drawn across it and the tap in the corner and the bucket underneath and the stained bedspread on the single bed and the Ganpati idol to the side and the shaving mirror and pegs for his clothes on the wall and the urchin with the clean strip of towel and the condom and the soap and his hand outstretched for his tip and then, by and by, they were done and lying side by side and Ravi thought, I'm sure this is a well-trodden path, but it's sure as shit new to me.

She told him her name and she told him where she was from and she told him that if this place were ever to be found closed, there was a sister establishment on Kittredge Road. His little booth shared one light in the larger room with three other booths, and he rested in the darkness and listened and smelled her powdered and sweating pits and knew, with a sudden clarity, that he needed to shake the newness of this out of his system or he'd be doing it the rest of his life, and in that effort lay the seed of its own failure, for who in the wide world has ever shaken that particular habit by practicing it too much? And even as he thought this he chased the thought away, because a rubber or three and a woman who is visibly a woman and a sinning ground that is even ostensibly of one's own choosing is always armor enough for one as young as him.

So he asked her to knead his shoulders and as he lay there, her hands warm upon his skin, he wondered who owned the place. I don't know who owns it, but I know who runs it and keeps us safe, she replied. Akbarzeb. That man out there, asked Ravi. No, said the woman dismissively. You'd know him if you saw him. He's like a tree. Is he violent, then? What do you mean? asked the woman. Does he hit you? He never touches us, she said. In that or any way. Sounds like a prince, said Ravi.

A hand softly turned his face toward her own, and she said: In our Mumbai, he is.

When he came out, it was finally raining.

As the monsoon entrenched itself on the land, the city Ravi had grown accustomed to took on new shapes and shifted behind the silver and the gray of the rain. One night, returning from a dinner, as great walls of water scudded down across the road lights and across his windshield, he took refuge behind a long line of SUVs that sped, their red lights blinking, toward Colaba. Up the causeway the convoy roared, Ravi and a few other cars gratefully in its wake, until, arrived at journey's end, the whole train pulled up to the curb. As Ravi drove slowly by, he saw the man at the convoy's heart stepping out under an umbrella, while a mountain of a man waited, bareheaded and oblivious, to embrace him. His hug enveloped the man of consequence while the rest of the entourage pressed around them, and then they were lost to sight and Ravi drove on, thinking, in some obscure way, that he'd been present at a coronation carried out under the cover of the pouring rain.

Ravi did his best—said the drunk, a glass still in his hand and still emptying rapidly—that month and the next, to wring every last bit of flavor from the whores of this island. He visited the health and beauty centers of the Fort and had a nodding acquaintance with every pimp from Colaba Post Office to Leopold Café. He knew the walk-up brothels of Pasta Lane and the Strand and even old Cuffe Parade. He met girls from the northeast and from the south, from UP and Maharashtra, and wherever he went, they all claimed the protection of Akbarzeb. At times his aura let them down and they sported visible scars, but their belief in him was undimmed and they had faith that his long arm would visit retribution on their tormentors, in this world or the next.

He went about his regular clean-cut business too. He played squash and squeezed in a round or two of monsoon-rules golf and went to work and partied hard, as is the way of young men of his stripe in Mumbai, and he became friendly with a nice little Punjabi girl, formerly of Cathedral and always of Malabar Hill, proud bearer of a set of tits that made you think the world was a kindly place. She was a willing conspirator in love and he thought, more than once, that she could cure him of his wandering in the dark, but her calls and flirtation and warmth were no match for afternoons, postworkout, spent searching for porn on the pavements and alleys of the Fort and perhaps a quick hand job after and the thrill—the thrill, for what is it if not that?—of an anonymous tryst with a nameless woman never before glimpsed who will clean you off before and after and send you on your way. And everywhere he went that season, in the parlors, up the stairs, down the sidewalks and through the stalls, stepping over the bodies of migrants and junkies, in the mud and the clinging motor oil and the ever-present sludge, he walked in the shadow of Akbarzeb.

The monsoon was a vehement one that year, making up for its late arrival. The days were dark and the nights spectral with lightning and the rain seemed set on washing the city back into the sea. But there wasn't enough water in the air and in the sky for Ravi. Sometimes, he thought, when he looked in the mirror after he shaved, that his very eyes were darkening. The dirty water that washed over his feet in the streets seemed freighted with more than just bacteria. He didn't know, anymore, whether the city stained him or the other way around. The thought of another anonymous whore, another windowless cubicle, another lineup against a wall, occupied his waking thoughts and consumed his vision till he could see nothing else, and he knew himself to be addicted. And he wondered, again and again, how a man who lived in that world and drew sustenance from it could still stand apart and not be infected.

Akbarzeb? inquired the tourist.

Who else?

Did you know Akbarzeb means "very big dick" in Arabic? said the tourist.

The drunk looked like he was accustomed to burying just this sort of unverified and unsolicited little nugget till an opportunity arose for its exhumation in a situation such as the one he and his interlocutor were in, and so he—feigning nonchalance—continued. Akbarzeb's immunity to the virus that was consuming Ravi began to haunt the latter man. He wanted to meet him, to talk to him, to expose him for what he really was and not as all the other creatures of the dark saw him. For is there a man in the world—declaimed the sodden drunk—who can rise above measuring other men against his own mean self?

You know who Akbarzeb is, don't you? he asked suddenly.

Of course, said the tourist. He's famous everywhere. But I didn't know he'd been a pimp.

Legislators don't start out as anything but, claimed the drunk. The listener kept quiet and waited.

So: Later that season, on a night that was relatively clear, Ravi and a friend set out on a night of genteel slumming. The bar girls of Mumbai were just becoming well known, and there was one place in particular, Manik in Lamington Road, that was hugely popular. Young girls danced in mirrored air-conditioned halls and their patrons, boozy perverts mauling their whiskeys to the side, showered them with currency notes. The bouncers enforced a strict no-touch policy, the girls flounced and shook their asses and flipped their hair, and the men dropped their earnings on the dance floor in a choreography of anodyne excess that was, for many in the city, the only taste they had of decadence. It became de rigueur that year for young men to take their dates there at the end of the night, so a frisson of darkness and danger could run up and down their well-bred backs. So that they could claim, however temporarily, that they had known Mumbai, that other one, the harbor bitch they'd all been told about but never been introduced to.

But Manik was closed that night, and so they were directed to Heera, a smaller place that lay just across the Chinchpokli Bridge, over which the dead mill stacks of the previous century still loomed. They drew up in Ravi's car to a closed door guarded by a few thickset men who smiled and waved them through a gap between two shops, over an open drain, and beneath a hanging air-conditioning unit, whose runoff was indistinguishable from the slowly falling rain. Another man waited there, a door to a kitchen open, in which men sliced cucumbers and shook out peanuts into bowls and bow-tied waiters lurked with trays, and then a swinging door and another world, of smoke machines and stairs and a deejay console and loud film music and lehenga- and sari-clad girls dancing on a glass floor under which fish deranged by the music swam manically and around that monstrous arena, men drinking and watching and considering on who best to drop their money.

The staircase led ever upward. Ravi and his friend rose through the various levels of heaven, each one smaller, more private and quiet and with fewer men to share space with, till finally they arrived at a closed door. The bouncer there gave them the once-over, nodded, and let them through. On the walls were the standard-issue mirrors, and on the ceiling an ugly chandelier turned down low. But everything else was different. There were no chairs, no sofas, only white linen-covered mattresses and bolsters. There was no aquarium dance floor, but rather a polished wooden surface. There was no deejay, only a soft playing of the soundtrack from *Pakeezah*. There were no dancing girls either, save one, a smoothly moving houri dressed as a kathak dancer all in white, the bells at her ankles tinkling and winking in the light. Ravi looked at her and then he looked again, for she was beautiful, a woman well past her first youth, but lovely despite or perhaps because of her experiences. She seemed to glide about that space as if she were above it and its sordid moorings and Ravi would have been happy to indulge her in that, till he saw the only other man in the room. He sat there, a huge presence against the wall, his feet alone enough to take up the space of a normal man, his eyes fixed quietly on the woman and with no mind to the new entrants, and Ravi knew it was him, and he knew why the dirt of what Akbarzeb did didn't stick to him. "*Mausam hai ashiqana . . .*" crooned Lata over the speaker, to countless millions of men then and since, but for Akbarzeb, she spoke only to him.

Ravi and his friend stayed there, across the room from Akbarzeb, for the time it took the record to replay itself and come back to the same song. They dropped their drinks and ordered more and gave their money to the dancing woman with a courtly flourish, which she accepted with a grace intrinsic to a ceremony as foreign to the girls downstairs as was courtesy to their patrons. She wept when the soundtrack wept, flirted when the right song came on, danced with abandon when it was appropriate, and always she spoke to him, to Ravi, with her kohl-lined eyes and her fluid body and her mobile face and once, when he handed her the tribute that was her due, their fingers touched and it seemed to him that this, only this, was what separated men from beasts.

Just once, in all the night, did Ravi catch Akbarzeb's eye. That orb stayed and studied him and then, in a moment, was gone, on its inevitable return to its rightful place, satellite to the dancer's sun, and even as they got up and left, almost bowing their way out of that temple, he didn't look nor did he stir. Outside, through the bedlam into the suddenly heal-

ing, quiet rain, walked the two friends. The city slept under
its blanket of rain and it struck Ravi that the monsoon was
indeed the time, at least in this latitude, for a young man's
fancy to turn to thoughts of love, and he hummed the chorus
to the song as he drove the two of them back to their homes
to the south.

Did you know that the word *mausam* is actually the root
for monsoon? said the tourist. Originally from the Arabic.

The drunk raised an eyebrow politely and made no reply.

Ravi became an habitue of Heera. He didn't need any company to go there. He drove through the pouring rain and occasionally through the evening calm and always made his way
to the top floor. He had no time for the commerce of the lower
floors, where each man had his own favorite and expected,
if the money he dropped was to her satisfaction, to have his
attentions returned. Not for him the laborious scrawling of a
phone number on a currency note in the hope that the girl of
his choosing connected it to him. He knew what he wanted,
and they were both at the top of the stairs. Occasionally, he'd
have the woman to himself, but as the night progressed and
the demands on his time slackened off and then ceased, Akbarzeb himself would arrive from his dominion to the south, a
heavy presence through the door and across the mattresses and
then down, his hand already returning the adaab the dancer
threw his way. And always, he ignored Ravi, even as he stepped
across his feet to his own accustomed place by the wall.

Sometimes the two of them shared her with some other
enthusiasts. Once there were two friends who thought that a
chat with Ravi was indicated as well, and so positioned themselves one to each side of him. Much better than Kennedy
Bridge, said one with the air of sharing a confidence. The

other leaned across Ravi, nodding judiciously, his elbow prac-
tically in Ravi's crotch. Much better. Have you been? they
asked him. No, he allowed. You must make your way past the
sluts on the bridge itself, they pointed out. Then you have
to descend a putrid set of stairs. Then you must wake up the
musicians and the girls and the madam herself. *Then* the musicians tune up, the madam calls out the beat, and the girl, if
she's in the mood, dances.

Really, said Ravi, trying to sound interested.

Yes. The closest Mumbai still has to a real mujra. And
what a parody it is. Half-hearted dancers, tone-deaf musicians, and that toothless harridan with her hair still crazy from
the mattress.

This is much better, said the other one. No pretense.

No, agreed his friend. The music is canned, but what music. *Pakeezah!*

And the woman. Isn't she something?

Ravi had to agree.

She calls herself Meena. She's obsessed with *Pakeezah.*
That's all she dances to.

Is that all she does? he asked.

They looked at him slyly, and then with real interest.

Clearly you're a shaukeen, they said. But of what?

They spoke, as friends will, into the silence that followed
that question. There's no better dancer in Mumbai. Not one
who dances for our money, at any rate.

All you want is the dance? asked Ravi.

That's it, they said eagerly. We're disciples of beauty. In
music. In dance. In women. We don't need to touch it. It's
enough for us to know that it's there.

Ravi looked at them as at aliens on furlough from a distant planet. Besides, they continued, you know that man in

the corner? Ravi could only nod. If he can't touch her, what chance do we have?

You mean, he isn't?

Apparently not. But you didn't hear it from us. Anyway, we don't come here as often as we'd like. He's not the sort of man you want to offend.

Clearly not, said Ravi.

But she is a dancing girl, mused one of them, while the other one nodded.

She's also a woman, said Ravi. She can choose who to give it away to.

The other two drained their drinks and then went away, but not before they shook their heads and muttered shaukeen again, half-admiringly.

That night, sitting through the second and then the third loop of the soundtrack, he thought he detected an extra smile from Meena. She looked at him from under her lashes as she swung and twirled to "Inhi logon ne," seemingly beckoning him to sing the male part to "Chalo dildar chalo." And, so bidden, he did what he thought he never would. He slipped away to the bathroom and wrote his number on a currency note and held it out to her; and as he did so, he held it in his hand a moment longer than was necessary and permitted himself a long, slow look into her eyes. And then she was gone and ten minutes later, so was he.

Akbarzeb sat unmoving in his corner, and didn't even look in Ravi's direction as he left.

The drunk and his new friend were now almost the only inhabitants of their terrace area. The only other table was the one in the corner, and the earnest murmurings of the mismatched pair there had all but ceased. The rain had picked

174 // MUMBAI NOIR

up and the wind was whooshing away and it seemed obvious to everyone on the terrace that a lack of conversation doesn't equal silence, in this world or any other, and so they sat, semi-mute and deafened by their individual solitudes, looking at everything but each other, morosely putting their alcohol away.

Into the breach stepped the drunk.

No Arabic insights on shaukeen?

None, admitted the tourist glumly.

Pity, shrugged the drunk. Anyway, you're probably thinking: what happened to the whores?

The comfort of that world of naked bulbs and stained sheets, plywood partitions and idols in the corner and little slabs of soap on strips of clean towel, was suddenly a cold one. It had been alien and had spoken to that part of him that the Bombay Gymkhana and his flat with its view of the sea and his friends who'd all been to school and college together couldn't touch. But even that, now, was not enough. He wanted Meena.

And so he waited for her to call.

Did she? inquired the listener.

Of course she did. What did she have coming through her door? Young men committed to beauty? Aging reprobates in the revenue departments of the Maharashtra and central governments? Enormous gangsters groping toward some approximation of love?

The poor woman didn't stand a chance. He was the closest thing to normal she'd ever seen.

You think?

Not really, shrugged the drunk. Who knows why she called. She was a woman. She fancied him. Can't that be enough?

* * *

They spoke in Hindi, a language she spoke beautifully and he'd all but forgotten. She could only meet in the afternoons, she said, or the early evenings. That's okay, he told her, he'd find time for her, leave work early, make it possible. And as he said this, and the euphoria of her having called and his almost being home washed over him, came the realization: he could make the time, but could he make the place?

The uniformity of his own world was never as apparent to him as in that first conversation over the phone. English, ease, and entitlement defined his set, and Meena had none of those. He'd only seen her in the chastely sexy raiment of the kathak dancer. He didn't even know what she wore when she took the open air.

If she were just a friend, a curiosity, a trophy of a big night out, he could have taken her anywhere and been hailed as a hero. But the promise of intimacy carries its own weight and Ravi knew he would never be able to bear it in public. Not his public. It isn't just me, he reasoned to himself. She'll be humiliated too. But his own pusillanimity was stark in his own ear as he told her where to meet him. There was only a hint of a pause before she said, gracefully as ever, of course she knew the place, she would be there.

It was a bar just off Ballard Estate, where the sailors came and picked up their prey. In the early afternoon, though, it was still relatively clean. Ravi walked in and saw her immediately, sitting off to one side, dressed in a spotless white salwar kameez that gave the lie to the wet filth outside. She was sipping her lemonade with an air of quiet ease that brought a catch to his throat. He knew then that he could have introduced her as his young aunt from Pakistan or a dress designer friend of his sister, drumming up business for her studio in Lucknow.

Anything at all. But the die was cast and there she was and she smiled at him as he walked up to her and her hand came up in the adaab he'd grown accustomed to.

So they sat and they chatted and the waiters hovered and if she felt the weight of time slipping away, she didn't betray it. She hung on his words and touched his fingers with hers and once, just once, she leaned across and gently flicked an errant curl away from his face.

He didn't even think of Akbarzeb. No more than half a dozen times.

He owned that place, just as he did everything within five kilometers of Colaba, whether on land, out to sea, or in the air. The waiters knew who she was and they knew who she belonged to and Ravi knew that too. But she'd chosen him and so it had to be.

Finally, they ended up at that hotel on the dock road, a few hundred meters down from Ballard Estate. Where the sailors take their prey. Trucks outside, air conditioners in every room, a few hundred rupees an hour, and the boy with the condom and the soap carrying a whole towel instead of just a scrap. An actual bathroom, imagine.

You know the place? asked the drunk politely. If the tourist knew it, he didn't let on.

So: That's where it was done. And if she'd been there before, that poor darling in her spotless salwar kameez, she never let Ravi know.

Well? prodded the listener.

I don't know, said the drunk reflectively. As gracefully abandoned as her dancing, I'd like to think. But I don't know.

They pondered that for a space, long enough for it to register that the mismatched pair at the table by the corner were now gone.

Of course—said the drunk—he walked in through the door.

It was quick and painless. For Ravi at least. He was told to get his trousers on and get the hell out. He considered protesting and then thought better of it and as he glanced back, he saw, through the frame of Akbarzeb's muscular arm propping open the door, Meena in their freshly shared bed, the covers drawn up to her naked shoulders and a look of calm defiance in her eyes.

He didn't know how the time passed, that night or the next. He waited by the phone till he had to leave, and then waited by it again. He lived in Colaba and waited for the knock on his door but it never came and by and by, he found himself, later that week, at a party in Worli. In Samundar Mahal.

You know it? asked the drunk.

I do, nodded the listener. The drunk raised his eyebrows, then continued.

Ravi was up near the top, looking away toward Mahalaxmi and Malabar Hill. He was very drunk and it seemed to him that the city itself was reflected in the churning, crashing sea below. It roiled around the Vellard and broke across the thin line of Haji Ali and in the spray and the foam and the noise was Mumbai itself, lighted skyscraper and glistening slum, a mirror held up to every sinner in the world and only to him. It was a trick of the monsoon, a play of propinquity, an accident of being across from Malabar Hill at just the right time and place. But he was down the elevator in a matter of moments and heading toward Jacob's Circle and the beacon of Heera, past the jail and across the Chinchpokli Bridge.

The bouncers didn't stop or harass him in any way. He

made his fearful, courageous way up to the top room and the man there said it was closed, as he looked at Ravi almost with concern. Is Meena coming back? Ravi finally asked.

Probably not, said the bouncer.

Will Akbarzeb be coming?

This isn't his bar, replied the bouncer. But he's free to come whenever he wants.

Do you know where he lives?

The bouncer peered at him speculatively, as if trying to make up his mind whether to help him or not. Arthur Bunder, he said eventually. Someone there will lead you to him, if you want it badly enough.

Arthur Bunder, murmured the tourist. Over there, correct?

Correct, answered the drunk. Just over that parapet, away from the sea.

Ravi parked near the causeway and wandered down Arthur Bunder, knowing what he wanted yet not how to ask. The traffic at the late-night paanwallas and ittar sellers ebbed and flowed around him and the rain fell, first gently and then more and more insistently, and before he knew it, he found himself, wet and bare-headed, at the water's edge, down by the Radio Club.

Where he sat down on the seawall, his legs dangling over the edge, next to Akbarzeb.

He was truly a giant, that man. His wet clothes clung to him as one of his men tried, ineffectually, to hold a bedraggled umbrella over him. A couple more men hovered within a few feet, holding off a knot of late-night rubberneckers, who were all trying to peer into the bay.

What happened? asked Ravi finally.

She came by my office, replied Akbarzeb calmly. Back

there, he gestured over his shoulder, down the length of Arthur Bunder.

She told me that I didn't own her. That she wasn't mine to order around, that she'd take any man she so chose, if he'd have her. That she didn't choose me, at any rate, and there was no future in my holding my breath. That she danced for the music, for herself and for Meena in *Pakeezah,* and for any young man who walked in through her door with kind eyes and a warm smile.

All these things I already knew, said Akbarzeb reflectively. She'd told me all these things before and I'd made my peace with them. To love is sometimes enough, don't you think? You don't need for it to be returned.

So I asked her what she really wanted and she told me she wanted to be free of me. My presence and my shadow. Her life was dark enough without that as well.

So I said, Why? So you can fuck insects like that idiot who left you in that whore's room without a backward glance, with one hand on his pants and his dick in the other? Is that what you want? To be a tourist's whore?

She never cried, you see. She just turned around and left the room and the man I told to watch her was walking behind her and was too far away to stop her when she moved across the pavement and to the seawall and over into the sea.

An hour ago, friend, said Akbarzeb, as a heavy hand came to rest on Ravi's shoulder. Right here. And I'll have to wake up every day for the rest of my life knowing what my last words to that woman were.

Ravi expected at that moment to be pitched into the sea and truthfully he wouldn't have minded if that were to be his fate. There's no point in telling a woman like that that her feet are too beautiful to be put on the ground, continued

Akbarzeb. I wish I had, of course. But she was born with her feet dirty.

The sea broke around their own feet and the angry waves licked and spat at them and it came as no surprise to Ravi to find that not all the moisture on his face came from the wind and the sea.

Why cry now? asked Akbarzeb, reasonably enough, his reassuring hand still on Ravi's shoulder. You should have taken her home, to your clubs and bars and parties. All the places she'd never seen.

I should have. Then she'd still be here.

Don't flatter yourself, said Akbarzeb. She didn't kill herself because you showed her what she was. You weren't the first. You wouldn't have been the last.

But I was.

Akbarzeb glanced at him with his quiet heavy eyes, then turned away. She didn't choose to be what she was, he said. Did she tell you her real name?

No, said Ravi.

They sat there for a space, long enough to gaze into the dark sea, dark as only the monsoon can make it, where even the lights of the street behind and the boats in the harbor and India beyond the bay are dimmed and die. The dark is a powerful draw and Ravi heard its call. But he stayed on the wall next to Akbarzeb, who finally stirred and said: Go away. Leave the city, or I won't be responsible for my actions. And then this can all end.

And you? Ravi couldn't help asking.

I have a world to take care of. I won't even have time to grieve.

That was fifteen years ago, said the drunk. Fifteen years. The bar girls are gone, Akbarzeb's a legislator, cell phones are everywhere. Ravi disappeared, and his absence was only re-marked upon for a fortnight at the most, at the club, around the bar, by his wondrously endowed Punjabi friend: then he too was smoke on the water of Mumbai. He went on to be-come a realtor or a consultant or a banker or a shipping agent someplace else, and doubtless he wrestles the dark there as well.

But, prompted the listener.

Yes, agreed the drunk. *But . . .*

Imagine if you will, said the tourist, two men at the sea-wall. Those two, at the table by the corner: is that them down there? He gestured at two men, one large and one slim, who walked slowly across the street to the pavement and the sea-wall beyond, the sea a liquid churning devoid of light. Is that the story? That they meet every year to remember her and then walk down to where she jumped into the sea, humming "chalte chalte" to themselves?

The drunk looked at him appraisingly over his glass and then laughed. What kind of story would that be? he asked. What kind of hack do you think I am? Why can't that be Akbarzeb and a random crony, and the sight of them triggered the memory of that time in me?

Or why can't I be Ravi? he said. How else would I know the story so well?

He lurched to his feet then, did the drunk, and for the first time the listener grasped his size, the scale of him. Why can't I just be a drunk you met in a bar and you a tourist look-ing for a story, and a story all that it is?

He came over to the listener then, a huge hand gentle on the other man's shoulder. Who then felt himself being led to the parapet to where the building slid off to the street below in a torrent of falling rain and the wet pavement beyond that and then the dark sea and finally:

Imagine if you will, said the drunk. Two men at the seawall.

PART III

AN ISLAND UNTO ITSELF

THE WATCHMAN

BY ALTAF TYREWALA

Worli

Someone is going to die today.

When I arrive on duty at seven a.m., I see a cat with blood-smeared whiskers sneaking out the building gate.

While sipping my morning cup of tea, I spill a drop on the C of *SHIV SECURITY* embroidered on my company uniform.

Then the milkman arrives wearing a blue shirt.

I close my eyes. I don't need to see anymore. I know what will happen next.

One: a pigeon will come roost on the gate's lamppost.

Two: the third-floor youth will return from the pool on his motorbike.

Three: the vegetable lady will set up shop on the pavement outside; and nestled in her hair bun will be a single bloodred rose.

Without verifying the sequence of events, with my eyes still closed, I turn around and enter the security cabin.

Pandey, my fellow dayshift watchman, is breakfasting from a tiffin box. He looks up in alarm. "Who's watching the gate, Mishra?" he asks. Pandey's tone is without rancor. The gate isn't to be neglected even for a second.

"Someone is going to die today," I say.

I return to my position at the gate.

Let me be wrong. I stare at the gravel on the ground. *Please?*

I look up and around.

No!

There is the pigeon. Parked *there* is the swimmer's bike. And pinned to the just-arrived vegetable-lady's hair bun is a maroon, blossoming . . .

Yes. Someone is going to die today, and I can do nothing about it, just wait to be proved correct.

Pandey takes up position beside me at the gate. We are trained to stand with parted legs, raised necks, and hands locked behind our backs; to not smile like doormats or frown like jailers; to guard with a detached alertness. *STRONG & COURTEOUS. SHIV SECURITY. PROVIDING SOUND SLEEP FOR 21 YEARS.*

One would think we were trained for a more profound purpose.

"What . . . what happened? Tell me," Pandey asks.

From the milkman's blue shirt down to the rose in the vegetable-lady's bun—I exclude nothing. "These same things happened the morning Paresh-bhai . . ." I trail off.

"Are you absolutely sure?" Pandey asks.

"Yes," I reply. I glance at him. "Don't look at me that way. You know I'm no seer."

Pandey mutes the fearful awe in his eyes.

One morning several months ago, right about this time, Paresh-bhai, the second-floor resident, had hailed a taxi. Right about then a passing truck burst one of its tires. The vehicle buckled, skidded across the road, and mowed down Paresh-bhai like a stalk of walking, talking human weed.

That morning, when I heard Paresh-bhai squeal, I was studying the red rose in the vegetable-lady's hair. And before that I was watching the third-floor boy park his bike. And before that I was awed by the pigeon roosted precariously on the lamp-post. And before that . . . on and on, identically, unmistakably.

"We must do someth—"

"No!" I cut Pandey off.

What could we do? Signs had lined up like the dots children join to complete a picture. I have tried not to look at things. But if a watchman won't watch, what else will he do? I have tried to ignore patterns, only to learn I have no control over memory—it remembers everything: beautiful or ugly, consequential or not. Some days I dream of working in a mine. I imagine myself chipping off rocks deep underground, where there will be nothing to see and no designs to remember. But today, someone is going to die. And, unfortunately, I know.

I know.

"Mishra, what are you doing!" Pandey cries out.

I have placed a blob of white lime on my left palm and sprinkled flakes of tobacco on it. Pandey doesn't notice till I begin grinding the mixture with my right thumb.

I roll the paste into a ball and jam it between my lower lip and teeth.

Pandey watches with shock. "That's too much! You'll be stoned for hours!"

"That's the whole idea," I say—to be out of my mind for hours; hopefully, by then, whoever is to die will have died.

The narcotic blend stuns my mouth.

My salivary glands shut down. White lime slithers across my gums. Tobacco flakes fuse with my teeth. And then . . .

And then cautiously, little by little, saliva begins trickling in again. Once spit meets lime, tobacco flakes dance. The uproar of intoxication numbs my senses in seconds.

Now I am only a thing standing by the gate. The person in me won't be back for a while.

The Sunday morning grows busier. People start to go in and out the gate of Sea View Apartments. Pandey begins call-

188 // Mumbai Noir

ing out to residents as they come and go. *"Take care, sir! Take care, madam!"*

What a fool. As if you can tell people not to die.

"Mishra!" Pandey nudges me urgently. Through my blurred vision I can sense a huge orange object zooming toward us. Its edges are glinting. When it is almost upon us I . . . I raise my trembling hand and salute.

Whew! It was only the seventh-floor resident's Santro on its way out.

Several more false alarms ring through the day. Each time Pandey winces and runs to save some child or woman or man who he fears might be run over by a reversing water-tanker or might fall into an open gutter.

By late afternoon, I stop slurring and swaying.

"Welcome back," Pandey says.

I spit out the narcotic cud. My senses may have cleared, but with clarity comes a physically excruciating sense of dread.

Pandey retreats into the security cabin, this time for lunch. No tobacco, alcohol, or drugs for him. Pandey's opiate is food.

Standing alone at the gate, I survey the scene: at eye level, the cemented compound; overhead, the wind-beaten twelve-story building; outside, the street with nonstop traffic; and people everywhere—all these people oblivious to constantly lurking death.

"Aahhrrrp!" Fifteen minutes later Pandey announces his return with a loud burp. He bounds up beside me like an excited animal. "Anyone die?"

I look at his wide-eyed, eager face. Hadn't he considered the possibility?

"What if it's you?" I ask.

An intense wave of terror passes over his face.

And then he says, "What if it's *you?*"

I chuckle tiredly.

In five more hours, at seven p.m., our duty will end.

The wait begins.

Two-fifteen.

Two-thirty.

Three p.m.

At three-thirty, Baadal, the cycle-mounted tea vendor, rides into the gate veering to the right to counter the can slung on the left side of his bike.

He leaps off swiftly, rests the bike on his bony hip, and pours us two cups of tea. Pandey takes his. He refuses to hand me mine. The petty man. Baadal pours a cup for himself. We start slurping at the syrupy brew.

"Someone is going to die today," Pandey blurts. He glances at me with a vicious triumph.

Baadal continues to drink the tea.

"You heard what I said or no?" Pandey raises his voice. "I said someone is going to die today!"

"Ya, so? Someone dies every day," Baadal says.

He takes our money, mounts his cycle, and goes away.

"Stupid punk," Pandey mutters under his breath.

A hot breeze sweeps through the compound of Sea View Apartments.

A silence descends upon us.

Pandey and I stand side by side without a word.

The afternoon's dead heat stills the air. Now every movement around us, even the tiniest of motions, takes on an unbearable gravity. That coin slipping from someone's hands. The downward spiral of that sparrow.

"Ui . . ." Pandey makes a strange guttural sound.

I look at him.

He is shortening his neck. Widening his eyes. Ballooning his cheeks.

"What happened?"

Pandey runs to the side of the security cabin. I hear him heave. *Hoowyack!* And then I hear the splash of vomit hitting the tarmac.

Pandey takes a bottle of water from the cabin. He gargles his mouth and clears his nose. When he returns he looks exhausted, harassed.

"Bad food?"

He doesn't answer. He takes up the guard position.

"Pandey?"

"You're a bastard," he says. He doesn't look at me. His throat sounds sore from the heaving. "We can't do anything. What's the point of knowing something if we can't do anything?"

"Why'd you vomit?"

"I couldn't take it," he says. He looks at me, then looks away. "The tension was too much for me."

Vapors from his vomit reach us. Now even I could vomit.

"I just want this to end, Mishra," Pandey says. "I've been waiting since morning. You've spoiled my whole day. Now I just want someone to die. I've had enough."

Four-thirty.

Four-forty-five.

Five.

Five-ten.

Five-fifteen.

Five-twenty.

Five-twenty-one.

Five-twenty-two.

Five-twenty-three.

Five-twenty-three.

Five twenty-three.

Pandey sees me tapping my watch. "What?"

"It stopped!" I shout. I knock on the dial. "I was just looking at my watch! The second hand suddenly stopped!"

I remove the watch from my wrist. I tap the dial several times. When I press it to my ear I hear a tomblike silence.

"Let me see." Pandey takes the watch. He mimics my motions. He hands it back. "The second hand is on twenty-three."

"Very strange," I say.

I hold the watch at a distance. This old metallic object suddenly seems dangerous, like a treacherous best friend. I throw the watch on the ground. After a moment's hesitation, I bring my heel down on it. Hard. Over and over and over. The dial is destroyed beyond recognition. I kick the heap of junk aside.

"You could have saved the strap," Pandey says.

He doesn't wear a watch. And now, neither do I. Without time, without hope, terrified and anxious, we stand with parted legs, raised necks, and hands locked behind our backs. But Pandey and I forget that we are to neither smile nor frown. Instead, we do both. Smiling, frowning, as we struggle to conceal a knowledge too significant to remain hidden, each of our faces contorts into an amused, quizzical grimace. Like schoolmasters who've shat their pants.

Residents of Sea View Apartments start emerging from the building for their Sunday-evening constitutionals. As they walk in and out the gate, Pandey and I are given odd stares, strange glances, lingering looks. A child points at us and starts to cry. The child's mother looks at Pandey and me. She gasps and hugs her child.

"Act normal," I whisper to Pandey.

"What? *How?*"

192 // Mumbai Noir

"Smile. Just smile," I say. I force my lips into a smile. I glance at Pandey. His grimace gives way to a sad, constipated grin.

Residents form groups of twos and threes in the compound. Something is being discussed very seriously. Worse, Pandey and I are being looked at repeatedly.

A man breaks away from the group of residents and approaches the gate. "Mishra! Pandey!"

"Ji, sir?" I say.

"Haan, sir?" Pandey says.

"What's the problem?" the man demands. "You two are scaring everyone! Have you seen your faces? What happened? Why do you look so scared?"

I peer at Pandey, hoping he will say something. But he is staring at the ground. As usual, it's all up to me. "No, no problem, sir. We are just doing duty."

The man studies my face closely. "Why are you smiling like that, Mishra?"

Now more residents, about fifteen to twenty of them, approach the gate.

"What happened?" a woman asks the man who approached us first.

"I don't know," the man says. "These two won't tell. Look at their faces."

"Mishra, Pandey," another man says. "What is the matter? Your faces are pale!"

A woman yells, "Call up their head office! Their supervisor will make them . . . *Oh my god!*"

Pandey's legs have given way. He has collapsed on the ground.

I am jostled aside as the residents rush to nurse Pandey. He is thrashing his head side to side.

Someone throws water on his face. Pandey comes to and sits up. A doctor in the group checks his eyes. "It's okay," the doctor announces, "he's all right!"

Pandey nods in agreement.

The residents of Sea View Apartments crowd around Pandey. Now they *must* have an explanation. "Don't be afraid, son, tell me what's wrong," an old woman says.

Pandey starts to weep. He buries his face in his hands and begins heaving. The old woman caresses his head. "Shh, it's okay, just tell us what's wrong . . ."

Pandey raises his teary face. He looks at me. He points his finger and shouts, "Don't ask me, ask him! Ask him!" And then he turns inconsolable.

Nineteen sets of eyes glare at me. My face starts to twitch.

A man says, "Mishra!"

"Mishra!" two women shout simultaneously.

Another man says, "Better say something, Mishra! Tell us what's going on here!"

Pandey is shaking his head to warn me. But silence is no longer an option.

"Someone is going to die today," I say.

The residents issue a collective, "*Haan?*"

"This morning a baba was passing outside the gate. He prophesied that today someone from this building was going to die."

A stunned silence. A dog barks. A bus rumbles by.

"Hmm," a man interjects.

Residents look at each other with raised eyebrows. They don't seem angry anymore. Their faces have a pensive, injured expression.

Now I am shaking and dry-heaving like Pandey. I too am weeping. "I don't want anyone to die . . ." I say. "Since morning

Pandey and I have been worried . . . going out of our minds . . . who will die . . . will that sir die . . . will that madam die . . . who will die . . . ?"

Residents are clucking their tongues and shaking their heads in pity.

The old woman who pacified Pandey now squeezes my chin. "Mishra beta, it is all destiny. No one can predict death. What is going to happen, happens."

"No, maaji," I say. "You are just saying this, but death is the worst thing to happen. No one ever wants to die . . ."

"I want to!" an old man says. Everyone looks at him and he smiles nervously. "I mean, not right now, but I'm not afraid of death."

"See?" The old woman nods and smiles. She expects me to be comforted by what that man said.

I smile back weakly.

What if I told these people the truth? There was no baba-vaba. It's me—I'm the harbinger of bad news, I'm the one who looks at everything and remembers everything and peers too deeply into the vault of reality.

A middle-aged man steps forward and smiles kindly. "Arrey, brother, death is not something to be afraid of."

I nod.

"He doesn't seem too convinced," a young woman points out.

And then, when I thought the day couldn't get stranger, events take a turn for the bizarre. The kindhearted residents of Sea View Apartments take it upon themselves to convince me of the insignificance of death. First, a show of hands is called for to see who isn't afraid of dying. All nineteen residents gathered around the gate raise their arms.

The old woman nods and smiles at me. "See?" she says.

I smile back weakly.

The young woman points out that I still don't seem convinced.

Next, all the residents are asked to describe how they would like to die. When they speak, they address me. "With a bang! *Bam!* I wouldn't even want to know!" "No, not me, I'd like to know in advance." "I want to go in my sleep, like my mother." "I want a heart attack." "I have cancer, so it's not like I have a choice." "Really? What kind?" "Liver." "I want to die on stage." "I at work." So on and so forth, till all the residents have had their say. After the last person describes how he would like to die, everyone looks at me, smiling, nodding encouragingly. The old woman has taken to stroking my sideburn. "See?" she says, "nothing to be sad about. No one minds dying."

Unfortunately, the effect these morbid testimonies have on me is contrary to what was intended. Not only does my dread deepen, I now begin doubting the sanity of these men and women. "I appreciate all this," I say, "thank you. I am sorry for spoiling your Sunday evening. I will pray for you all. I will pray for your safety and for a long life for all of you. God willing, no one will die."

The old woman's face droops and she pulls her hand back. The residents seem irritated.

"Are you bloody stupid or something?" a man standing near me says. His face is flushed.

"N-no, sir," I stutter. "I . . . I just said I will pray that—"

"Oh shut the hell up!" the man says. "That's what we're trying to tell you. There's nothing to be afraid of. There's nothing to pray for. It's okay to die."

I try to smile. "No, I know, sir. I understand. Nothing to be afraid of. Nothing to pray for. I'm sure no one will die."

The man clenches his jaw. "You are *really* pissing me off, pal!" he shouts.

A woman standing beside him pats his shoulder. "Cool it, na!"

The old woman exhales noisily and shakes her head at me. I look around. Everyone seems disapproving.

I say, "But why is he getting so angry? I am not saying anything! I am agreeing with him. There is nothing to be afraid of. Nothing to pray for. Anyway, I'm sure no one will die."

"Unnhh!" The man tugs at his hair. "Stop saying that! Stop saying that! *I'm sure no one will die. I'm sure no one will die.* Why are you even saying that? So what if someone dies!"

Now this is too much. "But I don't want anyone to die!"

"Aaaarrggghh!" the man shouts. He jumps forward and grabs me by the elbow. "You come! Bloody come with me!"

He starts pulling me and I look around for help. But the others are too stunned to react. The man drags me to the road outside the gate.

Now we are standing on the road, on the very spot where Paresh-bhai was crushed by the truck. Buses, cars, taxis, and scooters are whizzing past just a few feet away from us.

The residents have followed us out. All eighteen of them are milling behind me and the angry man clutching me by the elbow.

I lose my cool. "Sir, just let go of my arm. Don't make a scene. You are overreacting. I didn't say anything wrong, okay? Let me get back to duty. I'm sure no one will die."

"*Again?*" the man screams.

He slaps me hard on my left cheek.

And the next moment, letting go of my arm, he dives forward in the path of an oncoming BEST bus.

* * *

A balcony door slamming in the wind + Bus 65 passing outside the gate + someone shouting *Tunnu* + an itch on my left thigh = the arrival of a parcel from abroad.

A catfight across the road + a crying child + a woman in a magenta sari + the eight-floor resident's Palio entering the gate = a stranger trying to trespass into Sea View Apartments.

Children playing in the compound + the sixth-floor resident returning home early + a dog and bitch fornicating behind a parked car = Baadal veering into the gate, keeling over, and spilling his entire can of tea.

A girl in a black miniskirt + three crows perched on the first-floor window + a traffic jam + the sound of laughter = a seismic tremor.

I could go on. I also remember, for instance, the chain of events leading to a brawl on the street, a storm, and a pain in my chest. Some days I want to gouge my eyes out and silence my ears with molten lead. Maybe then all this remembering will cease. Or maybe then, and this is what I fear, my memory will latch on to some other unknown sense.

The man who dragged me to the road was merely trying to scare me. After diving forward into the path of an oncoming BEST bus, he jumps back, avoiding the vehicle by a few inches. "See?" he says. "Dying is that simple."

I say nothing. I realize I am dealing with a very disturbed man.

The man dives forward again, this time in front of an oncoming taxi.

"See?" he says again, having avoided the taxi by a millimeter.

I nod.

"Now, are you still going to pray that no one should die?" the man asks.

I shake my head.

"Good." He smiles. "You should never believe what those babas say."

The other residents break into spontaneous applause. But of course. A working-class superstitious watchman has been taught a lesson in high-class skepticism. I clap as well.

I follow the residents back to the gate. They disperse. Some return to their homes; some go out for a stroll.

Pandey is standing in the guard position. I go and stand beside him. My cheek is still stinging from the slap.

A few minutes later Pandey says, "Sorry, yaar."

We salute as a Tata Sumo exits the gate. No, no, *I* am sorry. I should have kept my mouth shut. The problem, I now realize, is in the telling.

A poor-looking man wants to visit flat 802. Pandey buzzes the flat on the intercom. The visitor is known and permission is granted. The man signs the register and enters the building.

The residents of Sea View Apartments are luminaries in their own right. There is a millionaire who owns the entire top floor. There is an actress on the sixth floor. And throughout the building is a sprinkling of very wealthy businessmen. Security was lax till a decade ago. But the country was poorer back then. And the residents of Sea View were like their countrymen. As the country grew wealthier, so did these residents. Now their lives are impossible without people like Pandey and me protecting them from people like Pandey and me.

Could I be wrong? Is it possible that someone will *not* die today?

The way the windows of floors three to six are aglow with a bright red, seeing how the sparrows are chirping and flying around like crazy, and sensing the relief of another sunset, I estimate the time to be about six-thirty.

Our duty ends at seven. I have just half an hour left to be proved right. But what if . . .

No, I cannot be wrong. Someone is going to die today. But what if . . .

How can I be wrong! There has to be a reason—some reason for me to remember so many idiotic, inconsequential details: A red rose in the vegetable lady's hair! A pigeon roosted on a lamppost!

Someone had better die in the next half hour. I see no motive to continue otherwise. If my memory and mind reveal themselves to be worthless, I might as well drink and drug myself to death.

No, if I can think, and if I can remember random sequences of events from weeks and months ago, there has to be a reason, some reason. Within the next half hour someone will die; and when it happens, I will remain calm. I will not celebrate. I will not grin knowingly at Pandey. I will keep quiet and go home, content with the knowledge that existence has its own plan, and that, watching-watching day in and out, I have somehow cracked that plan's blueprint.

The telephone in the security cabin rings.

Pandey goes in to answer it.

After a few seconds he shouts, "Mishra, take, it's DG-saab!"

DG is the Shiv Security supervisor for this part of the city.

Pandey emerges from the cabin. I go in and pick up the receiver. "Hello?"

"Haan, Mishra, DG here. Are you tired?"

"What, saab?" I say.

"Boss, are you tired?"

"Uh, as usual, saab. I've been here since morning."

"Could you, maybe . . ." DG says, "somehow stretch it till tomorrow morning?"

"Why!"

"Relax, brother, I'm asking for a favor. Rajkumar cannot come for duty. He has guests from village. If you can't do it, I'll have to fill in for him. Can you do the night shift with Sohrab?"

"But—"

"Ya, what?" DG snaps.

"Why didn't you ask Pandey?"

"Come on! Pandey just got married a month ago. It's too early for his wife to sleep alone. You know how women are in the beginning."

"Pandey told you this?"

DG laughs. "Don't be a nut. We have to understand such things."

"Tomorrow I will have to do the day shift as well?"

DG says he doesn't know yet, but most probably no. Either way, my overtime pay is assured.

"Okay," I say. "I'll stay."

What else? Do I have a choice? It is almost seven p.m. If I refuse to oblige, DG will have to do the night shift. But I don't care about that. It's almost seven, and if I refuse to oblige, I will have to go home a broken, hopeless man. I will have to admit that my memory and my mind have no purpose, and that all the events I see and remember amount to zilch.

This morning, after I saw what I saw, I was certain someone was going to die today.

Now "today" has become longer. The half-hour deadline has postponed itself. I thought I had grabbed existence by its horns, but the willful thing has managed to break loose again, leaving me hanging for another twelve hours.

Pandey is very sorry to hear of my double shift. He tells me to go eat something, to shit, piss, stack up on tobacco and white lime and whatever else will keep me awake through the night. "Go, go fast," he says. "I'll wait till you return."

I walk out the gate and cross the road.

Before entering the neighborhood eatery, I look back for a glimpse of Sea View Apartments. Against the backdrop of a dark blue sky, with the streetlights and flat-lights glittering, and the traffic zooming up and down the road, the setting seems poised for something momentous, something horrendous.

I exhale. It's going to be a long, long night.

LUCKY 501

BY SONIA FALEIRO

Sanjay Gandhi National Park

I

The Vihar Lake is an ink spot in the Sanjay Gandhi National Park. It is cool, dense, and dark green, shapeless yet distinct. It is infested with crocodiles and encircled by forest with spotted deer and owlets, minivets and magpies.

The dai lived somewhere on the banks of this lake. She lived on castration and so great was her skill she had transformed five hundred without suffering a fatality. Those desiring her services would make an appointment months in advance. They did so at her reed mat and bolster outside the Kanheri Caves, in the park, but quite far from where she slept. She could not write, but had a strategy that compensated. If a man was dark, she would mark his name with a circle painted black. A bulbous nose would find expression in a square. This way she remembered and, more so, was humoured.

Like the dai, the ones who came to her were neither men nor women. They were tragic, some thought, but mainly fascinating. They wore saris, applied lipstick, urinated standing up. Among them some were more beautiful than others. Their beards had subsided.

If they liked you enough, they would invite you home and tell you their stories. These stories were always the same. They were of a boy who dressed as a girl and was thrown out of home for doing so. Then the hijras recognized him and said, "But you are one of us! You share our soul." So the boy was alone no more. He knelt before the gurus and learned the laws. He knew the hijra anthem: One palm crack, "Hello!" Two, "Goodbye." More, "Beware." The years passed and the boy became a man who wanted to be womanly. So he surrendered his body to the dai nirvan. Like the one of whom it will now be told, the boy desired femininity he believed a doctor's touch could not realize. Soft skin, breasts. But when it was done, the castrated one was neither man nor woman. He was a third sex.

The one of whom it will be told, he called himself Shabnam. This is how it was for him.

The evening before the castration, Shabnam was asked what he would like to eat. A baby goat he didn't skin was roasted on a fire he didn't help prepare. There were breads and a fulsome daal. He concentrated on his food. He was asked: Which songs shall we sing? What stories would you like to hear? Questions made to one who should not die with regrets. He answered truthfully.

At night Shabnam's snores mingled with the gossip of the greylag geese. He slept well, perhaps because the day after was unimaginable.

At five a.m. he was shaken awake. It was stifling in the park, he realized, and in the muddy light his sleepy eyes saw a grove of trees beckon, their branches claw-sharp. He peered forward, but was unable to see clearly. The trees continued their rustling. A cold wind nibbled at his flesh.

The dai was squatting by his side, chewing sugar biscuits dipped in tea. She was ugly, concluded Shabnam. Wrinkles scrambled across her face. A coil of silver hair rotted down to her empty blouse. On as close inspection as he dared, he realized she could be of any sex but appeared of none.

This will not be me, he swore to himself. *I have chosen well. I am tearing out the root of my manhood before it is too late.*

II

Shabnam, then Sharad, had lived near the park all of his life. Its tranquillity was one of fits and starts, for there were slums within the park and without, and all along the borders of the main road that led straight to Aarey Milk Colony just outside of which he had lived. Cars sped past pots bubbling on twig fires. Women wrenched each other's plaits out in arguments over the communal tap.

Sharad wasn't as poor. He went to school, he had new clothes once a year, and although his room was not his own, it had a window and on this window a sill from which he could enjoy the pleasures of the park. His particular pleasure was bird-watching and some days his entire conversation might comprise sentences such as: "Another white-tailed stonechat!"

Sharad's parents were the Sharmas, and the Sharmas split the rent of their two-room, toilet, kitchen with a Muslim couple. The man and woman kept to themselves; they recited Rumi to each other. Their poetry, their detachment from all but each other, was romantic, and sexual, and his parents despised and feared them for it. His father would snarl, "What can you expect of people who pet their goats at breakfast and slaughter them for dinner?"

The Muslims were kind in the ways children appreciate. They spoke to Sharad directly, not through his parents. They lent him their precious Rumi. In time he could recite: *"Lovers don't finally meet somewhere. They are in each other all along."* He would echo the couple's murmurings from the room he shared with his parents. *"When I am with you, we stay up all night, when you are not here, I cannot get to sleep."*

And they introduced him to the hijras.

It happened thus. It was Friday, he was fifteen and waiting outside Ajantha Cinema. That night, as on most Friday nights, a stranger paused before him, and having appraised his reddened lips, the cinch of belt around his small waist, invited him in for a film.

Later, as Sharad raised his head from its accustomed position, he saw one of the Muslims, the woman, staring at him. Sharad was not embarrassed. This was how boys like him got by.

Then one evening, several weeks later, when his parents were at a wedding, the Muslims invited Sharad to the cinema. He wasn't interested in them in that way, he said. He liked them, just not in that way.

Yes, the woman said. Of course not, agreed the man. It was just the cinema.

Outside the theater, clearly waiting for them, stood two hijras dressed in nylon saris. One of them sucked on a joint as she fussed with her pleats. Another had wandering eyes and a lisp. *Thona re!* she mouthed to the knock-kneed black marketeer standing close, counting his wad of tickets with moist black fingers, *O mere thona re!*

The Muslims introduced Sharad. "These are our friends," the man said.

"They can help you," said the woman.

"You like boys?" the hash smoker cut to the chase. Sharad nodded. "Want to come with us?" she asked. Sharad shook his head. He had seen these hijras around. They begged. They stank. They were slum dwellers. And Sharad was no slum dweller, even if he did like boys.

The next Friday, as he neared Ajantha, he spied the hijras from a distance. He was about to turn back when the hash smoker beckoned to him with a paan-stained pout. The hijras bought the tickets, they watched the movie, no demands were made of Sharad.

Over weekends like these evolved something like friendship.

Sharad would look back at this courtship with a smile. If the hash smoker was to be believed, all hijras ever did was dance at weddings. All they ever spent their money on was the cinema. Then there was the casual introduction to their guru at a party. Had it even been someone's birthday?

His parents were told or found out.

No beatings.

His father was a civil man.

Sharad was locked in their bedroom.

Once he spied a sarus crane gliding above the trees. A park watchman had spoken of last seeing one two years earlier. His spirits soared. Then he remembered what he was.

The hijras came for him. Their thundering songs as they strode past Sharad's cowering mother recalled the determination of a pariah kite swooping down on a rodent.

As he stuffed some clothes into a bag, Sharad knew it had been a matter of time. The hijras of the slums understood him in a way his parents never could.

If his family wished upon him heterosexuality, the hijra guru he went on to share with the hash smoker wanted him to eradicate every sign of it.

Hira Bai had a square beefy face, a purple mouth, bitten-down nails varnished red. She knew everything, and one of the things she knew was this: "A real hijra has no chili." When this statement prompted no reaction, she petted Shabnam into submission. "You are *my* diamond," she growled over and over again. "And I want you to be flawless."

In time Shabnam accepted the logic of castration. Once a

nirvan, his hair would grow and his voice would soften. A nirvan is no better than an akwa, uncut; but he would no longer have to tuck it in.

So on Hira Bai's fortieth birthday, and at barely seventeen, Shabnam took his guru aside. Patting away her outstretched palm—he had, after all, said he had a present for her—he asked that she call the dai nirvan.

<h1 style="text-align:center">III</h1>

Stray images of years past now flitted through Shabnam's mind. Fearing agitation, he calmed himself as he knew best.

Favorites. The color blue. Kingfisher, quail, parrot finch, bee-eater. Swallow. Oh yes, robin chat.

He was offered no food, no water. He swallowed some opium and followed the dai and her two helpers to a pond thick with water chestnuts. Here, many years past, they had built a temple to the goddess.

As Shabnam prayed with the rest, the dai waited for the call. It could be a cock's crow. It could be a silence impenetrable. It could offer itself in minutes or be measured in the gathering of a cloud field. But once revealed, there was no going back.

A helper scratched his groin, a scraping sound like a cat pawing a shut door. The other, encouraged, quickly cleared his throat. Shabnam had been sweating in the sauna heat of the park and was heavy with drowsiness. A pintail duck quacked. Shabnam startled, said something. The helpers ignored him. The dai ignored them all.

They were all the same, she thought. Some barely eighteen. They believed the younger you were, the greater the feminizing effects of castration. Their gurus encouraged them, of course. The pretty ones were sought after as prostitutes. The more they earned, the richer their gurus became. So of course the gurus wanted nirvan for all.

They didn't encourage doctors either. A boy who went to Bangkok would work hard to save for the operation, but he might skimp in his offerings to his guru.

And there was such a thing as being too womanly, acknowledged the dai. It was one thing to chop off your chili. Another to get a vagina. What for to be so beautiful? A beautiful one wasn't a hijra, she was a woman. Next thing you knew, she ran off to get married and there was one less in the community.

The ways of boys were none of the dai's business. But she had reason to suffer discontent. She had recently turned sixty-five and she felt each day of her years. Her hands were spotted, lumpy; her limbs carried the weight of her age. And every slicing now turned her off food, her life's single greatest pleasure.

Yet each time she brought up the subject of retirement, the chief gurus would recoil. "But you're unbeaten at five hundred! Better than Tendulkar!"

For all their interest, what did they really know about her? Not one of the hijras she had sliced had asked whether she sterilized her knife. She did; boiling it over and over again in the water of neem leaves. They weren't curious about whether she herself was a nirvan. She was, although in her time there wasn't all this pampering and feasting. She was sliced with a thin piece of glass, nails were jammed into her urethra, three months later she returned to work, and if she peed while fucking, her customers, for what they paid, didn't complain.

Her guru had been a dai nirvan. Who knew that? When her guru died, she inherited the position.

The dai saw the sign.

She sighed.

Sure, a dai nirvan earned well and was respected in the community, she admitted, prodding the boy along. She was in a social class apart and on festivals received new utensils. Boys died and no one ever thought to blame the dai. It wasn't death, after all, that was an accident in this matter, but life. She was paid her full fee, irrespective. It was a good deal, she knew, and five hundred was a record unbeaten so far.

And yet.

Shabnam followed the dai and perhaps the opium had hit him, for he staggered and stopped repeatedly, as though performing a dance.

His testicles were knotted with twine.

In the slums of the park brewed the morning's hustle and bustle. Feet slapped the dirt road, bicycles pedalled on it, hands reached out to one another, vendors cried—*tea, vegetables, toys!* Children found plenty to laugh at as they ran about naked, feet kicking up pools of dust.

Shabnam heard all of this but softly, softly. He was so far away from them.

The poor continue submitting, he sneered.

What he meant, of course, was that not one of them cared for him.

Fear turned his bowels into water, *drip, drip, drip.*

Color? Flying? Flightless? Too easy.

First bird seen after running away to Hira Bai.

He paused, confused. A red-necked falcon? A black drongo? "Wait," he said. "Wait." The dai closed her eyes. Shabnam looked at her helplessly. "A water cock? A painted snipe?"

In the creamy blue sky sailed a kite and its colorful tail wagged this way and that. *Goodbye! Good luck!* it said to Shabnam drifting away to a happier place.

"A common teal?" begged Shabnam. "A kestrel?"

His knees gave way.

He felt water in his mouth, a steady stream that splashed his torso, rolling down to his feet. Now he cried, as they demanded, "Mata! Mata! Mata!" He cried, and the dai held up her newly sharpened knife.

How she enjoyed a good meal.

A hot-hot double rot. Methi ki daal. What she called vihar dai ki raita—curd sprinkled with chopped onions, tomato, coriander, and a handful of crisp boondi. In the summer she would spend days chopping and spicing vegetables for pickles. On her window stood an army of glass bottles and as the pickles ripened, friends would find excuses to visit her at meal times. Nothing beat homemade carrot pickle with hot roti and a fat glass of lassi.

These were small pleasures, she told herself. Not too much to ask.

Phallus, scrotum, testes.

He crumpled.

The blood was rubbed across his body; hot oil was drizzled on it.

A helper placed the severed parts in a plastic bag. Some liked to take them home to preserve in alcohol.

Shabnam awoke a few hours later and called out weakly to the dai. She hurried to his side. Picking him up like he was weightless, she carried him to the grindstone and thrust his naked body into a sitting position. She hugged him so tight. Blood trickled down his legs. Menstruation.

IV

When Sharad returned home after running away with the hijras that first time, his mother had cried into his shirt. They had walked up and down the colony, she told him, accosting every hijra they saw, demanding to know his whereabouts. "We went to the shamshan ghat," she wept. His father didn't speak to him. The neighbors had heard, and were pleased. For all their book learning, their protestations that they didn't share a kitchen with the Muslims, the Sharmas were no better than them.

The second time, he stayed away for weeks, dancing at weddings, travelling to Kalyan with Hira Bai to attend the urs of Haji Malang, a patron of the city's hijras.

This time when he returned, his mother's grasp had an unmistakable foreignness to it. It wasn't her fault. She was as full of longing as the first time she had held him in her arms.

V

After news of his castration spread, Shabnam became as popular as a cinema star. Hijras he had never met, and a few he had, visited him daily.

One would be so bold, having once lain on that same bed, to push aside the covers that swaddled Shabnam's shoulders down to feet. Here was a lemony yellow rib cage and a stomach uneven as upma. But above the womanly hips and before the small feet, their oval toenails a clear pink, was the reason why they had come to pay homage. A hairless mound of raw flesh. And crawling on it, a fresh puckered scar.

All the while he was being examined, Shabnam drifted between dreams.

On the fortieth day, the one who survived was celebrated with jalsa. He would be scrubbed with turmeric and dressed in the red sari of a Hindu bride. There would be flowers everywhere. The guests would jostle in high pitch. A few would be envious, he imagined, with a small shiver of pleasure. No doubt their masculinity would weigh heavier than usual and they would whisper that he thought too much of himself.

Hira Bai would be ecstatic.

And his parents? Would they come?

He giggled sleepily, imagining his father's reaction to his chili curled up in a jar.

And so the days passed, days that seemed like nights, nights of weeks that were a miasma of dreams, of bedside visits, of hot poultices.

Then broke a dawn destined to be his last.

When Shabnam awoke he did not know this and daydreamed again, perhaps aloud, as the dai fed him a broth of vegetables and chicken liver.

She said nothing.

Sometime between lunch and dinner, as she waited patiently outside the hut, Shabnam died.

Only a few minutes later, the dai entered and kneeled down to check his pulse. His flesh was cool. She straightened up briskly and walked toward the windows. Drawing back the curtains of sari cloth, she threw open the rotting shutters. December had arrived in the park. The sky crackled with the flap and caw of hundreds of migratory birds.

"How peaceful it is," murmured the dai.

The room would air out quickly, she thought, pleased.

Gossip churned like pepper in a mill.

What was it? Neither akwa nor nirvan but in-between.

"He wasn't fit to be one of us and so Mata took him," Hira Bai shrugged.

"He fucked women," the hash smoker lied.

His parents had forgotten him, the hijras said, and if they had not, who would be the first to tell them?

The dai's reaction was swift. She performed a puja of self-cleansing, then announced she would never again castrate. They begged her to reconsider. She was helpless, she said. Guilt had stilled her lucky left hand.

Death's rituals need no indulgence. Penis and testicles to the dogs. The helpers, faces disguised in shawls, feet anxious to leave the scene, disposed of Shabnam.

VI

In the Vihar Lake, a body watches a child slipping on his mother's bangles. He watches a teenager trying to escape something he's anchored to. He watches himself, his head on Hira Bai's lap, sighing as she runs a fragrant oiled comb through his hair. He spots a great eagle, a bristled grass warbler. He turns to share the sighting with his parents, only to find them standing behind him. His mother is crying, but it his father who surprises him. "Come back," he sighs heavily, so heavily. Now his womanly self wishes to be heard. She bends forward with a secret. Her chest is heavy with rolled-up socks. He leans in, pleased. Her face collapses into a swarm of wrinkles. The dai smiles at him with curious satisfaction.

THE EGG

BY NAMITA DEVIDAYAL

Walkeshwar

On the fourth floor of Tirupati Towers, an all-vegetarian building near Teenbatti, Anita Mitesh Shah heard the doorbell ring and instantly burrowed deeper into the comforter, her billowing pink cave. This is where she took refuge when she wanted to distance herself from the household's daily ablutions. Although her bedroom was at the end of the corridor, she could never keep out the gurgles and grunts of the servants, Tarini's whines, and the daily stream of terrorists disguised as broom vendors and fruit-sellers who came to her door. Everyone was trying to unhinge her in a sly, subtle way. She knew their game.

Some days, Anita felt threatened even by Rajkiran, the muscular sweeper, because she was convinced that he had stockpiled pictures of her in his head. Uncensored ones, accentuated with frozen nipples and blue toenails. As she lay there, she saw a flash of something being hit by a car in the building's driveway. She deleted the thought before it could completely unspool its menacing visuals. They didn't leave her alone.

Anita swung her legs over the bed and went through the ritual of double-clicking her feet, first the left one, then the right one, on the red line that ran through the carpet, over the gentle creeper that had been woven in by some kind Kashmiri to give her solace. She went into the bathroom, shut the door, delved into the corner of the cabinet behind the mirror, and took out the little pillbox with a green cap. Two capsules ensconced in her palm, she wrapped her gown tightly around herself and stepped out.

Suman, the maid with a slight hunch, was dusting, carefully working her way through the crevices of a crystal Ganesh.

"Get me water!" Anita barked. "Who rang the bell just now?"

"It was the maharaj, bhabhi. He had come to collect his clothes. He wanted to meet you, he came yester—"

"I don't want to meet him. Did you give him his clothes?"

"Yes, of course, bhabhi."

Anita was convinced the girl was being sarcastic. She glowered at her, hating even more how she always walked around with the bottoms of her salwar rolled up to just below her knees, revealing skinny white legs streaked with faint black hair, because she was endlessly washing clothes.

Fifteen minutes after Anita took her pills, the thoughts slowed down. She went into the bathroom and smoked a cigarette, blowing smoke out of the window and waving her hand in front of her face each time she did, so that the smell would go away. But the smoke merely curled its way back and seeped into her thick hair, lingering there like a halo of discontent.

The first time she had smoked was ten years ago, on her wedding night in Udaipur, where her family lived. She was in Hotel Marigold with the man who had suddenly transformed from stranger to husband after some well-meaning relative had fatalistically circled a *Times of India* matrimonial. He had handed her his lit cigarette with a grin. She'd felt flattered and strangely excited at the prospect of doing something so new and naughty. She had coughed and coughed, then vomited a week's worth of rich wedding food over the balcony, and finally lain flat on her back on the bed, and fallen into deep abiding sleep amidst the scent of stale tuberoses. In the morning, as they both sat on the balcony overlooking the lake, surrounded by low hills dotted with temples and mosques, he offered her another drag of his cigarette and she had breathed it in without any hesitation, like a pro. Then they made love. And she held onto that moment—the orgasmic skies and the temple chimes and the distant clanging of a Rajasthani brass band that applauded their union.

Ten years can change so much.

She vaguely knew that Mitesh had left very early in the morning. She had stirred, but not woken when she heard the shower go on and off. She had smelled the sweet incense that he lit in front of the little Laxmi photo in the corner of their room, a ritual he followed just before he left every morning, and she knew he was gone. The doorbell woke her up to that familiar paralysis of loneliness.

Back in the bathroom, she sat on the toilet seat smoking her second cigarette, and absentmindedly called his number. The first line of the Gayatri Mantra screeched into her ear before she heard his voice.

"Hello?"

"So, what are you doing, Mr. Mitesh?" she asked. Playfully. Hopefully.

Mitesh reminded her that it was budget day and a busy time for Paypal, his subbroking office. It was a brief conversation. She put the phone down, popped a minty Kushal Kanthil into her mouth, and went outside into the dining room. She stood at the window. The sounds of an angry street swam up through the dazzling summer heat. Car horns jolted with the chants that emanated from the Jain temple on the street corner. A reverse horn plaintively belted out the *Titanic* theme song. Two people were fighting, perhaps over a parking space, or the price of onions, or maybe it was just the way they spoke.

Anita sat on her dining table sipping tea out of a melamine mug. She scratched at a dried-up patch of yellow daal on the clear plastic table cover and contemplated the day that loomed in front of her. She had to go to Dr. Jain, who kept changing her dosage, taking her on a merry-go-round of emotions which she didn't mind. It had become her new reality. She'd long forgotten what it was like to feel normal. She also had to pick up two new muslin dhotis for Mitesh. He wore them every morning to the temple and they grew thin quickly, probably because the cursed maid spent all her time washing them too hard. Taru needed a new box of HB Natraj pencils. Anita also had to interview the new maharaj. She felt overwhelmed and weakened by her task list.

A few minutes later, she picked up the telephone handset and dialed her husband's number again.

"Actually . . ." She paused, clutching the phone tightly. "Actually, I just wanted to tell you to bring home some money." She waited, desperate, wanting him to continue the conversation. But obviously that was not to be. The stocks must have been flickering like little green aliens in front of him. *Soma Cement. Alpine Industries.* He was in another world. So she put the phone down after a weak, "Don't forget."

Those were the conversations she now thrived on— money and food and which social event they had to attend that weekend. They were distant dialogues, but they gave her immense comfort because they took her away from the diabolical dramas that banged around all day in her head during the times between the pills. She thrived on the quotidian. Her daughter's schedule of school and classes, her husband's routine of work and home. The food that had to be ordered, bargaining with the vegetable vendor, visiting the family jeweler to break and remake the same necklaces, bangles, rings. Once a week, they ate out. She was grateful that he no longer nudged her in the middle of the night, because she would slip into a deep sleep after her last pill. It had been three years since they had touched each other.

Some time back, she had popped into his office in Bhuleshwar, after stopping by Pannalal Jewelers on the next street, where she'd dropped off a kundan necklace to get its clasp repaired. When she pushed open the tinted glass door that had *Paypal Finance* painted in red letters, she was surprised to see that the old man who sat at the front desk had been replaced by a young girl. The girl had curly hair with blond highlights and a big pink mouth. The girl looked at her strangely, as if she were an imposter, not the proprietor's wife. Mitesh had come out of his cabin and seemed surprised to see Anita. He turned to the girl and asked her to bring madam a cup of tea, just a little tenderly, she thought.

That voice stayed on in her head and kept coming back, in startling ways, while she bathed, when she sifted through apples, looking for the nonbruised ones, when she walked on the treadmill. Sometimes she woke up to it. She kept nursing that moment, allowing it to enter her, letting it change volume levels. Sometimes that simple sentence—*bring madam a cup of tea*—was the only voice she heard for hours. Like now, as she sat at the dining table, her elbows sticking to the clear plastic sheet.

She called Mitesh. This time, she just heard his voice and hung up. He called back.

"No, no, nothing. I pressed redial by mistake," she said, gathering and regathering the little dried-up flakes of yellow daal in hurried finger movements.

A pungent lemony antiseptic smell pervaded the room. Rajkiran was swabbing the floor on the other side. When he reached the dining table, she lifted her legs onto the chair, folding her gown over them, so that he could get on with his cleaning. She watched him, moving in rhythmic movements next to her, and felt fearful again. *Bring madam a cup of tea.* She shut her eyes and the feeling went away. Maybe the three of them could go and have veg sushi at Cream Centre; it had been awhile since they had taken Tarini out. They could leave at seven after she returned from her abacus class. Anita was about to pick up the phone again, then decided against it.

The bell rang. When Suman opened the door, a light automatically went on and illuminated a photograph in the hallway. It was laminated, frameless, and enormous, covering almost half the wall. In the picture, they looked like any other happy family—a man, a woman, and a little girl, smiling on a beach, frothy ocean at their feet, with a balloon seller walking away from them. There were no dead bloated fish; no maimed characters smelling of urine. There was no other woman, no scent of a stranger in the medley of sweat and perfume and aftershave and stale cigarettes. The print ensured that the memory museum meant for public viewing would be filled with happy Kodak moments. Maybe loss showed up in the negative, or in dreams, or in an act of violence that would be passed on like a family heirloom.

That was the time the three of them had gone to Kovalam, to a timeshare beach resort. Mitesh had complained that there were not enough vegetarian dishes on the menu and he'd hated the smell of fish that lingered like a bad conversation and followed them everywhere, even into their room. They had not fought, but he had been on the phone most of the time. The market never sleeps.

It was the dhobi at the door. Suman walked in, hunched, with a pile of freshly ironed clothes. Anita then remembered that she had to interview the new maharaj that afternoon. Her sister-in-law had promised to send a candidate who was known for his exquisite undhiyo. Perhaps she could do a trial meal with him, but only if he was willing. She knew the breed; they could be quite difficult.

A week back, when Anita was out shopping, her household had turned upside down. She heard the story later from Suman, dramatized in her high-pitched voice. The maharaj was in the middle of cutting long yellow ribbons of khandvi and he couldn't find the coriander. He accused Suman of hiding it and started rummaging around in the refrigerator. That was when he made the discovery.

Deep inside the vegetable drawer, hidden under a sheaf of spinach, there lay a candy-striped paper box that said, *Pom Pom Wafers*. The Maharaj wondered what it was doing there, so he opened it. Inside, there sat a solitary, oval, faintly cracked egg. He held it for a split second, with a look of horror on his face, and then dropped it as if it were a ticking bomb. He stared at the yolk spreading slowly across the white Granamite tiled floor, then gathered up his dhoti and ran out of the kitchen, cursing the bhabhi loudly in his native language, cursing her parents—Suman repeated this detail twice over—and left the house.

Later that evening, Anita's mother-in-law came upstairs and confronted her about the egg, her green-brown eyes blazing, her two-carat solitaires sparkling furiously.

"Do you know we could be thrown out of the building? The only reason no one has said anything is because Papa is so close to the builders and they have their accounts with Mitesh."

"Mummy . . ." Anita was in tears, shaking. She could hear them. The mean voices started moving and knocking about in her head. She contained herself and told her mother-in-law what Dr. Jain had said. Little Tarini was not meeting the growth charts and she had to supplement her diet with something more substantial. He was the one who suggested eggs, she pleaded, only one a week.

Her mother-in-law's voice softened: "At least ask my permission next time you want to do something like this. We could have thought of something that would not go against anyone's feelings, na?"

Anita did not look up. She heard the word *feelings* and drew in. When she did look up, she saw Suman lurking behind the kitchen door, watching the scene.

She took an extra pill that day. She did not dare bring up the incident with Mitesh. All she told him was that the maharaj had left and her husband smiled and said, "Well, you didn't like him much anyway, no? But he was a good cook. Ask Parul-behn to help you find a new one."

It was true. Anita was not entirely unhappy that the maharaj was gone. She had never liked this man who tyrannized her kitchen with his overbearing disgruntled manner. She abhorred his rasping voice and the little gold studs in his ears. She hated the way she could see his striped shorts under his white kurta and dhoti. She used to find him muttering to himself while kneading dough, a strange smile on his sunburned face. He terrorized her. Once, he dared to sneak up to the bedroom door and saw her holding an unlit cigarette. He stared at her as if he had caught her naked and she spent the rest of the day hiding in her bedroom. She was convinced he would tell her mother-in-law or discuss it with the other cooks when they gathered in the evening at the street corner.

She had meant to talk to Mitesh about the evil maharaj, but by the time he came home, she would slowly be entering her pink cave. She would only remember again in the morning when the maharaj asked her to order the food for the day, staring at her breasts while she gave her instructions: chana daal, doodhi, thepla, and your chopped-up penis, you son of a bitch. After a while, she let him decide what to make so that they didn't have to interact.

The phone rang. Anita's sister-in-law Parul said that the new maharaj could only come the next day. Anita felt despondent and desperately wanted to call her mother. But her mother was dead. Anita put on her black tights and a new white kurti with silver crochet at the end of the sleeves. She slipped on a diamond bangle. She then picked a pair of wedge heels and walked down the stairs. She hated the lift; its doors shut with a metallic clang, leaving her in a digital conundrum as it heaved up and down. She was always afraid that she would get trapped inside and the oxygen would run out.

In the building foyer, she ran into her neighbor Arti, and they hugged each other. They occasionally met for tea. Arti was always busy, going here and there with her Amway products, peddling enormous jars of vitamins, detergent, and protein supplements. She hardly ever had the time to sit and listen to Anita's nonstories.

"So I heard about your maharaj," Arti said with a smile. "And my maharaj told me that after he left your home, he was caught urinating on the road next to the governor's bungalow. He got into a fight with the police constable who caught him and spent a night in the Malabar Hill station lock-up. He has told everyone that it was all because of the egg that you brought into the house. He said you were cursed. What to say! These people will never change."

"I always knew he was trouble. I'm happy he has gone," said Anita. "The only problem is that we have to go downstairs and eat dinner with the monster these days."

They both laughed and walked out of the building together.

"See you at Gold's Gym tomorrow," Anita said.

"If I'm back in time, I'll come in the evening for tea. I want to see that new crystal Swarovski Ganesh you bought at the exhibition," Arti said. "And I'll bring you a fresh stock of hand sanitizer." She waved and walked off with her big bag slung on her shoulder.

Anita got into a taxi and directed it to Dr. Jain's clinic on the other side of Napean Sea Road, in a building called Doctor Center. It had been three years since she started going to him, after someone in their Lion's Club recommended him for migraines. He had diagnosed her with something that she didn't understand. And she had blindly started taking the pills he prescribed, never paying attention to what they were, never discussing them with anyone else. All she knew was that they made her feel better. Sometimes they slowed her down. Or they hyperaccentuated what was happening around her, making her feel like she was a part of one of the reality television shows she loved to watch, filled with drama and intrigue and dangerous people. They took her away from herself. They worked.

Dr. Jain's clinic was on the first floor, a small room with fake wood paneling that ran all around. She stared at the wood; a faint brown powder had begun to trickle down from it. It was exactly like the powder that had been forming a regular trail under the wood panel that ran the length of her living room, swept off every day by Rajkiran, only to return again and again. She was overwhelmed by the thought of termites taking over her entire flat, leaving only a sea of fine powder.

She had spoken to the Tirupati Towers manager about it, but the society did not permit pest control treatment because it went against the community's religious beliefs. *We do not kill living things,* she was told. She tried to argue with the manager, saying that the entire building could eventually collapse, but he called her a blasphemer and suggested that she stay out of men's business. What would he do if he found out that she had been secretly bringing eggs into their pristine society with its big marble statue-cum-fountain of Krishna in the foyer?

She was back home with a new vial of pills, staring at the wood powder for a long time, she didn't even know how long. She had already forgotten about the dhotis and the pencils. The bell rang and the photograph in the hallway lit up.

"Mummy has sent the food, bhabhi," said Suman, bringing three hot plastic cases and a tiffin to the dining table.

Ever since the cook had left, her mother-in-law had been sending food upstairs. One daal, two vegetables, and a dozen thin rotis slathered with ghee to keep them soft and smooth. Suman boiled rice, which was easy enough. At dinnertime, they went down to the floor below and ate with Mitesh's parents. The two men would sit on one side of the room and analyze the market's movements. Mitesh's mother would come out of her evening meditation and then try and coax her granddaughter to start attending Saturday-morning pathshala lessons at the temple. Anita would try and focus on Tarini's homework: Contour maps. English spelling. Marathi.

Anita continued to sit on her living room sofa, staring at the invisible termites. She felt them crawling all over her body. Suman spoke to her softly.

"Bhabhi, while you were out, the maharaj came to finish the hisaab and collect his dues . . ." She paused. "Bhabhi, he wanted to meet you this morning too . . ." Suman faltered.

She looked at her employer, a little concerned. "He said it's urgent. He said he wants to travel to his village and needs the money."

"Get ready to go to the bus stop, it's almost time for Tarini."

Anita headed to the bathroom, swallowed one of the new pills Dr. Jain had given her, and lit up a cigarette. As she stood at the window, waving out the smoke, she looked down and saw him. He was sitting on his haunches below the mango tree near the building gate, talking to the watchman. He had a cloth bag slung on his arm and his gold earring glinted in the sun as he abruptly turned around and looked up. She shrank back. But the wispy white smoke that had already wound its way out of the window could not be stopped.

Anita was fraught. She picked up the phone and called Mitesh. He told her he was in a meeting and couldn't talk. She went back into the bedroom and lay down on the embroidered pink comforter, growing more fearful. The room was closing in on her. She didn't know what to do. She picked up one of her daughter's coloring books on the bedside table, reached for a box of color pencils, and started filling the empty picture furiously, indiscriminately, the hair red, the shoes green. It kept her focused and she felt strangely intimate with the picture of the girl carrying a bucket down a hill. She thought she saw Rajkiran's shadow outside, entering her daughter's room. But he had long left, so who was it? She put down the book and dialed Mitesh, but it rang incessantly, bleating the Gayatri Mantra over and over. She tried again; there was no answer. After the seventh attempt, she knew that something was terribly wrong. *Bring madam a cup of tea.* The words reeled in her head, almost like a record playing on a low speed. She stormed into the bathroom and washed down one more pill with tap water. Diarrhea? Cholera? She didn't care. She didn't care what, where, when, how, who. She just needed Mitesh to . . . The doorbell rang. Anita rushed out and stood near her bedroom door while Suman went to see who it was.

The three people in the picture lit up and, for that brief moment, there was a happy family. Then Anita heard the familiar rasping voice: it was her previous maharaj.

"Please call bhabhi," he was saying to Suman, in some distant drama down the corridor.

Anita sat on her bed, letting him spray his spittle on the world and flay his antennae. The commotion outside grew louder.

"I know she is inside. Call her!" He ordered Suman the way he used to when he still worked in this home. Anita heard Mitesh's voice echoing in the middle of the maharaj's commands. *Bring madam a cup of tea.* She picked up a pink pencil and jabbed it on the bedside table. The nib broke. She tried calling her husband again but the phone was switched off. No Gayatri Mantra. No Mitesh. No Tarini. No Arti. Just a long empty beach with a priest walking toward her, his dhoti billowing, never managing to reach her. And the seashore littered with thousands of broken eggshells.

Anita went back into her pink cave and let out a long low wail. She got up. She was walking on eggshells toward the kitchen, away from the priest, her gaze set on the distant horizon of her kitchen countertop. She picked up an eggshell shaped like a vegetable knife with a brown handle. Was it a knife or was it a dead crab? She looked around the kitchen. Where did the priest go? *Call madam a cup of tea, bhabhi. Bring madam a bhabhi. Madam is a cup of tea.* Holding the knife-shaped eggshell in her trembling hand, Anita tried to trace her footsteps on the shore back to her bedroom. Left? Right?

She wandered out of her home, past the giant photograph of her family, into the darkness of the corridor.

A spray of blood flew onto the faces in the photograph. She stabbed him a second time, straight into his soft belly. Suman screamed. The maharaj managed to grab Anita's arm, push her down, and then fell on top of her. The seashore vanished. The priest disappeared too. As Anita lay beneath the cook's writhing body, her white kurti soaking in his blood, she could smell his fresh Lifebuoy soap. He was howling with pain and cursing in guttural Rajasthani. Suman didn't stop screaming.

The cook let out a bark like an angry animal and bit at the bhabhi's nipple. Anita did not flinch. She heard the lift door open. She peered at the spray-painted photograph above her, the crimson tide forming at the little girl's feet. Anita shut her eyes. The priest had brought madam tea. In a broken eggshell . . .

COOK COOKS OWN SOUP
by Staff Reporter

In a shocking incident, a Teenbatti housewife, one Anita Mitesh Shah, was attacked by her former cook yesterday afternoon at her flat. Police investigations revealed that the cook, Ratilal Rathod, was upset about being thrown out. He returned and first attempted to molest the maid, Suman, who hails from Jharkhand. When Mrs. Shah tried to save her, the cook created a ruckus, attacked his former boss, and bit her breast. In self-defense, she stabbed him. Rathod, who is originally from Rajasthan, is in critical condition at J.J. Hospital, and criminal proceedings will be initiated against him after his recuperation. Mrs. Shah, who is married to a subbroker, lives in Tirupati Towers, a Jain society at Walkeshwar Road. Her condition is said to be stable.

The newspaper lay unopened on the dining table. Anita sat there nursing her bandaged breast. In front of her stood an empty glass of water with a pale pink lip mark on the rim. The bell rang and rang but the picture did not light up. A gust of wind blew into the room and a half-empty pillbox rolled out from under the table, the little black pills scattered around it like so many dead flies.

AT LEOPOLD CAFÉ

by Kalpish Ratna

Colaba Causeway

When Ratan Oak looked up, the man he was expecting had arrived. He sat down against the mirror, a bullet hole above each shoulder. A third, between them, would have drilled right through his heart.

At half past nine thirteen days ago two men had lobbed a grenade in here, then stepped in and let loose with AK-47s.

Everyone at Leopold's this morning stared at those bullet holes, and the man got in the way. He tipped back his chair and considered their stares with polite disdain.

Ratan seemed to know why he was here—but dimly—and only in the dark looking-glass of his mind.

Ishrat Syed

* * *

Ratan hadn't meant to step into Leopold Café. The signboard had caught his eye. A '50s blue-and-white Coca-Cola "good times" poster that said *Since 1871*. He'd never noticed that before. The old one had been white, with squat black letters. It was something of a memorial to Prema. Their first quarrel had erupted over that sign.

She wanted to go in. He didn't.

"I'm not eating in a place named for a butcher," he said.

"How do you know that? Maybe Leopold's the owner. Maybe Leopold's his uncle?"

"It's Irani, Prema. They don't have Leopolds in Yazd. It's named for Leopold of Belgium, butcher of the Congo."

"Why Yazd? Why not Tehran? Maybe they don't know he was a butcher, maybe they don't even know where the Congo is. Why should they? All they need to know is bun maska and chai and that's all I want. Not everyone bothers about useless stuff, like you."

That peripatetic quarrel had lasted nearly a decade. Their parting had done him good. He hadn't heard from her since.

They hadn't gone into the café after all, that awful day. Twenty—good heavens—twenty-six years ago. A long while, to keep a quarrel going. And all she had wanted was bun maska and chai.

Ratan entered Leopold's with the feeling of walking into a mirage. He expected the restrained grief any house of death exhibits the week after—a quiet decency, with an attention to detail that marks the return to life. Leopold's was nothing like that. It was—blasé. The cheery red-and-yellow checked tablecloth, the single rose, the slotted steel napkin holder, all disowned chaos.

It was surprisingly crowded, considering the hour. European tourists at breakfast, with the relaxed air of having checked in at the oasis the night before. For all its tragic present, the café conveyed the comfort of a haven. It felt like the last stop on the Orient Express. Empire still lingered here, and not just in the naïve mural where pink ladies chatted brightly with gentlemen in sola hats and chocolate-brown waiters hovered, bearing trays.

The backpacker consulting his *Lonely Planet* and the two French girls examining him furtively, the British couple intent on their sausages and the American woman writing postcards—they could all have been here since 1871.

The rest, all Indian, were here because of November 26 and paying the uneasy homage of curiosity when the time for aid and condolence was past.

This irritated Ratan. Ratan bristled when the waiter pointed out the bullet holes. Nonetheless, he looked. They were in the large mirror across the room. Four, each nested in a bright nebula of fracture lines, sucked deep into the black continuity of glass. The space beyond made the room around him shimmer. The tangible, the fungible and familiar, and the sentient lay beyond the glass.

Something was still missing.

It would come now, in the next ten minutes, before half past eight. Once settled in its expected place, it would alter this geometry of light and shadow. It would complete the picture, and make the place familiar again.

It was not unusual for Ratan to experience the familiar in an unfamiliar place. It was useless telling himself he had never been inside Leopold Café before. All he had to do was wait.

He looked away from the mirror, frowning. Fisticuffs

pounded the inside of his skull. His other life, awakened, was clamoring for liberty.

The pain no longer frightened him, but he still flinched from it. Sometimes, as now, he couldn't be sure if it was pain— or excitement. Everything was heightened. Color grew more intense, smells stronger, and vision more acute. Conversations buzzed annoyingly about him. His skin was raw with anticipation, as if the lightest touch would unleash a convulsion. Time accelerated. He was about to enter his other life—the life of Ramratan Oak.

All he had to do was wait. He gritted his teeth and waited for the man to arrive.

That was it. There should be a man at the table by the mirror. But he wasn't here *yet*.

The waiter took Ratan's order without comment. Why, what else had he expected?

Sorry, sir. Europeans only.

Ratan actually heard the words. But he couldn't have. Here came his coffee.

I must request that you move to the back of the room.

Ratan turned, though the waiter hadn't spoken at all. When he looked at the mirror, the picture was complete.

The man was there now, sitting, as expected. He leaned forward a little and his back loomed in the mirror, drilled neatly with a bullet hole. The spidery cracks around it radiated brightness into the space beyond.

There, in that dim interior, was Ratan's table; and there he was, stealing a glance at the man; then quickly looking away and smoothing his mustache—

His *mustache*?

Perhaps it's time I grew one, thought Ratan.

Don't. It is a—

—plant of great cultivation, Ratan finished the sentence with irony.

His own eyes twinkled back at him from the mirror as Ramratan Oak polished his spectacles to take a better look at the man. Next to Ramratan, Ernest Hanbury Hankin, shielded by a newspaper, was halfway through the man's story.

"He's growing immortal just sitting there," murmured Hankin. "Year by year by year every minute."

"How can he possibly do that?"

How can he possibly do that? Had he just said it?

The waiter seemed to have heard him. He followed Ratan's eyes.

"Takes all sorts, doesn't it? That's his table, and he won't sit anywhere else. Who are we to object? He's here like clock-work. Eight-fifteen, every morning. Made big noise because we were closed four days. After the attack? Orders breakfast and eats in great hurry—before his friend turns up."

"Oh, that isn't his friend," said Ratan.

"No? Business contact, maybe. Not *our* business. Anything else, sir?"

Recollecting why he was here, Ratan asked for bun maska.

The waiter smiled.

"We keep changing the menu, but Indians only ask for bun maska."

"At least these days you allow Indians. In the old days you would have refused to serve me."

"Impossible!"

"Not to worry. Times have changed now."

"That's good, then."

* * *

The man looked exactly as Ratan remembered him. Exactly as he looked now to Ramratan in the mirror.

Ramratan had polished his spectacles twice in ten minutes, as if that might help his disbelief.

Immortal? He hadn't seen anybody looking this *mortal* of late. The man's face was like crumpled parchment, his pale blue eyes brilliant chips of ice. He was tall, taller than Ramratan, but with a curious laxity of limb. His large hands were covered with tortuous veins tensed in blue knots against startlingly white skin. In contrast, his white ducks looked yellow. The many layers of linen beneath his khaki jacket were limp with perspiration. He removed his sola and dabbed preciously at his beaded forehead.

Ratan noticed the man was dressed differently, in kurta pajamas now. His long exquisite feet stuck out in beautifully crafted kolhapuris. In Ramratan's time it was called "going native."

He was waiting, as Ratan had seen him wait before—

Ratan's bun maska arrived.

The waiter was a young man. He couldn't know the dish was iconic, and with it should come a syrupy cup of Irani chai. Also, it was clear Leopold no longer baked its own biscuits. In his childhood, Iranis served biscuits with their chai for free. Nankhatai, Shrewsbury, ginger, coconut—

"Coconut biscuits," said Hankin. "These really are the best in the world."

Ramratan bit into one. Rough and dry, but that might just be the waiter.

"Disregard the waiter," murmured Hankin. "I'll break his skull for you another day."

The thought of Ernest breaking anyone's skull was so implausible, Ramratan couldn't help but smile. Meanwhile, the waiter had retreated, mollified by Hankin's largesse.

"There, he won't trouble us anymore. He isn't a bad man, really, Ramratan, just—"

"Just a victim of the times," Ramratan preempted Hankin's words.

"Sorry I had to bring you here. You did want to see the man."

"Yes, Ernest, I do. Forget the rest." He stole another look at the man near the mirror. "How old did you say he was? He looks about a hundred to me."

"That I can answer with accuracy. He's exactly seventy-four years, two months, and two days old this morning. I've seen his papers. Patton Prescott. Born October 5, 1829."

"Looks older."

"He'll look younger the next time we see him. If the rumor is true."

Ratan no longer had any doubt. This was the same man. The man Ramratan and Ernest Hankin were talking about. The man whose shoulders were on the other side of those bullet holes.

Today was December 8, 2008.

In the mirror, Hankin was reading the *Times*. The date on the masthead was December 8 too. But the year was 1903; Ramratan had just turned forty, and Hankin was younger. Ratan rummaged for a sense of what it had felt like then, wondering what the moment's sting had been, and why it had marked him thus, with memory.

Prescott. The man's name was Prescott.

"Patton Prescott," said Hankin.

Could Ramratan see him through the bullet hole? Was

that all it took to be able to see through the mirror? As if in answer, Ramaratan took off his spectacles and looked at him. And, all at once, Ratan was there.

Patton Prescott had been evicted from Watson's Hotel for creating a disturbance. Naturally, Mrs. Biggett took him in.

In the world of lodging houses, Biggett's had a reputation for dullness. A neat narrow building in Byculla's Clare Road, it had once been a baniya's pleasure house. Bankruptcy, and a strong attack of religion, had forced the baniya to sell the place. Mrs. Biggett, recently widowed, bought it for a song. It had few graces and she ensured none of its former airs endured. There was no drunkenness, no lechery, no conversation, and nothing to eat. And whenever he was in Bombay, Hankin boarded here.

"It's a well-kept secret, Ramratan, but the woman has a kind heart. I've never known her to turn away rejects. She'd heard of the incident at Watson's, and asked me to vet Prescott's papers. Everything seemed in order, so there was no reason to turn him away."

In the dead hour before dinner, when Mrs. Biggett serves no aperitif and hungry boarders shuffle between carom and planchette without hope, Hankin began a conversation with Prescott.

Initially, Prescott wasn't forthcoming, but it did emerge he wasn't here on a pleasure trip. He was in Bombay for his health.

"He began questioning me about native medicine. A misleading label, I told him, and—"

"—lectured him for an hour about Unani tibb and ayurveda—"

"I did no such thing! I merely answered his questions."

"Right, right. Go on."

"He was undergoing a native treatment, he said, which would be of great interest to European scientists. I wanted to learn more. He was reticent at first. Then said he had been given an elixir. You know, Ramratan, I'm always suspicious of terms like *elixir* and *tonic*—"

"Balamrut. Liver pills. *Tono-Bungay*."

"Exactly! The market's thick with them. I asked him if he knew what this elixir was. The elixir of youth, he recited with a trusting smile. All done very scientifically. His doctor had shown him rats that were two hundred years old. He said they were tireless."

"He meant they fucked like crazy."

"No. I don't think it was that—but he's signed up for the elixir. Said he felt twenty years younger already, and all he'd had so far was the introductory dose. Is it a pill? I asked. He smiled. Nothing like a pill, he said. It was a curry, a delectable curry. And the coin dropped. Goat's testes! This hakim has fobbed him off with gurda kapoora. Have you tried it? Very popular among the bucks in Agra."

"Here too. This nation's eaten it for centuries. Yet look at us. No. Prescott's doctor has something more exotic on offer. The next phase of therapy will probably involve rhinoceros urine."

"Well, he did say the treatment goes from solid to liquid to gas. He's ready for the liquid phase now. The hakim administers the dose right here. Every morning at exactly half past eight."

"Why here? And not in his dawakhana?" Ramratan posed the question, only to answer it himself. "I suppose it would be undignified for Prescott to visit him there."

He stole another glance at Prescott, but couldn't for the life of him discern the faintest sign of youth.

"Why?" asked Ramratan. "Why is he doing this, Ernest?"

"I asked him that, in fact. His answer was peculiar. On his seventieth birthday he realized, at last, he was rich enough to enjoy youth."

"Someone else's youth, you mean. Are you sure he's meeting a doctor and not a pimp?"

"Heavens, I didn't think of that!"

Despite his raging battle with the Indian Medical Service, Ernest Hankin could never believe the worst of his fellow men.

"So that's the hakim!" Hankin whistled softly.

A burly man in flowing muslin djibba and grubby churidar pajamas had joined Prescott. Something about him seemed faintly familiar. His back to them, he listened to Prescott, who had a great deal to say. The red tassel on his fez swung a fraying pendulum, like time dispersed to the frequency of his approving nods.

Holding up a finger for silence, he ceremoniously measured Prescott's pulse. Charisma or coincidence, he induced absolute silence. The air seemed to congeal, and then his voice was heard.

"One drop of semen, Prescott sahib," he said, "one drop of semen is equal to seven drops of blood."

Then that finger again, this time cautionary.

"Count your drops, Mr. Prescott. Count—your—drops."

Hankin reddened with suppressed laughter.

"Mustaches," murmured Ramratan in mirth. "Mustaches, Ernest, were invented for moments like these."

Was Prescott embarrassed? He didn't look it. Oblivious to all else, he was tuned to the hakim, as if mesmerized.

The hakim stood up and walked around to Prescott's side of the table. A small vial gleamed in his right hand and

Prescott leaned his head back as he bent over him. When the hakim stood upright again, Ramratan saw his face for the first time.

He leapt up and would have rushed at the man if Hankin hadn't gripped his arm and forced him back into his chair.

"I know this rascal!" Ramratan was furious. "I've seen him hang about the mortuary. That wasn't goat he fed Prescott! Hurry, Ernest, before it's too late—"

"Anything else, sir?"

Ratan returned to the present. The bun maska sat untouched before him. He ordered another coffee to get rid of the waiter, then turned anxiously back to the table by the mirror where Prescott still awaited his guest.

In the mirror Prescott's hakim now had his back to Ratan. The vial put away, he was taking his leave.

He glanced over his shoulder behind Prescott and through the bullet holes into the room. His light brown eyes sparked carnelian as they focused on Ratan. He ignored Prescott's farewell and hurried out.

Ramratan and Hankin had disappeared. Only Prescott kept his seat, back to back with his twin, on Ratan's side of the mirror.

Ratan sipped the coffee. It helped steady him. He became aware of a soreness in his calves. Odd. He'd barely walked a mile. No, not odd at all—it was very long since he'd raced on a bicycle.

Ramratan was peddling hard with Hankin weighing down the Raleigh. Still, quicker than a tram! They reached the mortuary in half an hour.

Eight-thirty on Saturday morning. The place was deserted. Ramratan peered into the autopsy room. The four cadavers from the day before lay exactly where he'd left them.

"Bhiku!" he thundered.

An alarmed clerk from the coroner's office popped his head out and retreated hastily.

"Bhiku!" Ramratan bellowed again, louder.

This time, Bhiku's son Mangesh slunk out. He was a gangly lad of sixteen, with a taste for chandol. Twice in the last year Ramratan had hauled him out of Liang's chandol-khana, the sleazy opium den in Safed Gali.

"Where's Bhiku?" he demanded.

"He's ill."

"Get him! I'll cure him when he gets here."

The boy did not budge. Last night's revels showed in his pinpoint pupils. "He said I was to do his work today."

Bhiku, then, was too drunk to even stand up.

Ramratan snarled and strode past the boy's inane smile.

Hankin followed him into the autopsy room. The air smelled of carbolic and bleached blood. Tall windows, fierce with morning, blazed over the four dead men. They stared straight up, sightless. The marble slabs gleamed in milky opalescence.

"Lock the door, Ernest!"

Ramratan was already bent over the first cadaver, a mason who had fallen off a scaffold and died on impact, the contre-coup shearing his brainstem. He looked young in death, the burden of life lifted off him.

Ramratan whispered an apology that would never be heard and dipped his hand between the man's legs to heft the scrotum. It settled cold and soft in his palm. He pressed down with his thumb. It sank right in.

Hankin met his eyes; Ramratan nodded.

So too the next. The one after. And the last.

"All?"

"All four. Cotton wool."

He strode out and collared Mangesh.

"Come on!"

He half-lifted, half-dragged the terrified boy, bumping his knees along the sloping corridor.

"Walk, will you? Take us there!"

Mangesh led them, as Ramratan expected, to one of those green-curtained cubicles that line the pavement on Shuklaji Street.

"He won't be here," said Hankin. "May still be at Leopold's."

But Ramratan was beyond counsel.

Above the green curtain a neat sign in English announced: *Clinic of Confidence.*

Clinic of Confidence!

Ratan laughed out loud. Why, he knew that! He remembered staring at it from the upper deck of the 4 Ltd. in Dongri. Never those local trains for him, he was a BEST man all through his undergraduate days when traffic inched its way along Mohammad Ali Road giving him time enough to memorize the blackboard list outside the Clinic of Confidence. He recalled it now, verbatim.

Hydrocele, piles, fistula, small size increase, weakness, lack of interest, debility, thin semen, thick semen, semen block, semen loss, all kinds of venereal diseases.

And then in tall red capitals:

LIFELONG GUARANTEE OF FULL TENSION
SATISFACTION TO EXTREME OLD MEN
AND
MIDDLE AGES.
HAKIM ARIF KHAN DEHLAVI B.U.M.S.

The Medical College knew him simply as Bums and Cums.

Ratan hadn't seem that board since the flyover opened to traffic. Like many things that had lasted a century, it did not cross over into the new millennium.

But Prescott was here. Patton Prescott. He could be nobody else.

It had worked then, the elixir of youth!

That wasn't how he remembered it. They had kept it from Prescott, hadn't they, after they burst in on the hakim?

Into the Clinic of Confidence, then up a staircase. No—a *ladder*, wedged in a dark alcove. And above, way above, a skylight that glared like a malignant ocellus. His fingers hooked onto Mangesh's collar, Ramratan urged the boy forward as Hankin lumbered slowly behind them. They trudged up five stories to emerge on a loft right beneath the tenement rafters.

This was no attic. It was a laboratory busy with flasks, angled glass tubes, stout jars, alembics, and shelves. Rows and rows of wooden shelves, all ancient, cracked, bursting with secrets in the frigid stagnant air.

A blue flame leaped, and there he was, their quarry, and if the signboard was to be believed, Hakim Arif Khan Dehlavi. His agate eyes, dilating over the wild tangle of beard, stabbed Ramratan with fresh rage.

A small alembic hissed and sputtered over the flame. In

its blue flicker the table shimmered spectral, as if covered with nacre. But it was something else.

The table was heaped with testes—big, small, gray, pink, glistening, dull. A mound of gonads crowded and jostled for space, as if a massacre raged outside these walls and a maniac loosed upon the dead had cached his spoils in here.

Strange, the cold air held nothing of the feral odor of dying tissue.

This registered in the blink before Ramratan sprang at the man. Hankin had to pull Ramratan's hands off the hakim's fat neck.

"I got these from the abattoir," the man rasped when Ramratan let go. "There's no law against that."

"I'll see you hanged even if I have to do it myself!" roared Ramratan.

The hakim turned to Mangesh. "There's no hope for you, boy, opium's got your soul." He soothed his neck and mopped his face. "You must be Oak saab. It hasn't been easy getting past you."

"Where's the stuff you stole from the dead?"

The hakim pointed sullenly to the alembic. Its sinuous conduit led to the far end of the table and there it dripped into a thin glass flute. Tiny amber globules condensed on its sides and rapidly filled the flute with a clear golden liquid. Hakim Arif Khan sealed off the glass tube and held it out to Ramratan.

"Here! The essence of your dead. Take it! It has the strength of four men. Take it with my promise—I will stop making eunuchs of dead men. Out of respect for you, for I hear you treat the dead as your own."

Ramratan hesitated.

"Take it. Arif Khan Dehlavi is in truth Arif Khan Barmaki.

If you know what that means, you will take me at my word."

The name meant nothing to Ramratan. Nevertheless, he took the hakim at his word. What else could he do?

"Leave Prescott to me," said Hankin when they were out once again in sunlight. He took the glass tube from Ramratan and smashed it to pieces on the pavement.

The crunch of glass jolted Ratan back to the present. The table by the mirror now had a second occupant. Prescott's guest had arrived. Ratan had missed the opening act. Prescott had his face buried in his hands. His companion stood by and watched him with dispassion. Glass glittered on the floor between them.

"There!" the man said, and Ratan recognized the voice at once. "There! That's the end of it all."

"No!"

Ratan crossed the room in rapid strides.

"It didn't quite end like that. You didn't let him go that easily, did you? Don't you remember how it ended, Mr. Prescott? Hakim Arif Khan Dehlavi didn't let you off so easily."

They turned, not to answer Ratan, but to follow his eyes.

In the mirror, they were back at his table. Older, much older now. Scarred. Hankin had lost most of his hair, but the mustache still bristled gallantly.

And Ramratan?

Ratan saw himself, twenty years older.

The date was December 8 again. The year was 1923.

"Remember Prescott?" asked Hankin. "Hakim Dehlavi didn't let him off easy."

"Twenty years ago. To the day."

"Is it? Good god!"

"Whatever happened to Prescott? You sailed home with him, didn't you? It was the end of the hakim's elixir. I certainly had no trouble with him after that."

"No stolen testes?"

"Not another one. As long as I ran things there—"

"You still do."

"No, Ernest. Not any longer. Just fingerprints. Bloodstains. Fussy stuff like that. I only do police autopsies now. Earlier, till the end of the war, I checked every single corpse myself before I released it from the mortuary. Never missed any more testes. I put the fear of the noose in Bhiku."

"And his son?"

"Mangesh? Dead. Never woke up from a weeklong trance in Liang's chandol-khana."

"Pity."

Ramratan was silent. His city was built on opium. Libraries, hospitals, railway stations, and most other emblems of philanthropy—they were all built upon the wreckage of lives.

"Prescott came to a bad end, Ramratan. I am certain our hakim had everything to do with it."

Hankin had sailed back to England with Prescott. They parted at the pier. He never saw Prescott again.

Last year the name cropped up in a conversation. Prescott, he learned, had run wild. His family, torn between embarrassment and despair, had finally ceded all hope of reforming him. He ended up in the madhouse and died gibbering in a straitjacket.

"Reformed? Did he behave like those rats he told you of? Did he run around naked? Old men do terrible things. I worry sometimes over what lies ahead."

"I went down to Shropshire to find out. I visited the family—a son and a daughter. I told them I'd known Prescott in Bombay. He'd gone to pieces a year after his return from India, reeling about drunkenly with not a drop of alcohol in him. Lasted another six months in the asylum."

"Poor man! Ernest, could it have been something entirely unrelated? You destroyed that extract Arif Khan gave us."

"I asked them about medication. They were quite emphatic. No, he wasn't taking medicine. Of any sort. But I can be devious too! I asked about his general health. Headaches, colds, fevers, that sort of thing."

"Ah."

"Exactly. He was a martyr to the common cold, the daughter said, and never without his little flask of nasal drops. I was, don't forget, asking these questions nearly twenty years after. People can't be expected to remember details."

Ramratan pondered a long while.

"Even if Prescott kept receiving supplies from the hakim, why should the elixir drive him crazy? Any daughter would gloss over such embarrassments. Are you certain, Ernest, they didn't mean randy when they said mad?"

"Yes, yes. I made quite sure of that. I read all the notes at the asylum. No sexual excitement of any kind. I wondered about that *any kind*!"

"So it didn't work like that. It changed his behavior, his mentation, and his intellect. What do testes have to do with that?"

"Men often think with theirs."

Ramratan nodded. The war had made cynics of them all.

He couldn't let go of the story. It happened so soon after Prescott reached England. A yammering idiot in a year, and in six more months he was dead. He used nasal drops. That's as swift as injecting the drug into a vein. It had addled Prescott's brain.

* * *

"The elixir turned you mad, didn't it, Mr. Prescott?"

Prescott turned to Ratan in startled disbelief, and then laughed. "I've never felt saner. How would you know about the elixir, anyway?"

Ratan did not reply. He'd made a complete fool of himself. Prescott was *dead*. But this man—

"I think this gentleman is speaking about your grandfather, Mr. Prescott," said the hakim. "And also, about mine."

He scrutinized Ratan with astute eyes.

"Your name? Is it Oak?"

Ratan stared back, baffled.

"I think we better have a word, Mr. Oak—or is it *Dr*. Oak? I'm almost through with Mr. Prescott here. *Permanently* through. Please? Will you give me five minutes?"

Ratan nodded, walked back to his table and pondered the physics of breaking glass. It splinters in conchoidal fractures as shock waves ripple out. This was a mirror, not a windowpane. The dark space within it, he alone could explore.

Prescott—that Prescott—had gone mad from the elixir. This one might too. Madness is a convenient label for all things inconvenient. What exactly happened to Patton Prescott? Today it would be termed dementia, poor coordination, ataxia. A neurologist might not make the connect, but Ramratan Oak did—because he knew what the elixir really was. He lacked a name for Prescott's illness, because in his time it had no name.

He, Ratan, made the diagnosis because Prescott's illness now had a name. It was a prion disease, and the elixir had transmitted it.

Ramaratan's cadavers were never robbed again. Yet Hakim Arif had ensured that Prescott in England received enough elixir to last a year.

* * *

Hakim Arif Khan Dehlavi walked over to Ratan. He was very different from the man who had made a gift of the vial to Ramratan. His light brown eyes, though gentle and lustrous, yet recalled that carnelian flash. He drew up a chair and sat down next to Ratan.

"You're not Hakim Arif Khan, are you?"

"No. My name is Moinuddeen."

"Moinuddeen Khan Dehlavi. Or Moinuddeen Khan Barmaki?"

Moinuddeen's face lit up. "Your grandfather knew! We were told he didn't."

"So, it is family lore?"

Moinuddeen shrugged and suppressed a smile. Ratan felt a lance of anger.

"The name meant nothing to Ramratan Oak, and it doesn't to me."

"Barmaki is the ancient name of hakims who studied medicine before Islam. Charak, Sushrut, Jalinoos. And also— the medicine of the pharoahs."

Something glimmered in Ratan's memory but he couldn't place it.

Moinuddeen nodded.

"I see it begins to make sense. You are cleverer than your grandfather."

A hook.

What did a hook have to do with it?

Ask him for the hook.

Ramratan's urgent voice in his brain compelled Ratan.

"You have a hook, I suppose," he said. "I'd like to see it."

Moinuddeen gaped. "You knew?"

"He did. Ramratan Oak, the man who met your grand-father."

Ratan looked down. He didn't want Moinuddeen to guess what he had just realized. Vision or memory, call it what you will, he knew each word before Ramratan's broad-nibbed Waterman set it down on paper.

> . . . I can't help thinking we were wrong all along about that elixir. I continued counting testes, I became obsessed with that, and it kept me from seeing the larger picture. It had nothing to do with testes at all.
>
> I tell you, Ernest, it was the pituitary! Extracted with a hook, through the nostrils, in the ancient Egyptian manner, leaving no trace of intrusion. How am I going to live this down?
>
> Every one of those cadavers I passed as legit was missing its pituitary gland. God forgive my ignorance, because I never can.

"How many more victims, Moinuddeen?" asked Ratan quietly.

"Prescott's grandfather?"

"He died mad and demented."

Moinuddeen laughed. "He was mad and demented to begin with, wasn't he?" He nodded at the bullet holes. "Look at this Prescott! This one here, now. You think he looks mad or demented?"

"Actually, yes. He does."

Prescott had recovered his magisterial calm. His back obliterated the bullet holes.

"Men like Prescott live on the edge of time," said Moinuddeen. "No matter what age, they're always on the edge of time."

"What does that mean?"

"All they see is the abyss. Nothing registers but that emptiness. Nothing is real except their terror."

"And you cash in on it."

"Why not? The day after the Lashkar shootout, that very morning, he was waiting for me by the door. The corpses were still here and blood was everywhere. He didn't seem to notice. Nothing mattered but his fix."

"You were here too, weren't you? Vial in hand, to offer him his fix?"

Moinuddeen lowered his eyes. "Yes, I was. Demand and supply."

"Why did you break the vial just now?"

"Because I broke with him."

"Why?"

Moinuddeen shrugged and looked back at the table by the mirror. Prescott responded with a quick grimace of pain.

"Look at him. Don't you think he's lived long enough?"

"He doesn't think so," said Ratan.

"Who is he to decide?"

"Who are you?" asked Ratan.

"I'm his timekeeper, that's who I am!"

Despite himself, Ratan asked, "Does it work?"

"How old do you think I am?"

"Thirty-five?"

Moinuddeen smiled. Ratan noticed a craquelure of gray on his pale skin, as if its depths abjured light.

"Was that your grandfather? Mortuary Oak?"

"Great-grandfather. Dr. Ramratan Oak, pathologist."

"Your *great*-grandfather? There's your answer! Pathologist, mortician—what's the difference? They're both doctors of death. We, on the other hand, are doctors of life. The elixir allows you life. You'll want to know how it works. You're a doctor too? Like Ramratan Oak?"

"Microbiologist."

"Then you'll know. I'll make you a free gift of the idea—in apology to Ramratan Oak." He patted Ratan's shoulder in farewell. "Tell the world when you find out."

Prescott intercepted Ratan at the door. "Do you know any others?" he asked in an urgent whisper.

Ratan looked at him with contempt.

"Any other hakims?" persisted Prescott. "He broke the vial! I have just enough for five more years."

He stayed Ratan with a trembling hand.

"What's five years?" He snapped his fingers. "Gone, like tomorrow."

Ratan shook him off and stepped out into the bustle of Colaba Causeway.

Moinuddeen was astride a Bajaj Chetak. Morning light gilded his brown hair. He raised a hand in salute to Ratan.

"It's goodbye to all that now. I'm done with the whole tamasha!"

"What will you do now?"

"What do you think?" He laughed. "I'll live!"

THEY

BY Jerry Pinto

Mahim Church

These things don't happen in Mahim," Milly said angrily. "What things don't?" Peter asked mildly. He knew that his wife was not a morning person. She had never been. But now she was not an afternoon person either. Slowly her citric rages had begun to spill across the day. Eventually, she would not be a day person or a night person. The logical conclusion? She would not be a person at all.

"Murder," she said, and waved the tabloid at her husband.

"It's here already?" he asked, slightly disturbed. When he was a boy, the tabloids had come out in the evening. When he was an adolescent, they had shifted to the afternoon. Now they arrived, it would seem, with morning coffee.

Milly was reading the report with the concentrated attention of the dyspeptic.

"In your gym too," she said, throwing it down amid the debris of the dining table's morning meal. "In your very own gym."

"EverFit isn't my very own gym," he replied. "I only exercise there."

"Forgive me, senior copy chief," she said. "I should be more accurate in my diction."

She was laying a little trap for him. She wanted him to say that she had used *diction* in the wrong sense. Peter sidestepped it neatly. He knew the original meaning of the word.

"It's time to go there anyway," he said.

"I can't see what a man your age wants with a gym," said Milly. This was more formula than complaint. "Anyway, it's probably closed. Scene of the crime," she added. "I remember the time there was a body found in a gunnysack outside this very building."

Peter did not point out that she had just remarked that murders did not happen in Mahim.

"A woman, no?" she continued with relish. "Cut into pieces, the paper said. But no one ever marked the spot or anything. They just arrested the gurkha. But now maybe they've got modern. Maybe they have yellow tape and lumen lights. Like *CSI*."

Peter shrugged and made for the door.

"So where are you going?"

"I'll walk around the park then."

"Keep your eyes on the dogs," she said, and grinned suddenly. "As if you ever could."

"Looking is no sin," he countered.

"And if thine eye offend thee, pluck it out: it is better for thee to enter into the kingdom of God with one eye, than having two eyes to be cast into hellfire," said Milly, but her tone was mild.

"Hell must be crowded then," he responded, as he picked up his mobile, his hand towel, and the bright blue identity card that certified him as another poor simp who had bought a complete health plan, valid until the end of the year.

There was a bunch of people standing around EverFit (*Where Fitness Lives*). When Peter was growing up there had been only two gyms in Mahim: Talwalkar's was the big one; Slimwell was the little one. Neither had had a tagline. Now there was Cloud Zen (*For Mind, Body, and Spirit*) and Zai's Health (*From A to Zai*) and Barbaria (*Unleash Your Inner Conan*), all fighting for the Mahimkar's time and hard-earned. And then there was EverFit for those, like him, who wanted a treadmill and a patch of ground on which to do surya namaskars when the rain came down and turned the park to red soup.

Inspector Jende was standing outside the gym, wearing his habitual expression of carefully cultivated expressionlessness. The day had begun to heat up, sucking sweat from its citizens to turn into the acid rain that would be unleashed in a month or so. The gym was cordoned off. The paanwalla's shop that stood to the left of it was open for business but the keysmith who had a little stand to the right of the gym had given up the fight and closed for the day.

"Pittr," Jende said, "what you're doing here?"

"Jay," said Peter, "are you finally considering getting rid of that paunch?"

"Don't be silly. Late last night. Body found. Don't read papers now?"

"Who is it?"

"You're not on the crime beat."

"You came home for a drink the day I took voluntary retirement, remember?"

Jende beckoned to him and they walked into the gym together. Kalsekar, at the reception, looked shaken. It was the first emotion Peter had ever seen on his face which was usually set in surly uncommunicative lines, the face of Indians everywhere who found themselves in dead-end jobs. The only other time Kalsekar had shown any sign of emotion was a month earlier. He had been wearing a rather nice watch. "Great watch," Peter had said. Kalsekar had smiled and shown it to him. It had three faces on it; one for local time and two for other time zones. What did Kalsekar need three time zones for? It was not a question you could ask. Perhaps Kalsekar had a son who lived in Los Angeles. Peter reached for the kind of question he could ask: "How much did you pay?" The smile dropped off Kalsekar's face like a maggot off a corpse. "Khari kamaai ki hai," he had said, sweat-of-the-brow earnings. He had not worn it again.

Now Peter was about to hand over his wallet when he realized he would not be actually working out and did not need a pouch into which to put his pocket contents. He nodded at the old man. Kalsekar tried to nod at him now; Peter saw that he was actually shaking. Death could do that to you; and murder was death rubbing your nose in your mortality.

They walked through the deserted gym, a long rectangular room. At its far end was a door that led to the changing rooms, a massage room, a sauna, and a couple of pots. The body was in the massage room. The back of its head had been smashed in, a fine mess of red and black. No gray matter, Peter noted, just streaks of yellow. That would be body fat. Ubiquitous: body fat. Ubiquitous, too, the war against it. The young man had been a foot soldier in that losing battle.

"Vishal," Peter said. "Works here. Trainer."

"The old man identified him."

"Family?"

"Doesn't seem to have any. Orphan."

"Weapon?"

"I don't know. We have to wait for the medics."

Peter looked around. It was all very ordinary. The posters of Arnold snarling on the walls. The rows and rows of dumbbells. A sign that said, *Please bring deo to the gym*, and another that informed members that the establishment would be closed every fourth Sunday for maintenance.

"Come," said Inspector Jende. "Thaane chal."

"Am I under arrest?"

"Don't talk nonsense. You will know when you're under arrest. Come and have one cup chai."

They headed to the police station across the road and settled themselves at Jende's desk.

"Chai!" shouted Jende. "Maadherchod," he said comfortably and meaninglessly when it was served. The man who brought it smiled pleasantly and sheepishly and left.

"Line pe rakhne ke liye," said Jende. Peter wondered at how the city had slowly leached the meaning of these potent abuses. Now Jende could call his tea supplier a motherfucker simply to keep him in line. Peter also wondered whether the tapriwalla was a Bihari. He decided to let it go. The man looked pleased enough to have the police account. Then a thought struck him: *Do the police pay?*

Jende interrupted this line of thought: "Bola."

Peter shrugged. "I don't know much about the victim."

"Who is asking about victim? I am asking about anything, everything. Full story of gym. Tell everything you know. I will see what-what to use."

"Okay. It seems to be owned by Muslims but run by Hindus."

"Jesus!" said Jende, unconsciously adding another dimension to the problem of religion in India. "Please, nothing like that, haan?"

"I hope not. Enough we have had. But there seems to be a Christian somewhere in the mess as well."

"*Jesus Loves You?*"

"Indeed. Why would they have that sticker above the door?"

"*I am the light of the world?*"

"Yes. I saw that poster behind the reception."

"Not you, na?"

Peter thought this too bizarre to merit a response. Tea arrived.

"Aage?" Jende prodded.

"There are three instructors. One masseur."

"Aah."

"He's a sixty-year-old man."

"So?"

"Nothing. He's in his gaon."

"You know everything about this gym or what?"

"When you take a one-year membership, you're supposed to get five complimentary massages. I haven't had any because I was told the masseur is in his gaon."

"On the banks of the Ganga, no doubt."

"You too?" The city had had a parochialism seizure. A young political party had decided that too many outsiders had arrived in the city and were taking jobs from the locals. Out-of-townies had been beaten up. The boys from the banks of the Ganga had it especially bad. Many seemed to feel some sympathy for this stance, even if they disapproved, they said, of the violence.

"Arrey, where police has time to be political?"

Peter looked carefully at his old-school friend but Jende's face remained the stoic mask of the misunderstood man doing his duty. He continued, "Vishal was a trainer. The other two are Rahul and Sihon."

"Sea-horn?"

"So he said."

"Tera?"

"Mera."

"This is a name or what? Sihon?"

"I looked it up in the Bible. It's there."

"What did this Bible-walla banda do?"

"He was defeated by the Israelites."

"Why give name like that?"

"Why give name like Eklavya?"

"Arrey, he should be dutiful and obedient, like Eklavya."

Peter shrugged. He himself was a rock. Jende was Shiva, the blue-throated god. The names passed without comment. Everyone knew what a Peter was. Peter wasn't sure, but everyone else was; that counted in Mahim which sat across several communal and political fault lines.

"Three boys. One masseur. One old man. Members?"

"Many. Mostly college boys. And middle-aged ladies. And college girls."

"Means janta."

"Yes. Janta. Everyone. There is even one white girl."

"Chikni ya gori?"

"Full gori. She's from Poland, I think."

"In Mahim?"

"Shouldn't you know that? If she lives in Mahim?" Peter asked. An old rule made it mandatory to tell the police if you were having a foreign guest, even for just a night.

"Police should know everything. Then their work will be easy."

Peter recited gym schedules and holidays, talked about the sauna that did not work most days. Thought some more. "They divide them up. Rahul does the young college boys. Vishal does the middle-aged ladies. Sihon does the girls."

"*Does* means like . . ." and Jende waved his fist in a manner that suggested an infinity of lewdness.

"Bad verb. *Does* means *looks after*. Means when a college boy comes in, Rahul will give him a high five, ask him about his bike, his babe. Then he'll ask why he's late, what he's planning to do, maybe spot him. That kind of thing. Sihon will do that for the young women. And Vishal for the middle-aged ladies."

"Who does the old men?"

"No one."

"Means?"

"Means they come and say, *Hello, uncle,* once in a while, or, *Saab, first class?* But nothing else."

"Poor Pittr."

"Poor Peter, indeed."

They drank their tea.

"Come to think of it . . ." Peter said.

"Don't come to think. Just tell."

"I haven't seen Rahul in several days."

"Aah."

"Jay, it may be nothing."

"I said it's something?"

To which there was nothing else to say.

"More?" Jende offered.

"Marega. Acidity."

"Zindagi imtihaan leti hai."

Hindi film songs have various uses, Peter thought. One of them is to provide pop philosophy. And life does indeed require you to sit for several examinations.

Jende sat quietly for a while. "Yeh Vishal . . ." He framed his thought. "Not much fun, uske liye, na? Only fat-fat women in salwar kameez?"

The notion had occurred to Peter too. He shrugged. "These are only my observations, boss. Maybe there was no hard and fast rule . . ."

"Did you see exceptions?"

"When I was there? Never."

"And why do you think . . . ?"

Peter shrugged again. In his mind, he saw Shiva Jende, age ten, fighting a bunch of boys who were calling him kaalia. Victoria High School was not a kind place.

"Say."

Peter looked at him.

"Because he looked very blacky?" Jende asked.

Peter sighed. The color of your skin is always a marker in India. Always. Vishal would have been assigned the aunties on the basis of his darkness just as Sihon got the young women because he could speak a little English.

"Don't worry. I don't care now. Eklavya and Abhimanyu went on their mother's color, mere liye bas."

Peter smiled because Jende had mentioned his sons. One did that. One smiled at the mention of other people's children. But he hoped that Jende would construe his smile as one of friendly approval of another's offspring and not of the sentiment expressed. Was it a good thing that Jende rejoiced that his sons had taken on their mother's skin tone? Or was it a bad thing? Or was it anything at all?

"Yeh Kalsekar?

"I don't know. He just looks after the reception."

"Means?"

"He takes calls. And handles the membership renewals. And makes sure people don't come twice a day."

"Twice a day?"

"College boys."

"I can't go once a day. Where these boys . . . ?"

"You've joined a gym?"

"Police gym hai na? Compulsory."

They both thought about that for a bit.

The phone rang. The voice on the other side was shrill, hysterical. Jende turned matter-of-fact.

"Chhapar phaad ke," he said, invoking the metaphor that when God gives, He tears open your roof to pour it in on you. "One more."

He gulped his tea, burned his mouth, screamed, "Maad-herchod!" The tea man came in, assuming that he had been summoned. "Chal hutt," said Jende, waving him away. And to Peter, still sitting there. "Tu bhi."

Peter obeyed. You did not sit around a Mumbai police station if you were told to move on.

The park was quiet but Peter saw that a couple of EverFit regulars had also decided to walk.

"Hello," said Mrs. Vishwanathan, a retired schoolteacher. "What trouble this is."

He knew what she meant.

"They must refund," she said. "If they are closed, they must refund."

"Or extend," said Peter. "Give one more day for each day missed."

"Haan, like that they will do," replied Mrs. Vishwanathan. She was slowing him down but there was no way to shake her off. "Endless. First, that mobile went. Gone. One moment sitting there; next moment, gone. Then Zeenat, you know Zeenat?"

Peter indicated that he knew Zeenat. She was a schoolteacher and was getting married in three months. She needed to lose weight in a hurry and worked out with the kind of urgency that panicked the other women around her.

"Her house was robbed."

Peter looked puzzled.

"My mother said. In three. Everything in threes. In ours, three. Even in yours, three."

Peter nodded. He was still puzzled but he took her to mean the trinity, the triune godhead of Christianity.

"In yours, also three," he said.

"And then came Malini's house. That also robbed. Safaa-chutt."

Peter looked at her. "Malini?"

"Short lady? Got white-white skin from leucoderma? One pony she keeps?"

By which Peter understood Malini to be a sufferer from vitiligo who had a ponytail. "Her house was robbed too?"

"Like one panvati, this gym is," she said. "I told him, *You go somewhere else.*"

"Who? Vishal?"

"I told. This place will eat you. *They* will eat you."

Peter did not want to know whether she was going to identify who "they" were. He hastened his pace, but only a little.

Mrs. Vishwanathan gave a great sigh and asked: "But will one be able to go there?"

"Means?"

"Means without Vishal?"

Her voice actually wobbled. Peter started to look at her but decided against it. Vishal rose in his mind, as he had once seen him in the changing room. He had the body of someone who had devoted attention and steroids to it. He wore tight T-shirts and shorts to show it off. He had been turned loose on the several Mrs. Vishwanathans who came to the gym and here was the expectable result. He had noticed it himself, the restless hands that fluttered near the brawny young shoulders, the coquettish demands for help, the small gifts of specially prepared food. It was as much maternal as it was sexual.

"Very sad," he said, and meant it.

His mobile phone rang. Jende.

"Bola," Peter said.

"Just come."

"Where?"

"Debonair II."

This was a new high-rise on the sea face, at Veer Savarkar Marg, the road that ran past a crematorium, a mill, a monument, and a park. It began at the Siddhivinayak Temple, one of the city's most famous, and ended at the durgah of Makhdoom Ali Mahimi, the Muslim patron saint of the city's police.

"Which floor?"

But Jende had terminated the call.

At Debonair II, it was clear that the problem was on the fourth floor.

"Madhavi P. Twenty-four. Graphic designer. Dead," said Jende. "Not interfered."

By which Peter took him to mean that the woman had not been raped or molested in any way, peri- or postmortem. The victim had been young and female and pretty. Now she lay like a broken doll, her body oddly contorted.

"Why am I here?" he asked.

Jende pointed. A familiar blue card lay on the desk.

"Many people are members of EverFit," said Peter.

"A gym coach gets beaten to death. Then a female member is murdered. Too much or what?"

"Much too much."

"I am thinking," said Jende, "we are going to get more answers back at the gym."

Kalsekar was behind the counter. He was drinking tea as if it were gin. Perhaps he had spiked it with gin. His hands were shaking now.

"Let us sit together," said Jende.

"I don't know anything."

"This boy, Vishal . . ."

"All lies."

"I know that. But you must tell us the truth then."

"He was a good boy."

"Everyone knows that."

"Who would want him dead?" Kalsekar's face crumpled a little and suddenly he went from old to ancient.

"You tell me," said Jende.

"I don't know anything."

"Tell me what you know."

"It's all lies."

"Where did he live?"

"I did not even take rent."

Jende glanced at me. I'd had no idea. Vishal lived with Kalsekar?

"Food money I had to take. How much chicken one boy needs?"

"That is understandable. Anyone would take."

And so it came out, in fits and starts. The young man with the certificates who wanted a job. The discovery of some common village ancestry. The offer. The unlikely companionship between receptionist and trainer.

In the middle of it, the medical examiner came in. He held a dumbbell in his gloved hand. It had smears of blood on it. "Your weapon, I am thinking," he said to Jende.

"Come for lunch," Peter said to Jende.

"Mutton-chicken-fish?"

"I don't know," Peter confessed.

"Doll curry, probably," Jende said, mocking the Roman Catholic way of speaking of daal.

"I'm a poor man, Jay."

"Tell bhabhi, send a dabba. I'll be here interviewing all the boys."

Milly packed the dabba without too much complaint. She could see the need to keep an inspector sweet. "Never know when you'll need them," she said, while hesitating over a second piece of fish. Then she threw it in with the air of a woman making her final offering to the Fates.

When Peter took the dabba over, Sihon was being interviewed.

"This woman, she was yours to handle, na?"

"Nothing like that," said Sihon. He looked at Peter. "Means you tell him, uncle."

"Uncle only has told," said Jende.

"What has uncle told?"

"That you handle the young women, Vishal handled the aunties, and Rahul for the chiknas."

This made it sound far more dubious than it actually was. Sihon shrugged.

"*They* only told to do like that."

They did an awful lot of things.

"So tell us about yesterday. Did Madhavi P come yesterday? For workout?"

"She came."

"What she did?"

"Cardio."

"For how long?"

"Thirty minutes."

"What time?"

"Seven-thirty."

"And she left at?"

"Eight-thirty."

"So what was she doing for half an hour?"

"Means?"

"She did cardio for half an hour. But full one hour she spent in the gym?"

"Ladies are like that. They talk. They sit on the stairs and talk on the phone. Shower bath only takes ten-twenty minutes."

"Medical report says she was killed at nine o'clock. You were the last person to see her alive."

This was an unbelievable stretch and it could only fail.

"Arrey, sir, why you're talking like that? So many people must have seen on the road."

"Yes, that we will be checking. But where were you last night?"

A sly look came over Sihon's face for half a second and then it vanished. "At home."

"You were at home?"

"Yes."

"You're sure, na?"

"Yes."

Peter could hear the young man wavering.

"Okay. I will write this down and you will sign it. You were at home last night."

"Sign?"

"And we will check this with your parents."

"Arrey, no, saab, please, why all this?"

"Because you are lying to me."

"Lying?" But he was already caught.

Peter stepped in. "Sihon?"

"Uncle?"

"Tell the truth, baba."

Sihon looked terrified for a moment. The truth was a loaded weapon.

"Sir, I am not like that. But he said. They could not. So I said. But I was there."

"You're on drugs or what?" Jende demanded.

Peter stepped in again. He realized suddenly and uncomfortably that he and Jende were playing Good Cop, Bad Cop à la Mahim.

"First say this: what are you not like?"

"Means, sir, I would not do. We are told. Don't even look at the ladies. Means, they are your sister. We are told."

"And you looked on them as your sisters, yes, yes," said Peter soothingly.

Sihon seemed uncomfortable.

Jende pounced: "No, he is not looking on them as sister. He is going to Madhavi's house for sex."

"No, sir," Sihon almost howled. "Not Madhavi. Chanda."

"Chanda?" Peter asked.

"My setting is with Chanda," Sihon repeated.

Peter tried not to respond but he knew his surprise was showing on his face. Chanda was one of the yuppie women at the gym. She wore designer trackpants and carried a water bottle that looked like it had been designed for intergalactic travel. She took tiny sips from it, as if the liquid inside were rare and precious. Sihon was having an affair with Chanda? They might be about the same age but it seemed as odd as Mrs. Vishwanathan and Vishal.

"Chanda? What you're doing with Chanda?"

"Her husband told."

"Her husband told you to fuck Chanda while he

watched?" Jende asked, but he was already losing steam.

"Means not like that. He doesn't have."

"What doesn't he have?"

"Means no children."

Peter could feel shock seeping through his face but Jende didn't seem particularly surprised.

"He didn't have brothers?"

"His brother is not like me," said Sihon, extending a forearm and turning it for them as if displaying it.

Peter raised his eyebrows.

"Means I have color."

Sihon obviously believed that Mr. Chanda had chosen him as surrogate father on the basis of the color of his skin. A few minutes later, he was allowed to leave. His alibi was watertight. He had been doing his duty with Chanda, and Mr. Chanda had also been present. Jende received this information with no change of expression. Peter hoped his own face was as expressionless.

"I told my parents I was studying for IAS. Please don't tell, aahn?" Sihon said as he left.

"Haan, one more mystery cleared," concluded Jende, pointing to the *Jesus Loves You* sticker. "That boy's work."

Rahul was up next.

"Vishal was a good guy," he said. "He was a good guy."

"Did you know Madhavi P?"

He had known Madhavi. But he had not even been in the city until that very afternoon. He had been on an Ashtavinayak yatra, visiting the eight Ganesha temples of note in the state of Maharashtra. The young men at EverFit had had to fend for themselves for a couple of days. Twenty other people could vouch for him.

The door opened a crack—it was Mrs. Vishwanathan. "Excuse, please," she said to Jende. "May I have a word with the manager?"

The constable on duty outside poked his head around the door. Jende raised an eyebrow and the constable looked like he had been struck by a bolt of lightning.

"Chalaa," he said, and Mrs. Vishwanathan vanished.

"Odd how you meet people again and again," Peter said. And he told Jende about their walk around the park. "And yes, I wanted to mention this: two robberies have happened. Three, if you count the mobile phone that vanished."

"Who-who was robbed?" Jende asked.

Peter could not remember. And so he stepped out where Mrs. Vishwanathan was still squabbling with the constable, and in triumph she entered in and gave the details of the robberies.

When she finally departed, denied of her request to see Vishal's body one last time (her voice wobbling again), Jende turned on Peter.

"And when were you going to tell me this?"

"I told you."

"By mistake. If maami had not come barging in, you would have forgotten. There is something going on in this gym. We find out what, we crack this case. Luck by chance, you come here for exercise. Tell me everything."

"What do you mean, everything?"

"Everything means everything. Anything you saw. Anything you remember. Anything you do. Anything anyone else does. Make a list."

So Peter made his list:

Rahul looks after the college boys.

Sihon looks after the young women.
Vishal looks after the aunties.

"Same to same things don't write," said Jende, looking over his shoulder.

No one looks after the uncles. (Including me.)
Gym timings are from 5 a.m. to 10 p.m.

"These also you told," Jende complained.

You have to wear separate shoes for the gym.
Mr. Kalsekar is the first person who greets you when you come into the gym.
He gives you a pouch into which you put your spare change and your money and your phone and everything else so it won't bother you.
He gives you a token for your stuff.
This system was started when an elliptical trainer broke down because a five-rupee coin slipped inside and jammed it.
No one claimed the five-rupee coin.
The sauna works on Mondays, Wednesdays, and Fridays.
There is a masseur who works part-time. He is in his gaon.
The gym charges Rs. 500 per massage.
No one takes massages.

Jende picked up the list, although Peter felt he had barely finished saying what he knew.

"How did the mobile get stolen if it was in a pouch with Kalsekar?" Jende asked.

"I think the guy was talking on it as he went in and so he

didn't put it in his pouch," Peter said. Then he paused. "But I think it was found later."

"These robberies. This murder here. That murder there. These are three faces of one coin."

Peter kept from commenting. Perhaps the rim of the coin might be considered a third face, he thought. Sometimes things can have three faces. Like the Shiva at Elephanta and the three faces of Kalsekar's new watch.

"Kalsekar had a new watch," he told Jende.

Jende froze. "Show me your keys," he said.

Peter was nonplussed.

"Your house keys. Show them to me."

"What do you want with my house keys?" Peter asked, but he reached into his pocket and produced them nonetheless. He wished now that he had not agreed to attach them to the Our Lady of Perpetual Succour key chain, but Milly had insisted. "She won't let you lose your keys again," she had said. And so far, she had been right.

"Did you ever give them to Kalsekar to keep in a pouch?"

"Yes. Many times. When I went to the gym."

"And this pouch-shouch. How is it sealed?"

"Sealed? What sealed?"

"Means: how do you know they haven't taken something out?"

"Who is going to take anything out? Everyone knows how much money they have."

"Money is not the only valuable thing, na?" Jende held the keys out against the light. He grunted a little.

"What? What?"

"Tell bhabhi she might have had a lucky escape." He pointed to a tiny blob of blue sticking to the teeth. "You can go now, Pittr," said Jende.

* * *

Later, he came to see Peter. He knew that his old friend would be up, reading. But he also knew that Milly would be asleep so he did not ring the bell; he only whistled, long and low. Peter let him in.

"You solved the full case. You and Mrs. Muthuswamy," Jende said when he had drunk a glass of water and was slumped back in an armchair.

"Vishwanathan."

"That only."

"How?" Peter asked. "How did you figure it?"

"You know what *they* do when they get money?" There were many *they*s in every city, thought Peter, but Jende continued: "They buy 555 cigarettes. They buy Black Label and they buy a new watch."

"Kalsekar?" It seemed incredible. "Kalsekar?"

"The mobile phone started it," Jende explained. "Vishal robbed that one. They gave it back when the owner made a noise. Kalsekar figured there must be an easy way to rob everyone. And when the pouch system began, they found one. The house keys. Kalsekar would take them out and press them into clay molds."

The blue blob on the teeth of the key.

"Then he would get duplicates cut," Jende continued.

"The keywalla outside."

"Haan. He was part of it."

"Picked him up?"

"Like in the films *Faraar* and *Nau do gyarah*. When the first cops came only."

"Involved?"

"Something they must have given him. He must have known. How many keys people can lose?"

Peter thought about that. "Then the two of them would rob the house?"

"No, only Vishal. Only this time, that woman Madhavi came back. She found him there and began screaming. He hit her to shut her up. Hit her too hard. Broke her neck. Then he went back home and told Kalsekar. Kalsekar told him to run away, to go to his gaon. Vishal didn't. He went to the station and then came back to the gym."

"Why?" Peter asked.

"The maal. The loot. He wanted his share of what they had taken from Madhavi's house. He told Kalsekar that."

Peter was still a little confused. "That upset the old man so much that he picked up a dumbbell and beat the boy to death?"

"No, worse. Vishal said he was going to the police. He said he was going to tell them that Kalsekar had done it all. He told Kalsekar he had left Kalsekar's fingerprint back at Madhavi's house."

"That's not possible . . . is it?"

Jende grinned, a rare occurrence. "See, even you don't know. You're not sure if your fingerprints can turn up in someone else's house. Kalsekar believed Vishal. That was the problem. That was what killed Vishal. That Kalsekar believed him."

"A little knowledge is a dangerous thing."

"Waah waah."

"Not me, Pope."

"You Catholics bring your pope into everything. Do you know where we found him?"

"The pope?"

"Why we'll be looking for your pope? Where we found Kalsekar."

"Where?" Peter braced himself. Surely not another dead body? Things come in threes . . .

"In the market. Apna Gopi Tank Market. He was trying to get one of the kassais to cut off his fingertips."

Peter looked carefully at his friend. He couldn't be sure whether this was a joke or not, but Jende had his police face on. "You're giving me some daaru-shaaru or no?" Peter took out his bottle of Royal Challenge.

"Chhee. RC still?" Jende protested.

"I am one."

"You are a Royal Challenge?"

"Jay, your brains have gone on bandobast or what? I'm a Roman Catholic, RC. Royal Challenge, RC? Got it?"

"Anything you'll say to save money. Cheapda," said Jende, but he seemed to relish the first fiery swig.

"Besides," said Peter, "you might arrest me if I serve you Black Label."

GLOSSARY

The following glossary provides simple explanations of select (though by no means all) Indian terms used in *Mumbai Noir*. These words come from Hindi, Urdu, Maharathi, Punjabi, and Gujarati.

Abba/Abbu: father
Abbe: friendly, informal word to refer to a man
Accha: okay; good
Adaab: a Muslim greeting
Adda: a group hangout
Adhan: Islamic call to prayer
Adrak: ginger
Ammi: mother
Arrey: hey
Baba: father; older man; holy man
Baccha: child
Bakr'a Eid: the second Eid holiday when goats are sacrificed
Banda: colloquial term for a man
Bandobast: arrangement
Baniya: trader; shopkeeper
Bhabhi: sister-in-law (brother's wife)
Bhai: brother; gangster (colloquial)
Bhen: sister
Bhenchod: sisterfucker
Bhuna-gosht: roasted meat
Biryani: a rice dish which usually contains meat and saffron
Boondi: small fried chickpea flour balls

Bun maska: a Parsi snack consisting of a roll and butter
Chal hutt: get out of the way
Challan: ticket from the police
Champi: head massage
Chana daal: split chickpea lentils
Chawl: tenement house
Chela: disciple
Chikna/Chikni: smooth; greasy
Chowki: police station
Churidar: tight pajama bottom
Chutiya: a pussy chaser; a moron; a loser
Crore: ten million
Daal: curried lentils
Daaru: alcoholic drinks
Dabba: box
Dawakhana: pharmacy
Dhobi: washerman
Dhoti: traditional sarong for men
Djibba: Muslim attire worn by men
Dupatta: a long scarf women wear with a salwaar kameez
Durgah: a Muslim saint's shrine or tomb
Faltu: extra; useless
Firang: foreigner (slang, slightly derogatory)
Gali: small street; alleyway
Gaon: village
Gayatri Mantra: Hindu prayer
Ghagra: a long, flowing skirt
Gharana: household
Ghat: riverbank
Ghungroos: small bells, usually attached to anklets
Goonga: a mute person
Gori: a white girl

Guthkha: an intoxicant made of tobacco, betel nut, and other spices

Haan: yes; also can mean "what" when used interrogatively

Hafta: a week; weekly protection money paid to police or gangsters

Hakim: indigenous doctor

Halkat: a mean person; a person without any values

Handi: a cooking vessel made out of clay

Haramzadi: a female born of unwed parents; a disgraced woman (colloquial)

Havaldar: policeman

Hijra: a transgender person

Hisaab: account

IAS: Indian Administrative Service

Ittar: natural perfume

Jab: when

Jalsa: festivity

Janta: the public; the people

Jehennum: hell

Ji: respectful suffix meaning "sir"

Kaajal: traditional eyeliner

Kaalia: black

Kasaai: butcher

Kathak: traditional classical dance

Khala: mother's sister; aunty (colloquial)

Khandvi: a snack made out of gram flour and yogurt

Kholi: small apartment; hut

Kolhapuri: traditional sandal

Kundan: purified gold

Kurta: a loose shirt

Kurti: a contemporary, casual, and shorter version of a kurta

Lathi: a stick

Lakh: one hundred thousand
Lehenga: long, flowing skirt
Maadherchod: motherfucker
Maal: stuff; goods
Maharaj: specialized cook; chef
Maibaap: parent
Mandir: temple
Marathi: the language of Maharashtra
Marega: you'll kill
Marg: street
Masjid: mosque
Mata: mother
Mausam Hai Ashiqana: a romantic atmosphere (song title)
Mera: mine
Mere liye bas: I've had enough
Muezzin: the person who leads the call to prayer at a mosque
Mujra: a form of dance originated by Mughal courtesans
Nakli: not real; counterfeit; false
Nan khatai: a biscuit
Naqaab: a mask
Neem: a type of tree
Paan: betel nut
Paanwalla: a person who sells paan
Pathsala: school
Pav: a traditional Bombay fast food dish served with a bun
Pooch-taach: inquiry; investigation
Qurbani: sacrifice
Raita: spiced and garnished yogurt
Rehmat: mercy
Saab/Sahib: a superior; during colonial times, a white man
Salwar: baggy pants
Sandaas: toilet; latrine

Senti: sentimental
Shaukeen: a connoisseur
Surya namaskar: in yoga, a sun salutation
Tamasha: a show; a dramatic event
Tapri: a type of local tea
Tel: oil
Tera: yours
Thaana/Thaane: Police station
Thepla: a savory pancake
Undhiyo: a savory vegetarian dish
Upma: south Indian breakfast dish
Urs: a Muslim holiday
Uske liye: for him or her
Ya: or
Yaar: friend; dude; man
Yatra: journey
Zindagi imtihaan leti hai: life gives you tests

ABOUT THE CONTRIBUTORS

AHMED BUNGLOWALA is the creator of the cult Indian private eye Shorty Gomes—short, sardonic, and at times exasperating. *The Days and Nights of Shorty Gomes* was published by Rupa & Co. in 1993. Ahmed grew up in Mumbai's Nagpada and studied at St. Xavier's College at Dhobi Talao. He later moved to Pune to take up a corporate job as a spin doctor. He now lives in Goa with his wife and three dogs.

Kavi Bhansali

NAMITA DEVIDAYAL wrote the award-winning memoir *The Music Room* and the best-selling novel *Aftertaste*. She is a writer with the *Times of India* and has covered a wide range of subjects, from being a "yummy mummy" to music to personal finance. She graduated from Princeton University with a degree in politics. Devidayal lives in Mumbai.

Gianfranco Mura

SONIA FALEIRO is a San Francisco–based award-winning reporter and writer. Her nonfiction narrative, *Beautiful Thing: Inside the Secret World of Bombay's Dance Bars,* has been published worldwide and translated into several languages. For more information, visit www.soniafaleiro.com.

Donna Hopkins

SMITA HARISH JAIN grew up in Mumbai and, despite having twenty-three addresses since leaving, still considers it home. Her earliest recollection of the city is of ragged beggar boys playing cricket under a canopy of neem trees. After publishing a number of short stories, she is working on her first novel, also set in Mumbai.

Arijit Datta

DEVASHISH MAKHIJA spends his life driven to manic curiosity about little things (such as why the butterfly is not called the more befitting "flutter-by"). To distract himself from such insomnia-inducing questions, he tells stories, writes screenplays, makes films and graphic art, scribbles poems, stands on his head each morning, and sings songs to the Mumbai pigeons each night. His alter ego resides at www.nakedindianfakir.com.

RIAZ MULLA was born in Mumbai in 1969. He is a trained electrical engineer, and has worked in the power and IT industries. He is currently in the education field, leading the Mumbai training division at Tech Mahindra, one of India's leading IT firms. He is married with a son and a daughter. "Justice" is his first published fiction.

Chirodeep Chaudhuri

JERRY PINTO lives and works in Mumbai. He is the author of several books and is executive secretary of MelJol, a non-governmental organization that advocates for the rights of children.

Mohsen Masoomi

R. RAJ RAO calls himself a queer writer, not because much of his work explores the theme of homosexual love in a way that no Indian writer has done before, but because his overall literary output is queer—he has written and published poetry, plays, short stories, novels, and a biography. His latest novel is *Hostel Room 131*, while his forthcoming novel is entitled *Lady Lolita's Lover*.

AVTAR SINGH spent seven years in Mumbai and two more in Goa before returning to Delhi. His last job was as editor of *Time Out Delhi*. His novel, *The Beauty of These Present Things*, which is set in Mumbai, is available from Penguin India. He lives in Delhi with his wife, son, and singing dog.

Ishrat Syed

KALPANA SWAMINATHAN and **ISHRAT SYED** are surgeons and they write together as **KALPISH RATNA**. Swaminathan also writes under her own name; her anthology *Venus Crossing* won the 2009 Vodafone Crossword Award for Fiction. Her most recent novel is *I Never Knew It Was You*. She lives in Mumbai.

Ishrat Syed

ISHRAT SYED and **KALPANA SWAMINATHAN** are surgeons and they write together as **KALPISH RATNA**. Syed is also a photographer; his last exhibition, *The Persistence of Memory*, previewed his pictorial project *Palimpsest—The Erasures That Made Bombay*. Their most recent book is *Once Upon a Hill*. Syed divides his time between Mumbai and Mississippi.

ABBAS TYREWALA is one of the most versatile talents in the Hindi film industry. His directorial debut, *Jaane Tu . . . Ya Jaane Na* (2008), was an award-winning critical and commercial success. He has written dialogues, lyrics, and screenplays for numerous highly acclaimed films, such as *Munnabhai M.B.B.S., Asoka the Great,* and *Maqbool*—an adaptation of Shakespeare's *Macbeth*. He was born in Mumbai in 1974 and studied at St. Xavier's College.

ALTAF TYREWALA was born in Mumbai and studied in New York. He is the author of the acclaimed novel *No God in Sight*, which was published across the world. His short stories have been included in numerous Indian and international anthologies and magazines. He has been awarded the DAAD Artists-in-Berlin Literature Grant for 2011, and he can be reached at altaf_tyrewala@yahoo.com.

Swati Bhattacharya

PAROMITA VOHRA is a filmmaker and writer whose work focuses on feminism, urban life, love, and popular culture. Some of her films are *Partners in Crime, Morality TV and the Loving Jehad, Q2P, Where' Sandra,* and *Unlimited Girls.* She has also written the Pakistani film *Khamosh Pani (Silent Waters)* and several documentaries, and published fiction and nonfiction in various anthologies including *Bombay Meri Jaan, Electric Feather, Recess, Defending Our Dreams,* and *First Proof.*

AM Faruqui

ANNIE ZAIDI is the author of *Known Turf: Bantering with Bandits and Other True Tales.* Her work has also appeared in anthologies like *India Shining, India Changing,* and *Women Changing India,* and in several magazines including *Frontline, Caravan, Tehelka, Pratilipi,* and *The Little Magazine.* She currently lives and works in Mumbai.

Also available from the Akashic Noir Series

DELHI NOIR
edited by Hirsh Sawhney
304 pages, trade paperback original, $15.95

Brand-new stories by: Irwin Allan Sealy, Radhika Jha, Ruchir Joshi, Meera Nair, Siddharth Chowdhury, Mohan Sikka, Palash K. Mehrotra, Hartosh Singh Bal, Hirsh Sawhney, Uday Prakash, and others.

"All fourteen stories are briskly paced, beautifully written, and populated by vivid, original characters ... Few books can alter one's perception about the state of a society, but this does, while delivering noir that's first class in any light."
—*Publishers Weekly* (starred review)

BROOKLYN NOIR
edited by Tim McLoughlin
350 pages, trade paperback original, $15.95
*Winner of Shamus Award, Anthony Award, Robert L. Fish Memorial Award; finalist for Edgar Award, Pushcart Prize.

Brand-new stories by: Pete Hamill, Arthur Nersesian, Ellen Miller, Nelson George, Nicole Blackman, Sidney Offit, Ken Bruen, and others.

"Brooklyn Noir is such a stunningly perfect combination that you can't believe you haven't read an anthology like this before. But trust me—you haven't ... The writing is flat-out superb, filled with lines that will sing in your head for a long time to come."
—Laura Lippman, winner of the Edgar, Agatha, and Shamus awards

BOSTON NOIR
edited by Dennis Lehane
240 pages, trade paperback original, $15.95

Brand-new stories by: Dennis Lehane, Stewart O'Nan, Patricia Powell, John Dufresne, Lynne Heitman, Don Lee, Russ Aborn, J. Itabari Njeri, Jim Fusilli, Brendan DuBois, and Dana Cameron.

"In the best of the eleven stories in this outstanding entry in Akashic's noir series, characters, plot, and setting feed off each other like flames and an arsonist's accelerant ... [T]his anthology shows that noir can thrive where Raymond Chandler has never set foot."
—*Publishers Weekly* (starred review)